Readers love
Laura Lascar_ _

When Everything Is Blue

"If you're looking for a great story about two young people falling in love for the first time, this is your next read. It's charming, earnest, and balances teenage angst with plenty of hope."

—Love Bytes

"*When Everything Is Blue* is a coming out and coming of age story that resonated with hope and possibility."

—The Novel Approach

The Bravest Thing

"Lascarso's writing is enthralling and stays true to the inner workings of a seventeen-year-old mind."

—Foreword Reviews

"I absolutely loved this book and can't praise it highly enough."

—Sinfully: Gay Romance Book Reviews

Andre in Flight

"*Andre in Flight* by Laura Lascarso is a beautifully written story about soul mates and eternal love. The author has done an excellent job in capturing the emotions, longing, grief and creativity which will leave you wanting for more."

—Gay Book Reviews

"…the writing is elegant and the characters well drawn and realistic, which is exactly what I expected."

—Prism Book Alliance

By LAURA LASCARSO

Andre in Flight
The Bravest Thing
One Pulse
When Everything Is Blue

CHARLIE SCHIFFER MYSTERIES
In the Pines

Published by DREAMSPINNER PRESS
www.dreamspinnerpress.com

IN THE PINES

LAURA LASCARSO

DREAMSPINNER PRESS

Published by

DREAMSPINNER PRESS

5032 Capital Circle SW, Suite 2, PMB# 279, Tallahassee, FL 32305-7886 USA
www.dreamspinnerpress.com

In the Pines
© 2018 Laura Lascarso.

Cover Art
© 2018 AngstyG.
www.angstyg.com
Cover content is for illustrative purposes only and any person depicted on the cover is a model.

Trade Paperback ISBN: 978-1-64080-741-9
Digital ISBN: 978-1-64080-740-2
Library of Congress Control Number: 2018935334
Trade Paperback published October 2018
v. 1.0

Printed in the United States of America

This paper meets the requirements of
ANSI/NISO Z39.48-1992 (Permanence of Paper).

To my daughter Leia,
for helping me translate the mysteries of a song to story.

CHAPTER 1

MY MOTHER always told me the most unlikely people can turn out to be criminals. No matter how charming or nice, a good personality doesn't clear you from a crime. Because as much as you think you know someone, you never really know the darkest desires of their hearts—vengeance, greed, lust, pride…. It's why you can't rely on your gut when solving a case. Only the hard evidence and objective facts.

That's what my mom does for a living, investigates homicides, and I help.

If it were up to me, I'd spend all my time sifting through police reports, studying lab analyses, and listening to witness testimony, but unfortunately there was this thing that kept getting in my way.

High school.

Which was where I found myself on a brisk November day—cold for Florida—awaiting one of the most torturous rites of passage for any introverted American teen: the high school pep rally.

The gym was not at all conducive to reading or reflection, my two preferred pastimes. The shoes of more than a thousand Frito-breath teens squeaked on the waxed gym floor, and the cinder block walls amplified their hyena-like laughter. Not to mention, the pep rally was essentially a parade of young, muscled flesh clad in spandex—compression shorts in the fall, wrestling singlets in the winter, formfitting baseball pants in the spring… and that was just the men.

Attendance was mandatory. Well, it was extra credit, which for an overachiever like myself was practically the same thing. And I'd arrived early—one of my many compulsions. As I was sitting in the juniors' section, waiting for the stands to fill up and the student-athlete hero worship to begin, I spied Dare Chalmers mounting the stands, taking them two at a time with his long, jean-clad legs. One part rebel, one part bourgeoisie, Dare would be forever minted in my mind as the Phantom of the Opera since he played the lead in last year's spring musical. I was brought in last minute for the very important task of holding the Phantom's bedchamber door shut. That is, until the Phantom swept through in his cape and mask and slammed it behind him with gravitas.

You see, the set crew never bothered to install the hardware so the door would close properly, and it kept wheezing open at inopportune times. Dare correctly identified me as being the one kid in high school with nothing better to do on a weekend night for the show's three-week run. And in return I got to nurse a hopeless crush on the most charismatic and popular kid at our school.

Correction: second most popular. The first most popular was his twin brother, homecoming king Mason Chalmers.

"Mischief and Mayhem" was the affectionate moniker used by the faculty of Eastview High for these two devilishly handsome twins. But they looked so different it was easy to forget they were related. Their family was of Irish descent with dark features and olive skin. Dare was tall and slim, with a face that could switch from tragic to comedic in the blink of an eye. Mason was a little more reserved, about my height and weight, with dirty blond hair he kept trimmed in a crew cut. Mason was strictly hetero—unfortunate because he filled out that singlet pretty well—while Dare…

Dare was a mystery.

It wasn't about who Dare had kissed; it was about who he *hadn't*. I'd seen several photos of Dare draped over drama kids who spanned the Kinsey scale—the Phantom's cheek pillowed by Christine's ample chest; Dare kissing Aaron Biserka, the stage manager, on the cheek; Dare dancing in some darkened room with a girl in front of him and a boy behind him, eyes black as a raccoon's mask in the camera's flash.

It was his combination of magnetism and ambiguity that caused my eyes to drift in Dare's direction whenever he arrived on scene. As though sensing my attention, Dare's head lifted, and he gave me his joker's grin. His floppy hair flopped with style over his eyes, and he pushed it off his forehead with one hand. And I stared, hopelessly devoted. Then, to my surprise and great distress, Dare switched course and made his way over to where I sat, causing my stomach to hippety-hop and my brain to go into hamster-wheel mode.

"Mind if I sit here, Charlie?" Dare asked. An embarrassing admission: after the musical's conclusion, I downloaded the *Phantom of the Opera* soundtrack. That past summer I'd listened to "All I Ask of You" on repeat like some crazed lunatic.

"Sure, but the seniors' section is up front." I motioned toward the sea of blank wooden benches, our designated area, which I was avoiding. Too much bad blood. "I'm sure they'd love for your ass to claim them."

Well, that came out wrong.

Dare chuckled and planted himself next to me. "I'll just keep this spot warm until your date gets here."

I couldn't tell if he was insulting me or flirting with me—which was often the case with Dare Chalmers—and it left me befuddled.

Dare sidled right up next to me, closer than normal, but normal enough for him. His personal-space bubble was significantly smaller than my own. Maybe it was a drama thing? Meanwhile, Dare's brother Mason and their shared best friend, Joey Pikramenos, took the bench in front of us. Daniela De Costa, Mason's girlfriend, broke away from the cheerleading squad to bound up the stands. She was diminutive in size but not in personality. In addition to her uniform, she was wearing Mason's letterman jacket—I knew it was his because of the patch on the right side of two men grappling. Daniela shot me a dirty look before planting a wet, smacking kiss on Mason's mouth. Then she climbed onto his lap and performed a little twerking number that made me blush, it was so overtly sexual.

"Get a room," Joey complained and shoved Mason's shoulder.

I scooted backward to give them space.

Daniela laughed, and having properly aroused Mason, leaned over his shoulder and said to Dare, "How's my makeup?"

Dare assessed her face. "Let me just...." He used the pad of his thumb to touch up a smear of gloss in the corner of her candy-lipped mouth. Daniela air-kissed him in response. It was such an intimate gesture, done so casually, that it made my own loneliness a little more biting.

Daniela then turned back to Mason and caught him looking a beat too long at the rest of the cheerleading squad. She grabbed his cheeks roughly between her manicured fingers, green and white for our school colors, and swiveled his face toward hers.

"Tell me I didn't just catch you looking up Kylie Crawford's *cheer* skirt," she demanded with a squirrely look on her face. I wondered at the specificity of "cheer" skirt. Was it worse to sneak a peek when a girl was in uniform?

"Don't they wear bloomers underneath?" I asked. Daniela's head slingshotted toward me so fast her ponytail sideswiped Mason's face. She looked me up and down like I'd just been beamed there from outer space. "Isn't that what they call them?" I glanced around for backup. "Bloomers?"

Dare and Mason shared a chuckle. The brothers looked nothing alike, but their laughs were exactly the same—a deep hiccupping *huh, huh, huh*. They probably thought my social awkwardness was done deliberately to save Mason from a sticky situation. Popular kids think everything is about them.

"You are such a freak," Daniela said to me. Each word was given individual emphasis, but what bothered me more was that she hadn't answered my question. She looked pointedly at Dare, as though some conversation regarding my freakiness had already taken place.

"Please excuse Daniela's manners," Dare said while patting her arm. "She's on a no-carbs diet and feeling a bit peckish. The correct term *is* bloomers."

"Whatever, Dare. Don't hate 'cause I'm beautiful." She fluffed up her ponytail for effect. "Two more pounds and I'm golden." She turned to Mason. "You are coming with me, Mason Chalmers." Daniela grabbed Mason's hand and pulled him up with her, no doubt taking advantage of the now-full gymnasium to remind everyone that he was hers. I kind of admired her for the way she claimed him with such confidence. I wished I had a tenth of her chutzpah. I'd been crushing on Dare for about two years now, crushing hard, and I still hadn't come up with the courage to make a move.

Mason stood, his ass now at eye level. I stared down at my backpack placed strategically in my lap. The parade of flesh hadn't even begun, and my ears were already burning.

"Aren't they adorable?" Dare asked aloud at their retreating forms.

Joey shook his head. "Things were so much simpler before the coupling."

Dare laughed. "She gives great makeovers. You could probably use one, Joey. Improve your own chances of coupling."

Joey narrowed his eyes at Dare, then glared at me like I was the one who'd insulted him. I steered my nose forward.

"So, Charlie. It's Friday. Whatcha got going on tonight?" Dare crossed his long legs and threw his arm casually around my shoulder. He spoke to me like we were old friends, which I supposed we were. We'd been in the same schools since elementary but never in the same social circles. With everyone packed so tightly together, our hips were touching as well. The heat of his body made me sweat, or maybe it was my nervousness. I could smell cinnamon on his breath and the expensive cologne he wore—not so much that it covered the smell of him, which I liked. Very much. I'd bet his bedsheets smelled the same.

Don't think about his bedsheets.

"Nothing much. Does your set have a door that won't close?" I asked, only half joking. If that was what Dare needed, I'd do it in a heartbeat.

He smiled, showing off his pointy canines. "You should have won an Academy Award for that performance, Charlie. Never have I seen a door operated with such finesse."

"I was upstaged by your door slamming," I told him.

He shrugged. "I had a lot of practice growing up. Did you know, Charlie-bo-barley, today is my birthday?" When we were in third grade, Dare played the name game with everyone in our class. My real name, Charles, wasn't "good for rhyming" according to Dare, so he switched it to Charlie. The nickname stuck.

"Oh… yeah, I guess I did." I said it as though it were only a vague recollection, as if I hadn't been obsessing all day whether to tell him happy birthday or not. And, if so, should I send him a text or post a birthday message to my Story on Snapchat or say it to him in person? Would knowing his birthday (and astrological sign) be considered weird, or would he be happy to know Scorpios (him) and Taureans (me) are very simpatico? "Happy Birthday, Dare."

"Thanks, Charlie." He squeezed my shoulder, and a shiver ran through me that was pure electricity followed by a roiling, nauseated feeling in my gut. "We're having this party tonight."

"Darren," Joey warned. I hadn't realized he was still listening.

"It's my party, *Joseph*. I can invite whoever I want."

"What about Mason?" Joey asked. I wondered how it worked having a shared best friend. When the twins had a difference of opinion, whose side did Joey take?

"Pfft. Bygones. That was *so* last year. Am I right, Charlie?"

Last year, I'd infiltrated a cheating ring led by my former best friends, the Geek Squad, who were posing as lovable dumb jocks in order to take their clients' SAT scores to unprecedented heights—for a profit, of course. I warned the Geek Squad I'd go public with their operation, but they told me there was no way I could prove it. That was a challenge I simply could not turn down. I offered my SAT-taking services to one Mason Chalmers, who enthusiastically accepted. With that recording of our negotiation, I persuaded Mason to tell the administration everything he knew, which he reluctantly did. Because of my meddling, I was now one of the few students abhorred by the popular kids and the nerds alike.

I didn't regret exposing the Geek Squad's scam, but infamy can be a bit lonely.

"It's a surprise party," Dare was saying. "Don't worry about any presents, though. We're spoiled rotten as it is."

I imagined some *Carrie* scenario where I was doused with pig's blood, running blindly while screaming into the yard. I'd managed to survive the past few months by lying low, but I felt there was a comeuppance brewing.

"And don't say anything to Mason." Dare glanced around to make sure we weren't being overheard. I assumed it was because Mason would kick my ass if he knew. "It's a surprise. He's going to flip." Dare shook his head and smiled as though we were sharing an inside joke.

Dare was throwing his brother a surprise birthday party? It was really... nice. Or it was his way to catch his brother off guard. The two of them were notorious pranksters, and their worst victims were often each other. During my freshman year, there was a video going around of Dare barfing on the indoor trampolines at the mall, followed soon after by one of Mason kissing his biceps and making faces at the mirror. During the first showing of *Phantom of the Opera* last spring, right after the chandelier fell, Mason and Daniela screamed like their heads were on fire and ran down the auditorium aisles wearing black capes and Phantom masks. Their antics were so well received that it became a staple of the show, which delighted Dare to no end. He thrived on drama.

"So, you interested?" Dare asked with an impish grin. His eyebrows were perfectly sculpted, far better than I remembered from when he was the Phantom.

"Did you wax your eyebrows?" I asked, unable to contain my curiosity.

He smiled sheepishly. "Daniela did them for me." He waggled them a bit for my benefit. "What do you think?"

You must be gay.

"They look great."

"So, I'll see you tonight, then?" he asked again. I was flattered by his persistence. And a little suspicious too.

"Yeah, probably not." I was a terrible liar, especially when it was for no good reason.

Dare frowned, and his expressive eyebrows pointed downward in the middle. I couldn't tell if his disappointment was genuine or if he was only acting. He was a better singer than actor but still pretty good.

"This is just like when you bailed on the *Phantom* cast party," he complained.

"I didn't bail," I argued. "I was there."

"Then why didn't I see you?"

Truth: I hid in a closet most of the night because I was too nervous to talk to him. I'm a compulsive truth-teller, but this was simply too embarrassing. Dare stared at me, waiting for an explanation.

"You were surrounded by your fanboys the whole night." I wasn't the only queer kid thirsting after the Phantom. The line started *way* back there.

Dare blinked, then beamed at me, and it was such a dramatic shift, like going from darkness to light. His hand tightened around my shoulder again. *Snap, crackle, pop.*

"You're adorable. Isn't he adorable?" He looked to Joey for affirmation. Joey rolled his eyes, probably immune by now to Dare's antics. "Come to my party tonight, Charlie Schiffer. You'll be my guest of honor."

He winked at me like some sly fox from the silver screen. This was the effect of being on the receiving end of the Chalmerses' charm, like being drunk without the hangover. I was utterly boring by comparison. I liked hanging out with my mom, reading books, doing homework, solving murders, and chilling with my dog, Boots. I didn't party; I wasn't much of a joiner; I'd never even gone on a date.

"Fine, yeah, I'll come."

Dare thumped my back. "Jesus, Charlie, you act as if I'd asked for your kidney. Remember, eight o'clock. That's when the wild rumpus begins. Tonight you're running with the wolves."

Dare braced his hands behind himself, arched his back, and howled. His face was one of rapture; his strong lungs carried the note with power, sending a familiar tremor through me, same as when I experienced him as the Phantom. A few of our peers spontaneously joined in, including Mason down on the gym floor and the wrestling team soon after. Their green singlets clung to their bodies like wet paint, chests thrust forward, shoulders back, muscles taut and straining as they howled like animals. Daniela started the cheerleaders going in a spontaneous a cappella harmony. Even our mascot was howling, and he was a ram.

Arwhooooooo. The sound was primal and edged with fear. The vibrations of sound rattled in my chest, and for a moment it didn't feel like a pep rally but the opening ceremony of some gruesome blood sport.

I glanced over at Dare, who was smiling at me like a maniac. Mayhem, the orchestrator of madness.

"Go on, Charlie," he whispered in my ear. "Join us."

I took a shaky breath, tilted my head back, and howled.

I DIDN'T expect to see Mason Chalmers again until that night for his surprise party. *If* I decided to go—it was still up in the air. But as I was getting ready to leave school, my passenger-side door opened and Mason slipped inside, shutting the door behind him with purpose. He still wore his green polyester warm-up suit, the jacket unzipped enough that I could see his sparse chest hair poking out the top. He'd been sweating too. I could smell his manly musk rising up in the shuttered cabin of my car.

"Hey, Mason," I said casually, while thinking *This is it*. Mason hadn't retaliated since my SAT sting because he'd been saving it up for one last annihilation. He'd let me think I was safe all these months, only to spring on me when I was unaware and defenseless.

"You and I need to have a little chat." He pivoted in the passenger seat so he could properly stare me down. His eyes were stony, his shoulders tense. His short buzz cut gave his face a severe appearance, and there was none of the amusement in his expression I'd seen earlier that afternoon at the pep rally. "It's been a long time coming, don't you think, Schiffer?"

"I guess it has." I exhaled the breath I'd been holding on to and resigned myself to whatever fate was to befall me. Back before my GPA dropped, I used to have this prime parking spot close to the school because of my academic achievement, but since losing that privilege, I've had to park in one of the dirt lots at the fringes of the athletic fields used as overflow for the sophomores and latecomers. I glanced around the desolate lot to see if Mason had brought reinforcements. He appeared to have come alone, but that didn't mean his burly gang of merry men weren't lurking behind the athletic portables, preparing to pounce the moment Mason gave the word.

"So, what do you have to say for yourself?" Mason crossed his arms so his biceps looked intimidatingly huge. He seemed to be fishing for an apology, but I wasn't going to give it to him. It wasn't fair to all those kids who put in the sweat and sacrifice and studied for the test. You shouldn't be able to buy your SAT score and therefore your placement at a university. The world is unfair enough as it is. Mason had been wrong to try to cheat, even if I was the only one to believe it.

"I'd say you got off pretty easy," I said at last. Mason got an in-school suspension. The Geek Squad, including me, had their school rankings dinged—straight Fs in "school decorum." The jocks also had to retake their tests and deal with their true aptitude. And I lost all my friends and severed any alliances I'd built over the years.

He squinted at me, confused or perhaps displeased that I was so impertinent. "Not that. This is about Dare."

Dare? What does he have to do with anything?

"I don't usually get involved with this sort of thing," Mason continued, "but Dare seems to be into you, and if you're planning to do him the way you did me…." He let the threat trail off, perhaps letting me imagine my own demise. Meanwhile my brain was glitching over the information that Dare might be into me.

"Well?" Mason growled.

"I wouldn't do that to Dare," I said in earnest and shut my mouth before anything more incriminating could come out.

"No?" His bullish face tilted. He didn't sound convinced.

"Absolutely not."

Mason scrutinized me. Despite his tough-guy persona, Mason was actually very smart. He was at the top of our class in middle school. It was only during high school that he'd traded his GPA for popularity and started hanging around a bunch of meatheads.

"Why not?"

I focused on my steering wheel, worried he'd see the full extent of my feelings. I could feel my face heating up, likely turning the tips of my ears a flaming pink. Luckily my complexion didn't allow for my blushing to be too obvious. Just my ears.

"I really like Dare. I'd never do anything to hurt him." I didn't elaborate as to how much or in what way—that might also be a trap. The seconds stretched on until finally Mason nodded as if satisfied.

"All right, then." He punched my shoulder a little too hard, like he didn't know his own strength. "Before I go, though, let me make it clear. Messing with me is one thing, but if you mess with Dare, I will fucking destroy you, Schiffer. Got it?"

If his words weren't convincing enough, the rumble in his voice definitely did it. I nodded and licked my lips. "Got it."

He pounded the dashboard lightly with his fist. "All right, then. Good talk." He climbed out of my car and rounded the front of it, using the two finger *I'm-watching-you* hand gesture like some high school bully out of an eighties movie.

I took a deep breath and let it out slowly.

"Good talk," I said softly to no one at all.

CHAPTER 2

BOOTS GREETED me the next morning by cleaning his tongue on my face until my cheeks were thoroughly wet and slimy.

"Boots, come on now," I fussed and gently pushed him away. His droopy eyes and *aw shucks* smile made it impossible for me to be mad at him. Instead of licking, he buried his wet nose under my chin and laid his muzzle on my chest until I finished waking. Usually my mom let him out for me on the weekends so I could sleep in, but she must have forgotten. While I sat up and stretched, Boots, a definite morning person, clambered off the bed, nearly tripping over his big hound-dog ears, and waited by the open door for me to join him. Then he led me out to the kitchen, which was also where his food bowl lived. He wasn't stupid.

My mom glanced up from her cell phone and looked me over. I felt guilty without knowing why.

"Did you go to the Chalmerses' party last night?" she asked, eyes narrowing ever so slightly.

"Morning, Mom."

Any other teen might wonder how the heck his mom knew about a high school party—a surprise one, no less—but not me. You can't catch a cold in this town without Detective Rebekah Schiffer knowing about it.

"Charlie?" she persisted. "The party?"

"No," I admitted. After a lengthy discussion of pro's and con's with Boots, I decided it was safer to refrain from attending the Chalmerses' surprise birthday party. Taken in large doses, my compulsions inevitably drove people away. Right now Dare thought I was adorable. I didn't want to prove him wrong.

And there was the whole other matter of Mason Chalmers.

"Why? What's up?" I asked. Mom's face had a pinched, worried look.

My own phone buzzed in my hand. It was an older model and, like me, it took a minute to rouse in the morning. I turned it over and opened Snapchat to see a picture of Dare and Mason posted to Dare's Story. It looked as though it was taken yesterday after the pep rally. Mason wore his green singlet and flexed his biceps, which were so stacked you could see the veins branching up his forearms like tree roots. He must have spent his summer in the gym. Dare was miming punching him in the gut, eyebrows slanted with devilish glee. Both of them looked cocky as hell, which stirred me up a bit. Daniela must have taken the picture with Dare's phone. Or Joey. Then I read Dare's message accompanying the photo:

Mason didn't come home last night. Anybody seen him? hmu

A cold, wet something slithered down my throat and coiled itself in my stomach. The hair on the back of my neck stood on end. "What's going on?" I asked Mom.

"The Chalmerses reported Mason as missing this morning." She studied me a little too closely. "Do you know anything about that?"

"No," I said reflexively. "Why would I?" She had a tendency to treat me like a suspect at times. It was pretty insulting. It probably didn't help that my mom got to know the Chalmerses a bit too well last year. After my SAT sting, there were some meetings with administration. I got in trouble for coercing Mason into telling the truth, if you can believe it. The Chalmerses used their family name like a get-out-of-jail-free card. They even wanted me to recant my story. Instead I played the recording for them and suggested we take it to the school board. Needless to say, I didn't leave the best impression on Dare and Mason's parents or Principal Thornton.

"I'm heading in now to speak with the parents," Mom continued. "The Chalmerses were on a weekend trip but were called back this morning by the boy's brother."

I thought of Dare making that call and posting the picture of him and Mason. He must be sick with worry.

Mom was wearing her black pantsuit, gathering legal pads and shuffling papers into her briefcase. Her gold badge was fastened at her hip, right next to her holstered Glock. Usually she wore a collared shirt with the Gainesville Police Department insignia and slacks. The business attire meant it must be serious.

"It's only been a few hours, hasn't it?" I asked with a sour taste in my mouth.

"Given the family's influence in the community, GPD wants this treated sensitively and expeditiously."

"And justice for all," I muttered. Her lips retreated into a grim line. I wished every missing teen were treated as sensitively and expeditiously. I looked again at the picture on my phone, the brothers' unbridled happiness. I'd always envied their freedom and arrogance at being rich, beautiful, and adored in a small town. Nothing bad could possibly happen to either of them. I'd have an easier time believing it was one of the twins pulling a prank, like Tom Sawyer spying on his own funeral to see what people were saying about him.

"You want me to come with you?" I asked. I'd often accompanied my mom as her assistant—taking notes and typing up reports; I even had my own GPD ID card.

"I don't think so, Charlie."

"I could ask Dare some questions. See what he knows?"

"I'm afraid not. This one has to be strictly by the book."

"I'm a professional," I reminded her, more than a little offended.

She came over and laid her hands on my shoulders.

"I know you are, sweetie. But this one… this *family*. You have history with them."

Mom stared at me until I reluctantly nodded. "I need to establish trust," she said, "and I'm afraid having you there might exacerbate an already delicate situation." She kissed my cheek. "This could take a while. You know what that means, don't you?"

"I'm making dinner," I said glumly. I hated being left out.

She smiled and patted my messy mop of bedhead hair. "I'm thinking Italian."

She downed the last of her coffee and placed the mug in the sink, gathered up her briefcase, and tucked her phone into her purse.

"He's probably just passed out somewhere, sleeping off a hangover."

She offered me a tight smile. "Let's hope so."

After my mom left, I poured myself a cup of coffee and stared at the picture of Dare and Mason on my phone, looking for any clues that might be hidden there, but I found nothing—just two unruly brothers horsing around for the camera. Bad things happened to good people, I knew that, but I couldn't imagine anyone harming Mason Chalmers.

The ill feeling in my stomach stuck with me for the rest of the morning, even after I'd eaten. Even though it was completely illogical, I couldn't help but feel guilty.

THAT EVENING, after running Boots in the woods behind our house, finishing up a paper for English, and throwing a pot of spaghetti on the stove, I mined my mom for information about Mason's whereabouts.

"Did you talk to Daniela?" I asked. If anyone knew where Mason was, it had to be her. She probably had multiple GPS trackers on him.

"The girlfriend? Yes, I did. According to her, the last time she saw Mason was at the pep rally. They each had athletic practice after school. She anticipated seeing him again later for this surprise party, but he never showed."

"What about his brother?"

"Darren Chalmers said he—"

"Dare," I corrected her. Her forehead wrinkled, probably because I'd interrupted her. She hated that. "No one calls him Darren," I reiterated. "It's Dare."

"O-*kay*." She started again. "*Dare* said he and his brother were supposed to meet at Waffle Kingdom and then arrive at the house together, but Mason never showed."

"Have you found his truck?"

"We're running the vehicle's tags. Hopefully we'll know something by tomorrow morning."

"Did they issue an Amber Alert?"

"No, Mason doesn't fit the criteria." She studied her plate of spaghetti. I waited for her to elaborate, but she didn't.

"The Chalmerses must not like that," I prodded.

"He's eighteen, and there's no proof of a struggle." Her face was placid, and I wondered if it was a point of contention between her and the Chalmerses.

"Are you leading up the investigation?"

"No, Hartsfield is." She was careful to keep her expression neutral. Hartsfield and my mom were the same rank, but Hartsfield was often appointed to take the lead on investigations, not because he was a better detective, but because he fit in better with the rest of GPD, meaning he was a man on a force that was 90 percent male.

Then I wondered if it might be my past confrontation with the Chalmerses that steered the appointment away from my mother. I hoped that wasn't the case. My mother wouldn't tell me either way, though. She took the department's snubs with a stiff upper lip.

"They're lucky to have you on the case," I told her. "If anyone can find Mason, it's you."

She smiled and flicked a loose curl that had fallen over my forehead. "Thanks, buddy."

I pushed my spaghetti around the plate with my fork, making little gullies in the sauce. I wasn't hungry. Usually I had no trouble discussing cases over dinner, but this time it was someone I knew. And the idea of Mason running away just didn't sit right with me. I worried they were wasting precious time.

"It just doesn't wash," I said at last, dropping my fork and sitting back from the table with my arms crossed.

"Why not?" She wasn't doubting me, necessarily; she was asking for me to back up my theory with evidence.

"If Mason were off on an adventure, it seems only natural that he'd take his partner-in-crime."

"That'd be his brother, Dare?" She paused, then seemed to have a moment of clarity. I'd seen this expression on her face many times before, whenever she connected the dots on a case. I waited for her revelation.

"Wait a minute. Was he… was Dare Chalmers the Phantom of the Opera?"

I swallowed tightly, feeling a familiar burning sensation in my ears and loop-de-loop in my gut. I'd tried to keep my crush under wraps, but she caught me a few times humming the music. It wasn't easy hiding your obsessions when your mother was a detective.

"Immaterial," I told her.

She folded up her smile and packed it away before the tension in the room became too great.

"Perhaps this is a means of separation and individuation common among adolescent twins," she posited, all business again. "Do you suppose this might be Mason's way of establishing his personhood, by physically running away from his brother?"

"That seems more likely if the brothers were identical or constantly being compared to one another, but they're so… different." They were both shining stars, each in their own right.

"I think there was a bit of comparison happening in the household," she said. I waited for her to continue.

"Are you going to elaborate on that?" I asked impatiently.

"I'm not."

I scowled at her, frustrated at her unusual caginess. I felt a little guilty too. Was it just the case, or was I looking for clues into Dare's personal life?

"How can you expect me to work with only half the information?" I fussed. She cleared her throat louder than necessary. My mother was all about boundaries. I went back to my original argument. "Even if that's what this is, Mason wouldn't let Dare worry. He'd at least tell him he was leaving or let him know he was safe."

"Perhaps he did, and Dare is only covering for him by acting desperate."

I thought again of the picture Dare posted that morning. "Did he seem desperate at the station?"

"Downright distraught," my mother answered simply.

"Anecdotal evidence?"

She motioned to her face. "He had bags under his eyes, said that he hadn't slept the night before. His clothes were rumpled. His parents found him searching the house and then the surrounding property with their four-wheeler. He kept drifting off midsentence and telling me we had to find him. He said…." She stopped and chewed on her lower lip.

"He said?" I prompted.

She shook her head. "You know how I hate relying on intuition."

"I won't let it influence me."

She sighed and rubbed her eyes. It had been a long day for her, I could tell. "He said he had a bad feeling that something terrible had happened to Mason. He related a story from a few years back. Mason fell off his dirt bike, and when Dare went into the woods behind their house, he found Mason with a broken leg. Do you remember that?"

"Yeah, it happened in middle school. Around the time when Dad…." I studied my plate. "You know." Neither of us liked to talk about my dad's death. Those conversations could quickly turn into therapy sessions, and we'd both been to our respective therapists already that week.

Mom picked up the conversation again. "Like I said, he seemed desperate for me to find him. Maybe he's a good actor—"

"He's a better singer," I said, somewhat randomly.

"The point is…." She looked at me. She really hated being interrupted. "He seemed genuinely concerned."

"Some kind of twin sense?" I asked.

She shrugged. She hated admitting to anything that couldn't be directly witnessed, tested, or dissected.

"What's GPD's operations plan?"

"We're organizing a search party tomorrow morning."

"Seems early for that."

She nodded. "Like I said, the Chalmerses are *very* important people." She sat back in her chair, her plate now empty. No matter the case, my mother managed to keep her appetite. "That was delicious. You added a bit of garlic to the sauce?"

"Just for you." She was trying to change the subject. We knew each other's tells too well. "So, where's the search being held?"

"Paynes Prairie."

That seemed grim. Dead bodies showed up in the swamps of Paynes Prairie more often than anyone would like to admit. The muck made for easy disposal, at least temporarily, and the tall marsh grasses meant you couldn't get a good look from above. The prairie stretched on for miles, so it was hard to search the whole thing. Plus the alligators and water moccasins were strong deterrents. I shivered involuntarily.

"That was the last signal from his cell phone. We think he may have thrown it out the window on his way out of town. That's the hope, at least," Mom explained.

"I'm coming," I told her. Yesterday I'd sworn to Mason, in my own way, that I'd look out for Dare. I imagined Dare making that call to his parents and searching their property, frantic to find his brother. I knew exactly what that felt like, and if there was any way I could help Dare, I wanted to try.

"You already know my feelings about it," Mom said.

"I'm still coming. The whole school will probably be there."

"Hopefully we won't find anything more than a phone," she said. "But if we do… if there's any proof whatsoever of foul play, you're off the case. Understand?"

"I understand your concern."

"And you're in agreement?" she persisted.

If something bad had happened to Mason, of course I was going to ask more questions. This wasn't like her other cases where the victim was unknown to me. This was the twin brother of someone I cared about, a lot. This one was personal.

"Seconds?" I asked.

She sighed, which I took to mean this discussion was on hold for the time being. She handed me her plate. "Just a little, and another piece of garlic bread too."

Lucky for me I'd figured out a long time ago, the way to my mother's heart was through her stomach.

CHAPTER 3

WE ASSEMBLED at the southernmost point of Newnans Lake, where Hawthorne Road met with 2082, just south of Kate's Fish Camp. It was just before dawn as people shuffled out of their cars and trucks; several others biked there as well on the Hawthorne bike trail. Cups of coffee were distributed as folks mumbled greetings to each other in the violet wash of predawn. We watched the sun rise over the marsh like blood seeping from a wound and woke a flock of red-winged blackbirds that zigzagged away, chattering their complaints at the sky. If it weren't for the somber mood, you'd almost think we'd gathered there for an early morning hike.

I thought we'd comb the swamps between 441 and I-75—the two most likely routes out of town—but Mom said this was where they'd determined the cell phone last communicated with the tower before the battery was removed or the phone died.

GPD told us we were looking for Mason's phone; they probably didn't want to say we were also potentially searching for a body.

Rangers from the Florida Fish and Wildlife Conservation Commission passed out waders and snake boots for members of the search parties, but there were only enough for a fraction of the people who'd come out to help, especially since most of the upperclassmen of Eastview High were there. For those of us who didn't have protection, FWC suggested we grab a big stick and knock the ground every couple of steps to "scare off the critters." The word *critters* made it sound like soft, furry mammals, not venomous snakes or twenty-foot alligators with bone-crushing jaws. Literally half a gator's length was its mouth.

My mother was with the operations unit, poring over aerial maps on a foldout table, so I joined the nearest group of classmates to form a search party. While we waited for supplies and further instruction from GPD, I overheard two girls talking about Mason's disappearance.

"Bet he ran off with that stripper from Café Risqué," one said. I recognized her as Tameka Thomas, a cheerleader from Daniela's squad.

"Is that what the fight on Friday was about?" said the other girl. My ears perked up at the mention of a fight. According to my mom, Daniela claimed she hadn't seen Mason since the pep rally, and she certainly didn't mention an argument between them.

"Mmm-hmm," Tameka continued. "Mason's fine as hell, but you know he's not faithful. Daniela just doesn't know how to handle him. I'd keep that boy sat-is-fied." Tameka made a slapping gesture and ground her hips in a motion that made my eyes go wide. The girls at my high school were more sex-crazed than the boys.

"When was the fight?" I asked the girls. They both turned my way and studied me like I was a bug and they were deciding whether to ignore me or squash me.

"Well, if it isn't old *Dick* Tracy," Tameka sneered. My SAT sting had burned a couple of the cheerleaders. They called me Dick for a while whenever they caught me in the halls. *Hey, Dick. How's it going, Dick? Screwed anyone over lately, Dick?* One time a whole hive of them swarmed me outside the gymnasium. It was pretty terrifying. "Are you on the case then, *Dick?*" Tameka asked, hands on her hips, coppery brown eyes studying me acutely.

"If the fight really happened, it could help with the investigation," I offered as my defense for being nosy. "I just want to help Dare find his brother."

Tameka pursed her lips and glanced over at her friend, who only shrugged. "Well, not that it's any of *your* business, but I saw them fighting outside the wrestling room after cheer practice. I didn't hear what they were saying because I don't put my nose where it doesn't belong, like *some people.*"

I sincerely doubted that, but instead of arguing with her, I only sighed and waited for her to get in her digs.

"But, then again, a girl's response to finding out her man's been cheating is pretty universal, so if I had to take a guess...." Here Tameka paused for effect, curling her upper lip a little and bobbing her head. "I'd guess she was giving him the business for messing around."

"What does that look like?" I needed more detail.

Tameka smiled at her friend. "Like this." She stalked up to me and shoved me back by my shoulders so I stumbled a little. Then she stuck her index finger right up in my face and pointed at me accusingly. "You good-for-nothing, lying, cheating dog. You think I'm stupid? *Do you think I'm stupid?* I saw that text in your phone. I know you were with someone else last night. Who was she? Who the hell was she? Oh no, son, don't you come at me now acting like you *looooove* me. You don't love me. You love yourself, you selfish sonovabitch. I hope you get a disease from that ho. Now, get out of my face before I beat you senseless, boy. I can't even stand to look at you."

She stuck her flattened palm in my face, spun on her heels, and walked back over to her friend.

"Wow," I said, reeling from her very visceral performance. My heart was racing and my palms were sweating. "End scene. That was brilliant." Where had I picked up that expression? Probably the drama department.

"Yeah." She brushed her manicured nails against her shirt and blew on their tips. They were painted alternating green and white, our school colors, just like Daniela's. I remembered the jacket Daniela was wearing during the pep rally—Mason's letterman jacket.

"Was Daniela still wearing Mason's jacket?" I asked Tameka.

She shook her head. "She took it off and shoved it at him, even though it was cold that day. That's how I knew she was pissed. She loves that damn jacket."

It was true. Now that Tameka mentioned it, I rarely saw Daniela without Mason's jacket, even on warm days. It was like the skin from her kill—proof to all her rivals that Mason Chalmers had been claimed.

At that moment a sheriff's deputy approached us and gave us all blue nurse's gloves and several two-gallon Ziploc bags. "If you find anything—and I mean anything—put it in a bag, seal it, and radio in." He glanced at the lot of us, seemed to have misgivings, and then shoved the walkie-talkie at me. "You're the group leader," he said.

I could tell from Tameka's expression, she didn't like that. "Because he's a boy?" she asked, shoulders squared, head tilted like a parrot. I felt the need to correct her that I was a man, not a boy, but I didn't wish to feed her ire. The deputy looked caught—he wasn't much older than us. Likely this was his first experience with organizing a search party.

"No, it's just because—" he started to say.

"You can be leader." I cut him off and gave Tameka the radio. "You've got the biggest mouth anyway."

Her eyes went wide and her mouth opened a little like she was about to retort. Then she smiled. "All right then, *Dick*. As team leader, I'm making you the gator getter. You walk ahead with that big stick of yours and *scare off the critters*."

I chuckled at her impersonation of the ranger. "My name's Charlie, by the way."

She smirked and shoved my shoulder playfully. "Yeah, I know, but you look more like a Dick to me."

FOUR HOURS and two water breaks later, we'd found two gators—both midsized—one tennis shoe, several plastic bags and bottles, and a pair of tattered underwear, men's. We bagged everything except the critters. Around lunchtime several pizza pies were brought in, and our group took a break to refuel. Over the course of the morning, I'd earned some respect in Tameka's eyes, especially after rescuing her from a gator that hissed at us from the side. We weren't attacked, but Tameka had to be soothed after that encounter. No one in our group found a cell phone or, thankfully, a body.

"What was it you were saying about an... exotic dancer from Café Risqué?" I asked Tameka while we drank our cans of soda provided by GPD. She was using my stick to scrape the muck off her shins and shoes while saying *nasty* on loop. I tried to sound casual about it, but I doubted I was very convincing.

Tameka shrugged. "I heard Mason went there a couple of times this summer."

"By himself?"

"No, with someone from the wrestling team. Big white dude with red hair."

"Peter Orr?" I often saw the two of them palling around.

"Maybe. Daniela was pissed. They broke up for a couple days, but it didn't last."

"Don't you have to be eighteen to get in?"

She gave me a disbelieving look. "Have you ever been to Café Risqué?"

"No," I squawked, indignant she'd think that of me.

"It's a dive, Dick. It's like a Denny's with strippers."

"What does the quality of the food have to do with anything?"

She rolled her eyes so hard it looked painful. "They'll let anyone in there. You could probably get in with a Bed Bath & Beyond coupon. Mason probably just splashed the cash."

Bribing your way into a strip club; that sounded like Mason's modus operandi. I considered telling my mom about it, but I didn't see how a couple of visits to a strip club were relevant to the investigation, and I didn't want to send her on a wild goose chase.

"You really think Mason was cheating on Daniela?" I asked. In our short time together, I'd come to rely on Tameka for her insider's perspective. She had her finger on the pulse of Eastview High. And I appreciated that she was willing to share her insights with me.

Tameka chewed on her lip. "That or she was pregnant."

Pregnant? That could certainly cause an argument, especially if Mason said something stupid, like "Well, whose is it?" I noticed Mr. and Mrs. Chalmers standing across the highway where GPD had set up operations between a mobile lab and the K-9 unit. The dogs were no doubt here to sniff out a body. Mr. Chalmers appeared dressed for a business meeting with everything but the tie, while Mrs. Chalmers wore stylish jeans, an oversized sweater, and tennis shoes. Her dark, graying hair was pulled back into a ponytail, and there was no makeup on her face. Dare was there too and looked as distraught as my mother described him yesterday. His hair was a mess, and he was gesturing wildly to the same deputy who'd tried to make me team leader.

A few feet away, Joey Pikramenos had his arms crossed, a UF ball cap pulled low on his brow. If Daniela was around, I didn't see her, but I did see Peter Orr in Ms. Sparrow's search party, along with Coach Gundry. Ms. Sparrow wore waders and a field hat with a sun shield, probably her own equipment. She taught science at Eastview and was the sponsor for the campus Environmental Service Program. Coach Gundry had his green Eastview High athletic pants rolled up to his knees, exposing his very pale and strangely hairless calves. They looked like two bowling pins.

My mom said Mason had gone to practice on Friday before he went missing. Someone should talk to Peter Orr and Coach Gundry to see what they knew.

As if my thinking of her had summoned her, my mom exited the mobile lab, spotted the confrontation happening between Dare and the deputy, and headed over to them. She placed a hand on the deputy's shoulder, essentially dismissing him, then turned her attention to Dare, doing her best to calm him. He looked to be on the verge of tears. Mom caught me staring from across the road. Either she nodded slightly for me to join them or I only imagined it, but I told Tameka I was going to check on him.

"Go easy on him, Dick. He's had a rough couple of days."

I frowned and handed her my stick. "Good luck with the gators."

She took it reluctantly. "It was your funk keeping them away."

I suspected she was joking but slyly sniffed my pits anyway—not too terrible—then headed across the street. There were officers directing cars to go around the hordes of people, even though there wasn't much traffic. Hawthorne was a four-lane highway, but 2082 was an old country road that split from the highway and led to the ghost town of Rochelle, not exactly a destination.

The Chalmerses lived on Newnans Lake, not far from here by my estimation, but this wasn't the route between their home and the high school. This was at least a mile out of the way. My mind turned over the possible reasons for Mason to be traveling this way on a Friday night, but I couldn't come up with one.

And why toss his phone out here at all? Why not just leave it at home or pawn it for some extra cash or, if he really wanted to throw us off his trail, put it on a bus. Either Mason wanted us to think something bad had happened to him….

Or something bad happened to him.

My mother was speaking to Dare in soothing tones when I arrived on the scene. She assured him they were doing everything within their power and there was no reason to panic. "We have no proof of foul play," she said, which was really the best she could offer. Gut feelings didn't translate to a crime being committed.

"Hey, Dare." I touched his shoulder lightly. Mom nodded and said she had to get back to the lab, clearly passing off the responsibility of calming Dare to me. Dare swallowed thickly and wiped the tears from his eyes. I'd only ever seen him cry before on stage, and those were crocodile tears. These ones made his eyes red and puffy. They looked very real and painful.

"How's it going, buddy?" I asked.

He shook his head and lifted his face to look at me. With his ashen complexion, greasy hair, and bloodshot eyes, he looked completely lost.

"It's not good, Charlie. Not good at all."

I didn't know if he meant for himself or his brother. Maybe both. I instinctively took him in my arms. He was a little taller than me but not as thick. His bones felt too sharp as he crumpled against me like a brittle leaf, leaning heavily on my shoulders. I hugged him tighter, knowing how desperate he must be to be held. After my father died, an officer came to the house to give us the news. I needed someone to hold me, and my mom was too much of a wreck herself. The officer, Sergeant Tallis, held me for a while until I could stand again. It wasn't like my dad hugging me, but it was what I needed at the time.

Joey lifted his head and watched us like a dog guarding its master. His face was splotchy and red—probably the reason for the hat. He looked like he could use a hug too. After another heavy moment, Dare gathered himself up and wiped his arm across his face, snuffling a bit. "Sorry about that."

"Don't be sorry. This is stressful. And scary."

"Yeah." Dare squinted and took a look around. "All these people came out here for Mason."

"And for you too."

He smiled, or tried to. "People really care, huh?"

"Of course they do."

"You been out here all morning?" His eyes crinkled in the corners like he felt bad for me.

"Yeah. I'm with the Eastview pep squad." I nodded in their direction. Tameka turned away like she hadn't been watching us.

"I hope they're treating you well."

"They're fine. We found a couple of gators but not much else."

"That's good, I guess," Dare said.

I nodded, even though not really. Clues were always a good thing, even if you didn't like the outcome.

"I should join a crew." Dare glanced around with a wild and desperate yearning in his eyes, almost like he was searching for Mason. I placed a hand on his shoulder.

"Have you slept lately, Dare?"

He shook his head. "Not much. I can't sleep in our house... knowing Mason is... out there...." He drifted off and cleared his throat again, seeming to disappear inside his mind for a moment. My mother said he'd been having trouble finishing his sentences.

I suspected he hadn't eaten anything either. He wasn't in any kind of shape to join a search party, and if Mason's body did turn up, I wouldn't want Dare to be the one to discover it. I surveyed the field. There were plenty of people out here already—GPD, the Alachua County Sheriff's department, FWC park rangers, parents, teachers, and most of our high school student body as well. They wouldn't miss me. Someone needed to take care of Dare.

"Why don't you come back to my house?" I asked. "You can take a shower, maybe eat something."

"I look like shit, don't I?" He stared at me, searching for the truth. Others might lie to him, thinking it was in his best interest, but not me. In this situation he needed someone to be straight with him.

"You've looked better."

Dare's shoulders slumped in surrender. "All right. Let me find my folks."

Dare handed Joey his keys—they must have driven here together. Joey gave him a bro-hug, and Dare kissed his cheek. Then Dare went over to where his parents were interfacing with Lieutenant Hartsfield. He seemed to have taken on the task of handling Dare's parents so my mom could get some work done. Just from my limited interaction with the Chalmerses, I didn't envy Hartsfield one bit.

Dare's mother barely acknowledged him, and I recalled what my mom had said about the comparisons taking place in the household. I wondered if his parents were just focused on finding Mason or if their interaction spoke to a larger pattern of behavior.

Dare followed me back to my car. He was a physical person—both the brothers were—but with Dare his movements reflected his mood. When he was joking around with friends or performing on stage, his posture was expansive, and he gestured grandly with his arms, his face always miming for laughs or tears. Now, as we walked along the road's shoulder to where my car was parked, his back was hunched and he rubbed along the outside of his jeans almost compulsively. His attention alternated between jumping at any little noise and long stretches of silence. The leaves crunched under our feet like potato chips. It hadn't rained in a few days and the weather was dry, which meant whatever evidence was out there was still fresh. We arrived at my car, and I opened the door for him. It wasn't chivalry; he hadn't slept in more than forty-eight hours, and he wasn't processing correctly.

"You want to talk about it?" I asked once he was seated in my decades-old Acura. It smelled like Boots. There was always a fine layer of dog hair on the upholstery and my clothes as well—the downside of having a dog as your literal best friend. I didn't expect Dare to share anything with me, but I wanted him to know he could talk if he felt like it.

"The cops keep telling us he's probably fine, blowing off steam or whatever, but I know Mason. He wouldn't cut me out like this. He'd never just… leave me. Without even a text…."

I nodded; I'd assumed the same. "You think he's in trouble?"

"I spent all night looking for him. It wasn't even that cold outside, but I shivered the whole night through. And even now…." Dare gripped his upper arms, which were covered in goose bumps, the fine blond hairs standing at a slant.

What an odd thing to say. "What do you think it means, Dare?"

"Mason is cold. Freezing cold." His hooded eyes searched the landscape outside my windshield while his mouth twisted up in anguish, as though he were trying not to bawl. "I don't think he's in trouble, Charlie. I think it's already too late."

CHAPTER 4

I DIDN'T necessarily believe in ghosts, but when Dare said those words to me, I felt a chill race up my spine and settle like icy fingers on the back of my neck. I reached over and grabbed hold of his hand. It was slow to warm. I reminded myself this was not a romantic gesture but one of comfort.

"You're not alone in this, Dare."

He nodded and rubbed at his eyes again, as though embarrassed by his emotions.

Once at my house, Boots greeted us both with ample tail wagging and sloppy kisses. I rarely brought friends over anymore, so Boots was a little overwhelmed with whom to adore first. Dare solved Boots's conundrum by dropping to his knees so he could be properly venerated.

"I've always wanted a dog," Dare said, scratching Boots's back and turning his face so Boots could lick one cheek and then the other as though it were a slobbery shave. I let Boots love on him a bit more, then called him off.

"Your parents aren't dog people?" I asked.

"No, it's not that. Mason's allergic."

"Any other allergies?" I asked, trying to sound nonchalant about it.

"No, I'm the one with the bad allergy—stinging insects."

"Do you go into anaphylactic shock?"

"Yeah. I have to keep my EpiPen on me all the time." He patted his jeans where there was a special pocket that ran along the outside of the regular one, long and narrow, one I hadn't noticed before. He must have had a tailor sew the pocket special into his pants.

"Not many people know about it. I got stung once when we were ten...." He stopped as though remembering. "Mason and I were out in the woods. He had to carry me home."

"You're lucky he was there."

"Yeah, he saved my life. After that our parents got us tested. Mason's allergy was dander, but he only gets congested and sometimes breaks out in a rash. That's probably why I went into theater after that, to stay indoors."

There was a far better chance of not getting stung by a wasp inside an auditorium than on a playing field. It was interesting to consider how something as arbitrary as an allergy might steer a person toward one passion or another.

"You were really good as the Phantom," I said, finally voicing the admiration I'd held on to for months now.

He mustered up a wry grin. "Thanks, Charlie."

I hoped desperately in that moment for Mason to return home safely. Dare's spirit would be irrevocably changed if he lost his brother. I should know. Losing my dad crushed mine.

Dare wanted to shower, so I showed him to the bathroom and gave him a fresh towel and a change of clothes. I told him to take his time, but he was in there so long I started to worry he might have fallen asleep and hit his head or something. I knocked on the door, and he said he'd be out in a minute.

He came out wearing my sweats and a T-shirt. His dirty clothes were rolled up in a tight ball. My pants were slung low on his slim hips, which caught my attention. His ankles were peeking out the bottom. I asked him if he wanted anything to eat, and he said he'd rather lie down if that was all right with me.

"Can you hang with me?" he asked, like a little kid who didn't want to be left alone in the dark. He stretched out on the couch, then curled around an afghan my grandmother had crocheted for us a long time ago. Boots settled in beside him, and Dare scooted backward to make room. I put on a PBS documentary about the Vietnam War and sat at the other end of the couch. Dare dug his toes into the outside of my thigh—I don't think he realized he was doing it. Ten minutes into the program, he was asleep.

I didn't want to disturb him, so I did some googling on my phone to see if the media had reported on Mason's disappearance. The *Gainesville Sun* had a story, which described the Chalmerses as a well-known and prominent local family. It went into the background about their large land holdings, including the spring they leased to Nestlé, a water bottling company, much to the ire of local environmentalists. The story mentioned past legal action taken against the Chalmerses regarding the effects of the water withdrawals on surrounding springs.

The reporter also dug up the fact that the brothers had recently been awarded access to their trusts and said the circumstances surrounding Mason's disappearance were suspicious. There was a quote from

Mason's father saying they were focused on finding Mason and bringing him home safely, and another from Lieutenant Hartsfield asking anyone who had information to call the tip line. I thought again about Mason's trips to Café Risqué. Maybe he was cheating on Daniela, or maybe he was mixed up in something criminal. It couldn't hurt to go check it out for myself.

While the documentary explained the chemical origins of Agent Orange, I stole glances at Dare to make sure he was resting comfortably and allowed myself the simple pleasure of admiring him while he slept. His long eyelashes curled over the apples of his cheeks, and his wide mouth pouted a little while he slept. His fingers curled in the stitches of the afghan, and the way he clutched the blanket made him look so hopelessly vulnerable. When the next episode began, I left the TV on as background noise and went out to the kitchen to see what we had for dinner. Ground beef, refried beans, taco shells… it looked like tacos to me.

I'd just finishing sautéing the meat when Dare appeared in the doorway, one elbow crooked on the doorframe, the other absently rubbing his sleek belly. With his bedhead and sleepy eyes, I could easily imagine what he'd look like waking up in the morning, and it stirred a lust that was entirely inappropriate for our current situation. I concentrated on chopping lettuce rather than mentally undressing him.

"Smells good, Charlie," he said in a husky voice, sitting heavily at our kitchen table and propping himself up with his elbows. His hair was in such disarray that I wanted to reach over and comb it out of his eyes, but of course, I didn't.

I opened the fridge and asked him what he wanted to drink. "We've got milk, orange juice, cream soda…." And a bottle of whisky, but I wasn't going to offer that.

"Water's fine."

I poured him a glass from the filtered jug. We didn't keep bottled water in the house. We were in the camp of the environmentalists who despised the bottling company. Their overpumping was killing our springs—that was undeniable—but Dare's family was only partly at fault. It was the politicians who refused to regulate the permitting who deserved most of the blame.

Dare's eyes alighted on the refrigerator door.

"That's your dad." He was looking at an old picture of my mom, my dad, and me at the Hoggetowne Medieval Faire. My mom had a wreath of flowers in her hair, and I was holding a wooden sword and shield. I was eight at the time.

"Yep, that's him." We still had a lot of pictures of him scattered around the house. It took us a while to clear out my dad's belongings, and most of his stuff we never got rid of, just stored his clothes and things in the garage to be decided upon at a later date. I wouldn't want Dare to have to go through the pain of packing away his brother's belongings into boxes and bins. It was an admission the person was never coming back.

"You look like him," Dare said. "So serious."

I glanced over to see if he was mocking me, but it didn't seem that way. I had my dad's square face, deep-set brown eyes, and pensive expression. My dad's hair had been much darker and thinning, while mine was curly on top and in need of a trim. In the summer my hair turned lighter than it was normally.

Dare was right in that my dad had always been a serious kind of guy. He was a visiting professor of criminology and sociology at the University of Florida when he met my mother. She'd taken one of his advanced classes in criminal profiling. He encouraged her to apply to the FBI, but my mother grew up in Gainesville and liked working in the community. That was one of the things that became a conflict later in their marriage. Dad wanted to move to a bigger city, and Mom didn't.

In any case, my dad loved a good debate, and from a young age, he always told me to "question everything." He really drilled that into me. That, along with my mother's ethic of only trusting hard evidence, made me a pretty big skeptic.

"I miss him," Dare said dejectedly, and it took me a moment to remember that we were talking about Mason. "And it's not like when he's away at camp. It's like this deep hollow pit, and I'm standing on the edge of it. If I look down, I get terrified I'm never going to see him again."

I couldn't promise Dare his brother would come back, so I walked over and squeezed his shoulders lightly. I didn't know where my confidence to touch him came from; it just seemed like the right thing to do. Dare melted in my hands, leaned back into his chair and sighed deeply. I brushed the long sweep of hair out of his eyes and imagined kissing him there on his forehead, a tender kiss, like you'd give to a child. Then I caught myself and slowly backed away. His eyes followed me, a curious expression on his face.

"Do you want to make your own taco, or you want me to make it for you?" I asked, somewhat stiffly.

"You make it. I'm not picky."

I had a moment of doubt, worrying I was going to give him something he detested, but the ingredients were all pretty mild, except for the jarred salsa, which I just put on the table for him to add if he wanted it. I prepared three tacos for him, thinking even if he didn't eat them all, he still had the option. I made the same for myself, even though I'd filled up on pizza not too long ago. I didn't want Dare to feel awkward about eating alone. Dare pretty much zoned out while we ate. He put food in his mouth, chewed, and swallowed robotically and didn't seem to give much thought to the act itself.

"This is good," he said as an afterthought.

"Thanks."

He glanced up at me. "Please don't judge me by my manners these past couple days, Charlie."

I smiled wanly. "You don't have to be polite for me, Dare, or anyone else. Just deal with this in whatever way feels right."

Dare sighed, shoulders caving inward a little. "You're better than my therapist."

"Maybe you should see my doctor." I had a great therapist. I'd seen Dr. Rangala every other week for the past five years. I'd cried in his office more times than I could count. I even developed a mild crush on him for about a year. It didn't matter that he was straight and married and much older and not at all interested. Thankfully, those feelings passed.

"I'm here for you, Dare. Whatever you need."

His gray-green eyes searched mine. He set his remaining taco to the side and wiped his hands on the cloth napkin I provided him. "Thank you, Charlie."

The way he said it, the seriousness of his tone, and his somber demeanor made me pause. "Of course."

He licked his lips and studied me. "There is something I'd like your help with," he said, as though testing my offer.

"Anything," I said, leaning closer.

"Do you think you could...." He glanced around the kitchen to make sure we were alone, which of course we were. "Do you think you could investigate this?"

It seemed premature and yet, I also had a really bad feeling. Mason had no reason to run off like that, and even if he did, maybe I could find out where he went.

The worst feeling was the not knowing.

I started to answer when Boots gave a one-bark salute, followed by the jingle of keys at the front door. My mom came into the kitchen a minute later and stopped when she saw Dare sitting at our kitchen table. He stood quickly, the chair legs squealing against the linoleum. He seemed nervous, which was unusual. I'd never seen Dare nervous in my life.

"Hello again, Detective," Dare said with a deferent nod in Mom's direction. His eyes darted around the kitchen, like a marsh bird's zigzagging trajectory, before landing on me.

"How are you doing, Dare?" Mom's tone conveyed compassion. She cared; she really did.

"Oh, you know… as well as can be, I guess. Find anything?" he asked hopefully. I held my breath.

"We didn't find Mason's cell phone. The lab is running tests on some of the other objects we found, but there's nothing yet that links us to Mason."

"Oh," he said. "Is that a good thing?"

She maintained a soft smile. "I think so."

Dare sighed and tugged at his shirt as though just realizing he was wearing different clothing. "I should go." He picked up his bundle of clothes. "I'll give these back to you tomorrow, Charlie."

"I'll give you a ride home." I stood.

"No, it's okay. I feel like walking."

"You sure?" I didn't want Dare walking home alone, even though he'd probably argue he was perfectly capable of defending himself against an attacker. But what if there was a serial killer on the hunt, targeting teenaged boys when they were alone and vulnerable?

"I can walk you home, then." I whistled for Boots, who was licking his empty food bowl as if that would deliver him seconds.

"No, it's fine. I need some time to think." He glanced again at my mother. "Thanks again for having me over, or… you know."

"You're welcome, Dare."

I walked him out to the end of the driveway. Boots ran off to chase squirrels in the neighbor's yard. It was a communal kind of neighborhood where kids and pets ran wild. The sun was starting to set behind the pines, its warm golden glow dissected by the tall, reedy trees. The pines were at times comforting, like wise old friends, and at other times ominous and brooding. I supposed it depended on your mood.

I wanted Dare to start home so he'd get there before it was completely dark. I gave him another hug. Overall, he seemed a little better off than when I'd found him earlier that day, so in that way, I'd done my job. I hadn't given him an answer yet on whether I'd investigate his brother's disappearance. I hoped Mason would be waiting for him when he got home.

"Thanks for taking care of me today," Dare said, running a hand through his hair as though he was shy all of a sudden.

"You're welcome here anytime." I meant it.

As if knowing this was goodbye, Boots bounded over and planted his front paws on Dare's thighs.

"Boots, down." He only wagged his tail more furiously. The dog had selective hearing.

"One more kiss goodbye." Dare leaned down so Boots could lick his chin, which he did with enthusiasm. I called Boots over to me; I'd not have him make a spectacle of himself.

"Take care, Charlie," Dare said with a little wave.

"You too, Dare."

He ambled down the road, the late-afternoon light shining on his chestnut-colored hair, his head hanging low, his clothes tucked up under his arm. He gait was a bit uneven, like that old nursery rhyme about the crooked man who walked a crooked mile. I'd text him in a few minutes to make sure he got home safely. For now I geared myself up for another round of cat and mouse with my mother.

I was going to find out everything she knew.

MY MOTHER was tight-lipped with me that night. Not even my tacos could soften her up to tell me much more about the investigation, though perhaps it was because there wasn't much to tell. The Chalmerses were not happy that GPD's search had proved fruitless and consequently were already making threats about suing the department. My mom had also been up since 4:00 a.m., so she was a tad bit cranky.

"I was surprised to see Dare Chalmers in my kitchen this evening," Mom said, taking a sip of chilled white wine. She'd brought the bottle of wine home with her. White wine was her choice of alcohol when she was working on a case because if she got called in, she didn't want to be too inebriated. Whiskey was for when the case got hard. When I didn't comment on it, she continued. "I didn't realize you two were so close."

"We're friends. And I understand what he's going through."

I didn't need to make the connection for her; we'd gone through the same thing with my dad. For two days he was missing. The only thing worse was discovering him in a seedy hotel room off US 441, dead.

Mom set her rather large glass of wine on the table and primly wiped her mouth with her napkin. "We were able to pull Mason's phone records."

Finally, I thought. *Now we're getting somewhere.*

"Anything interesting?"

"The last call Mason received was from Dare. It lasted five minutes."

"Is that suspicious?"

"Dare didn't mention it in his interview."

"Did you ask him?"

She sighed. She thought I was being obtuse. "Dare also couldn't account for his time prior to arriving at Waffle Kingdom."

"What do you mean, 'couldn't account for his time'?"

"He said he was out driving."

"That seems legitimate."

"He was driving on back roads—no cameras, no stops, no people. And his phone records show him in the same vicinity as his brother."

"It's a small town. Can't a guy go for a drive without being accused of murder? Besides, why are you even talking alibis? There's no proof a crime's even been committed."

"Confirmation bias," she said.

I harrumphed at her insinuation that I couldn't be objective. "That was a low blow."

"Maybe, but until this investigation wraps up, I don't want you spending any more time with this boy than you have to."

Ever since school started up again, my mom had been riding me to make new friends. *Not everyone at that school hates you, Charlie*, she'd told me countless times. Maybe not the freshman, but even those who weren't affected by my bust took it personally. No one liked a narc—I'd proven it. Now I had a friend who was in the middle of a real crisis, and she was telling me to abandon him?

"I'm old enough to pick my own friends." I stood and pulled Boot's leash off the back door. She had no reason to accuse Dare of anything. It was obvious to me he was hurting. Having compassion for his situation didn't make me biased; it made me human. "I'm going for a walk. I hope no one in a five-mile radius is murdered, or I might become the prime suspect."

"Charlie," she groaned as I left, somewhat dramatically, out the back door, holding it open for Boots to follow me and letting the screen door slam behind us. Dare would be proud of my theatric exit.

I took a dirt path that wound through the woods behind our property, using a flashlight to guide us and Boots's nose to lead the way. If my mother was being completely objective about this case, then I should be a suspect as well. I'd had a previous run-in with Mason Chalmers, I'd spoken to him the afternoon he went missing, and on Friday night I was home alone with Boots.

Dogs don't make for the best alibis.

But as the investigator, I could rule myself out. How easily I'd slipped into that role. Part of it was because I wanted to help Dare, but another part was because I wanted to be the one to solve the puzzle first. Other kids got a rush from winning wrestling matches or performing on stage or acing a test. For me, it was helping to solve a crime and doing my part to make sure the person responsible was caught.

An animal scurried away on the forest floor, breaking a twig in its path. The pine needles rustled in the wind. *Shhh, shhh, shhh,* they said, keeping secrets. Boots stopped and growled, his neck fur thick and stiff. I listened for anything suspicious but heard nothing. I calmed Boots with a reassuring pat, and we continued on. I probably shouldn't be roaming the woods at night with a kidnapper on the loose, but then, Mason could just as likely be marrying an exotic dancer in Vegas at that very moment.

I sure hoped that was the case, for Dare's sake.

CHAPTER 5

BEING AN International Baccalaureate kid meant I didn't have a lot of classes with the "general population," as the IB teachers called them. They were a bit elitist about the program, which only served to feed the perception that we were intellectual snobs. In any case, the only classes we shared with Gen Pop were electives, and I usually chose more advanced placement classes over the arts or athletics, so my mom and I could save money on college tuition. I'd already decided I was going to study criminology at the University of Florida, if I got in. Mom thought I should apply to a few other schools, even some out of state, but I didn't want to leave Gainesville, or her and Boots for that matter. The three of us were a good team.

In any case, being in IB meant I had no classes with Dare or his group of friends and not much opportunity to ask questions. I did manage to find Tameka in the halls between third and fourth period and ask her a favor.

"Have you seen Daniela?" I asked.

"She's not at school, but she's been posting pictures of her and Mason all weekend." She made a gagging motion with her finger.

I'd seen the photos as well. It was unnerving how they almost seemed like tributes, as though Daniela realized their relationship was over. Was it because he'd been cheating on her, or was it for some other, more sinister reason?

"Can you keep an eye on her for me? Maybe take her temperature on this whole Mason situation?"

"Am I on the case then, Dick?" Tameka asked with a sly grin.

I smiled. I was actually starting to like the nickname. "I'd appreciate your help."

She nodded. "I'll get the dirt, but I'm not working for free. And I will collect."

She made the motion of "making it rain," and I only hoped I could afford her fee.

At lunch I usually read a book on the couches in the media center or played mindless games on my phone in some lesser-traveled corner of campus, but today I wanted to check in on Dare. Despite my mother's warning, I wasn't going to abandon him, especially with so many unknowns floating out there. I went to their usual hangout spot, under the shade of a sprawling live oak tree where there were usually a dozen or more people, but the only person present was Joey, picking the crusts off his sandwich and feeding them to the squirrels and birds swooping in to collect.

"Hey, Joey." I ducked into his circle of shade, feeling a bit like an intruder.

"Hey." He pulled his hat down lower over his eyes. Hats were against dress code, but I doubted anyone had bothered him about it that day.

I didn't know if my mom had spoken to him, but Joey might know something about Mason's whereabouts, whether he realized it or not. It certainly couldn't hurt to ask a few questions. I took another step closer and sat down across from him in the grass. I'd always known Joey to be the sarcastic and somewhat grumpy sidekick to the Chalmers twins—the third leg of their table, with the power to approve or exclude someone from their ever-widening circle—but he seemed in this moment very fragile and not at all like the wise guy he portrayed.

"How you doing, Joey?"

He glared at me from under the hooded brim of his hat. "How do you think I'm doing?"

From past experience I knew Joey didn't like attention or talking about himself—he usually let the twins have the spotlight. He also had a very low tolerance for small talk. The thing about the twins, and Joey too, was that even though they were incredibly popular, they didn't get there by shitting on other people. They didn't bully others or put down people who didn't deserve it—they just made high school really fun and exciting, so you wanted to be around them to see what happened next. You could go to an Eastview party that was jocks mixed with drama kids and everyone got along fine. Which was why targeting Mason last year was pretty stupid on my part, because even while Mason and Dare seemed to have gotten over it, no one else at the school had.

"I heard Daniela stayed home today. Did Dare also?"

"No, he's walking the track." Joey jerked his thumb in that direction. Maybe Dare was trying to get out his nervous energy.

"Were you at the party Friday night?"

Joey glanced up briefly and then nodded. "I got there early to set up. Daniela was supposed to help me, but she was late."

"When did people start arriving?"

"About seven. We wanted everyone ready for when Dare and Mason got there."

I pulled out my phone and sketched a timeline. Mom told me the high school had footage of Mason pulling out of the student parking lot a little before seven. The cell phone was thought to be discarded by 9:00 p.m., which meant if someone had abducted Mason in that time period, it wasn't Joey. I didn't like to think of my classmates as potential suspects, but I also wasn't ruling anyone out.

"Where was Daniela?"

Joey looked at me warily. "Daniela didn't do anything."

I studied my phone without saying anything to contradict him. I hoped the awkward silence would balloon until he felt compelled to speak. Joey glanced around, looking uncomfortable. I waited.

"She got there a little before nine."

"And the party was supposed to start at eight?"

"Yeah."

"Where did Daniela say she'd been?"

Joey shook his head and threw another piece of bread on the ground. "She didn't."

"Did you ask her?"

"Yeah. I mean, she stuck me with decorating. I don't know how to tie a balloon or hang streamers. I did the best I could."

"So, what did she say?"

"She said *nowhere.*"

Nowhere. That wasn't very encouraging. "What was her demeanor when she got there?"

"I don't know. She seemed... out of it."

"Drunk?"

"No, just... weird. She wasn't acting like herself."

"Was she angry?"

"I don't know. I'm not a mind reader."

I backed off. Joey seemed protective of Daniela. Perhaps it was my reputation for getting them in trouble. Or loyalty to Mason. Or something else altogether.

"When did Dare get there?"

"A little after nine. Mason was supposed to meet him at Waffle Kingdom, but he never showed."

"And when Dare arrived, what was he like?"

"Freaked out. He kept calling Mason's cell phone. He sent people out to look for him. The whole vibe in the house was tense. Around midnight Dare sent everyone home except Daniela and me. He called his folks, and then they called the cops."

Either Dare was genuinely concerned, or it was a pretense to shift blame away from himself. I didn't like how so much of this case depended on my assessment of Dare's character. If he had a valid alibi, this would be so much easier.

"Did it seem unusual that Dare would worry so quickly?"

"Not really. Everyone we knew was at the house, so where would Mason be? And the two of them are like that. If Mason doesn't text him back, Dare will call me. Or Daniela. And Mason does the same with Dare's drama friends. Their parents are kind of hands-off, so they've always had to look out for each other."

Mason saved Dare's life when he got stung by a wasp, and Dare found Mason in the woods after a dirt bike accident. I thought of that expression, my brother's keeper, except that was a bad example because Cain was a killer.

A cold wind blew then, and my arms raised up with goose bumps.

"Was there anyone you thought should be at the party who wasn't there?" I asked.

Joey opened his mouth and then shut it again. "Some of the guys from his wrestling team weren't there yet, but I figured it was because they had practice."

I made a list of people to talk to: Daniela De Costa, Peter Orr, Coach Gundry, the staff of Café Risqué…. My finger hovered over my phone, hesitating. I added one more name to the list: Dare Chalmers.

"Is there anything else you can remember, either from that day or at the party that seemed unusual to you? Something that at the time you dismissed, but now, looking back, seems really strange?"

Joey pulled off his hat and traced the rim of it with his thumb. His lower lip jutted out, causing his chin to pucker.

"There is one thing," Joey said at last, obviously conflicted about it. I was okay with that. I could be patient. "Daniela was still wearing her cheerleading uniform."

I tried to find the significance in that; I'd seen her in her uniform at school more often than not, including the day of the pep rally. "Is that strange?" I asked.

"She wears it for games and stuff, but she doesn't, like, party in it. She always goes home and changes into something—I don't know—cute. And her makeup and hair were a mess. That's not like her."

Perhaps because she'd just found out Mason had been unfaithful and did something awful to get back at him.

"Was she wearing Mason's jacket?"

"No."

"Did she mention a fight between them?"

"No, but they fight all the time. And it's not like we talk about that stuff. Look, whatever you're thinking, it wasn't her. I mean, she's annoying as hell and petty, but she wouldn't hurt Mason."

I couldn't tell if he was trying to convince me of it or himself.

"Do you know if Mason was cheating on her?"

Joey's eyes cast downward, and he studied what remained of his sandwich. "I don't know anything about that."

"But you suspect it."

"Don't put words in my mouth," he said severely, eyes flashing with anger. Joey was loyal to Mason, and he wasn't going to say anything that might paint him in a bad light. I understood that. He was also worried for his missing friend, which probably heightened his sense of duty. I knew when to back off.

"Thanks, Joey. This has been really helpful."

"Does this mean you're going to help find Mason?"

He had that same hopeful expression as Dare when he asked. I didn't want to make any promises, unsure of what I could deliver. "I'm just asking questions." As an afterthought I added, "For Dare."

Joey nodded. "Good."

I told Joey to text me if he thought of anything else, then headed out to the football field, where Dare was drifting in and out of lanes and pingponging back onto the track when he hit grass. I sat on the bleachers and waited for him to come around again, hoping he'd notice me without having to call out to him.

About halfway around he glanced up and saw me. Instead of finishing the lap, he cut across the field and joined me on the bleachers.

"Any news?" he asked. I wasn't sure if he meant through GPD's efforts or my own.

"I talked to Joey. I want to talk to Daniela too."

Dare's brow furrowed a bit. "She's not here today."

I nodded. "You get any sleep last night?" If anything, the hollows under his eyes looked darker and more chronic. His clothes were wrinkled as well, like he'd picked up whatever was lying around on the floor this morning or slept in it overnight.

"No," he admitted. "I keep imagining the worst possible thing. And it just feels wrong to sleep or eat or do anything while Mason is missing."

"You have to take care of yourself." I thought back to the last time I saw Mason in the passenger seat of my car and the concern in his voice when he warned me not to harm Dare. I considered telling Dare about it, but I didn't want to complicate things between us. "Mason wouldn't want you to suffer like this."

Dare shrugged and squinted across the field to the athletic parking lot, where a police cruiser was pulling in. The car parked, and a deputy got out of the driver's side, shielded his eyes from the sun, and surveyed the field. A lady in plainclothes climbed out of the passenger side. My mother. She spied me and Dare across the track and said something to the deputy, then started to make her way across the field.

"They found him," Dare said and bolted toward her. It looked like he was trying not to run, which made for a ragged, hiccupping gait with his long scarecrow legs. I jogged after him and arrived at about the same time.

"Shouldn't you be in class?" Mom said to me with momitude.

"It's lunch," I said back with teenitude.

"Did you find Mason?" Dare asked.

Mom placed a hand on his shoulder. Only I knew that meant it wasn't good news. My stomach clenched, and I braced myself for whatever she had to report.

"We found some tire tracks," Mom said, "at the edge of Newnans Lake. We have a crew of divers out now investigating. Your parents are there. They asked that we come get you."

Dare swallowed, and his shoulders caved as a look of bleak understanding washed over him. "It's Mason," he said fatally.

"We don't know anything yet." Mom was trying to sound positive, which only meant it was as bad as I thought. "Why don't you get your things, and we'll give you a ride there?"

"I'm ready now." Dare glanced over at me. "Charlie's coming too."

Mom stiffened. "Charlie has class."

"Charlie can miss an afternoon," I said. Mom shot me a look.

"Please, Detective, I need him there. Please?"

It was the second *please* that got my mom; it was so desperate and sad. There was some quality about Dare that made you want to protect him. Certainly Mason had felt the same way. Mom just nodded tersely and turned on her heel. I jogged back and grabbed my backpack from the bleachers and Dare's too—he was ready to abandon it completely—and chased after them to the police cruiser. The deputy opened the door, and we climbed into the back. I'd done several ride-alongs with my mom, and I always knew a police cruiser by its smell—metallic, like biting a coin, mixed with the stress sweat of past perps who'd made the journey to the police station. The entire back seat was made of hard plastic, because people did strange and nasty things in the back of police cruisers.

Dare jammed his hands between his knees and rocked back and forth the whole way there. I placed a hand on his shoulder just to let him know he wasn't alone.

We were traveling on Hawthorne Road, not far from where the search party was held. The cruiser pulled off the road onto a path that was just rutted tracks from previous traffic. We were surrounded on all sides by towering pines, which in the moment felt quite claustrophobic. The "path" ended somewhat abruptly in a dead end at the lake's edge, where there were about a half dozen police cruisers, some unmarked, and a diving team with equipment. Dare's parents stood on the banks, behind the crime scene tape, tense and vigilant.

"I drove right past here," Dare muttered and then, as though realizing I was still standing beside him, he turned to me. "Friday night when I was waiting for Mason to meet me, I drove by here."

"What time was that?" I asked, pulling up my timeline.

"I don't know, quarter to eight?"

"Did you see anything?"

"No." Dare shook his head. "Nothing."

"Did Mason tell you he was headed out here?"

"No. He just called and told me he'd be late. Actually he texted me, and I called him back. I gave him shit for it, because I knew people would be at our house already." Dare drew his hands down his face. "God, I was such an asshole."

I was sure it was just Dare's annoyance at his brother for flaking. "Do you know why Mason would be out here?"

"No. He doesn't go for long drives like I do, says it's a waste of gas. His truck's a gas-guzzler. It's so strange...."

He trailed off and glanced back toward the road.

"What's strange?"

"I never come out here either. I just… had a feeling. You know?" He looked to me for validation, but I couldn't give it to him. I'd never followed someone based on a gut feeling. I also didn't like to think about what that meant: if GPD found something in the lake, Dare's admission put him at the scene of the crime.

Dare looked bewildered by it all as he walked over to his parents and greeted them. The head of the dive unit conferred with Lieutenant Hartsfield, who communicated that to his team via radio. Hartsfield then went over to Dare's parents to give them an update. I edged in a little closer.

"We found Mason's truck," Hartsfield said. "The license plate matches. We're getting a tow truck out here to pull out the vehicle and see what's what."

Hartsfield's face looked grim. Dare's mother turned away and folded neatly into Mr. Chalmers's chest like a bird nesting down for the night. His arms went around her to comfort her. Dare crouched down in a bed of pine needles and buried his head in his hands. I squatted next to him.

"He's dead," Dare whispered. "My brother is dead."

"You don't know that." I tried to comfort him, but my words sounded hollow, even to me.

"I know it, Charlie. I've known since Friday. Somebody killed my brother, and when I find out who…."

Dare's face reminded me of Boots's snarl when he sensed danger. The tendons in his wrists were taut and straining. His hands were two fists, balled up with tension. His voice was a growl when he said, "I'm going to fucking tear them apart."

DREDGING MASON'S truck out of the lake was a production. The first tow truck didn't have a cable long enough. Then, once a longer cable was secured, the muck acted like a suction cup, and the one truck didn't have enough power to get the job done. Its tires got stuck in the mud, causing the engine to keen in a terrible way. They had to use a second truck to tow the first one. Finally, with two trucks working in tandem, they were able to free Mason's vehicle from the swampy bottom. GPD didn't want to pull too hard and disturb potential evidence, so the actual towing of the truck went inch by devastating inch.

Dare alternated between rocking back and forth on his heels and pacing the outer perimeter of the crime scene. His concentration was focused on the activity in the lake, the tow trucks' slow progress, and Mason's F-150 as it slowly breached the surface like a whale coming up for air.

As soon as the truck was on dry land, the crime scene unit descended in full gear, and no one was allowed to cross the yellow tape, including my mother. She stood near their makeshift headquarters with a radio, giving orders and requesting information. A young woman in business casual clothing and waders stood next to her, taking notes. Normally I'd be doing that job, which I'll admit stung a little. Meanwhile the crime scene specialists worked with industry, dusting the door handles, the tailgate, the sides and hood of the truck. They filled vials and swabbed samples. I stood as close as I could get away with and made notes of my own. The truck appeared to lean to one side, though it was hard to tell whether it was the vehicle itself or the swampy ground.

When the techs finally got around to opening the driver's side door, a gush of water surged from the truck, and a spherical object rolled out along with it. At first I thought it was only a soccer ball.

It was not.

My stomach turned, and I had to fight down the urge to vomit. My first thought was to make sure Dare hadn't seen it. He and his parents, thankfully, were angled toward the passenger side. At the same time, the techs realized what they'd stumbled upon and took a step back. One lifted the radio and sent a message to my mother, who quickly activated her team to form a human blockade. The officers moved slowly but coordinated, trying their best to make it appear casual and accidental. Mom glanced my way, and without any instruction I strode over to where Dare and his parents were waiting.

"GPD is asking that we move back a little farther," I told them, making up something that sounded official. I spread my arms wide and herded them backward. They shuffled away, out of the line of sight, and then Dare's mother recognized me.

"You're that boy who got Mason in trouble last year," she said with an angry look on her face.

"Yes, ma'am. Charlie Schiffer."

She took the opportunity to tell me what she thought of me, which wasn't very much. I nodded along with her assessment, but I wasn't giving her my full attention because Dare had caught on that there was activity happening on the driver's side of his brother's truck. He broke away from his parents and strode in that direction. An officer tried to intercept him, but Dare pushed past. His tennis shoe got caught in the muck, and he nearly stumbled but regained his balance and continued on with purpose. I jogged after him, but I couldn't prevent Dare from seeing what was sure to give him nightmares for the rest of his life.

The forensics team was carefully bagging Mason's severed head.

CHAPTER 6

DARE WENT into shock. It happened so slowly that nobody noticed at first. His mother was hysterical, but Dare just… shut down. By the time I realized what was going on, the color in his face had drained away and his lips paled around the edges. Then his eyes glazed over and rolled back into his head. His body went limp. I caught him as he was falling and laid him out on a grassy patch of ground.

"Medic," I shouted to the EMTs on duty. Dare's hands were like ice as I tried to massage feeling back into them. "Dare." I shook his shoulders and felt for his pulse—sluggish but regular. A medic took over, checking his vitals and issuing commands. Dare's eyes slowly opened, then closed again as though he didn't want to face the realization that his brother was dead—not just dead, but murdered—and this was his attempt to stave it off for just a little while longer.

The medics wrapped Dare in a reflective blanket and massaged his arms and legs to get his blood circulating properly. They wanted to take him to the hospital, but Dare refused, so they set him up on the tailgate of the ambulance and gave him a juice box. He didn't drink it, though, just sat there with a vacant expression, the little plastic straw still attached to the box. I wanted to stick it in for him and hold the straw to his mouth, but I didn't want to treat him like a child.

My constitution was a little gray as well. Even though I'd looked at countless crime scene photos, I'd never actually seen a dead body in real life, or a severed head that had been in the water for three days. Mason's face had bloated so much that his jowls looked like grouper cheeks. His lips were purple and swollen as well, and his eyes had a bluish film over them like an early onset of glaucoma. He was almost unrecognizable, and it was hard to reconcile the waxy horror with the mischievous, smiling face I'd grown up with. It felt unreal, as though his head were only a prop in some theater production. Perhaps that was just my mind's way of coping.

Everything I thought to say to Dare seemed wrong, so I simply sat beside him and monitored his vitals. Neither of his parents came to check on him. His mother had to be medicated and taken home by a friend of the family. Dare's father paced back and forth in the muck, ruining his dress shoes and slacks. The sight of his pants all wet and dirty like that bothered me more than it should have, all things considered. My mother was doing damage control, keeping everyone extraneous away from the crime scene so it wouldn't be contaminated, while also consulting with the forensics team on how best to proceed.

Even though I felt sick to my stomach and wanted nothing more than to go home, I had to be Dare's eyes and ears. I figured that was why he'd brought me here in the first place. Having a job to do made me feel a little more in control and a little less unsettled. If I couldn't comfort Dare, I could at least take notes, so I listened in on the deputies' conversations and the radio traffic to deduce the following.

Mason had been murdered. They weren't sure if it was by decapitation or if he was dead already when it happened.

The keys were still in the ignition and the driver's side window was down, which meant the killer could have driven Mason's truck into the lake, presumably to hide it, and swum out the open window.

Mason's head had been lodged in the steering wheel.

His body had not yet been found.

In the hour since he'd discovered his brother was dead, Dare hadn't uttered a word and still looked ghostly pale. I wished there were a counselor present, someone who could say the right things to comfort him, but GPD was too busy collecting evidence and support staff had yet to arrive. I felt trapped between saying the wrong thing and saying nothing at all. Dare had discarded his juice box, unopened, and kept his hands clutched between his knees, rocking ever so slightly as though in a trance.

I debated for several minutes on the best course of action, but it seemed to me that Dare had had enough of the crime scene for one day. There was nothing to be gained by having him present. I hopped off the tailgate and stood in front of him, forcing his attention outward. Very slowly I stilled his knees with my hands, grabbed his fingers, and softly squeezed, similar to how I'd massaged them before when I was trying to help the paramedics circulate his blood.

"I should take you home," I told him.

Dare's eyes slowly focused, his chin lifted ever so slightly, and he blinked, still somewhat catatonic. "I… I can't leave Mason."

There was a crew setting up lights in the ashen twilight. I suspected they'd be here for several more hours, collecting evidence and photographing the scene. There were storm clouds gathering above us. I hoped the rain held off until they'd finished. A rainstorm would erase any tire tracks or footprints that could help us find Mason's killer.

"Why don't you come to my house?"

He stared at me for a while—minutes, it seemed—then his shoulders heaved and he sighed in resignation. Before he could change his mind, I called to a deputy for a ride, since both our cars were still at the high school. I told Mr. Chalmers I was taking Dare to my house. He nodded absently and looked past me to the rows of pines leaning over us like hunched old men in reproach. If only trees could talk.

"My boy," he said, broken-hearted. "Somebody did that to my boy."

DARE WASN'T hungry or thirsty. In fact, he was so out of it that he was barely moving on his own. I led him to my room and helped him take off his muddy shoes, thinking I could perhaps clean them for him before the stains set in. I built him a nest of blankets and pillows on my bed and turned on the classical radio station for ambiance—it was what I listened to at night before falling asleep. Boots seemed to know that Dare needed comfort and made himself available for cuddling.

"Can you stay with me a minute, Charlie?" Dare asked. His voice was muffled and his face mostly buried in a pillow.

"Sure thing, Dare."

I sat on my desk chair and tried to read a book I'd been neglecting with only my desk lamp for light so Dare could sleep. Really I just stared at the words swimming on the page and tried to make sense of it all. I was still in a state of disbelief. Mason Chalmers had been murdered, less than a mile from here, on his birthday of all days, and it was gruesome. It seemed like only a serial killer could do something so ghastly—someone seriously fucked-up in the head—but if so, why target Mason? Was he simply in the wrong place at the wrong time, or had his killer been stalking him, waiting for an opportunity when he was alone and vulnerable? Would the killer go after Dare next? That was the thought that chilled me to the bone and the reason I suggested Dare come with me to my house. At least here I knew I could protect him.

My mom got home around two in the morning. I was sleeping on the couch when I heard the sound of her keys dropping into the ceramic bowl in the kitchen. She groaned in exhaustion as her shadow on the living room wall stretched toward the ceiling.

"Charlie?" she asked, rounding the corner.

"In here." I turned on the nearby lamp so she wouldn't startle. Boots briefly made an appearance, then trotted back to my bedroom to be with Dare, leaving the door open behind him.

"Why aren't you in your room?" she asked.

"Dare's in there."

"Dare Chalmers?" she asked in a whisper that sounded more like a shout.

"He needed a place to crash. He didn't want to go home."

Mom sat down on the coffee table, her knees bumping up against the couch. Even though her voice was dampened, her gestures were at full volume.

"Charlie, what did I tell you? We're looking at a murder investigation here, and Dare is a person of interest."

"He didn't do it, Mom," I said tiredly and rubbed the sleep from my eyes.

"You don't know that," she insisted. "People lie, Charlie. People cheat and hide things—big things." She stopped there. I wondered if we were still talking about Dare or if she was referring to my dad.

I didn't want to argue with her. Until my mother found a better suspect, she was going to assume Dare was guilty. I couldn't blame her maternal instinct to want to keep me safe, and even though I was breaking one of my own rules, I knew in my gut Dare didn't do it.

"Did you find the body?" I asked.

She sighed. "No."

"Any ideas on where it is?"

"Hartsfield thinks the gators got it."

That was a disturbing thought, and one I didn't want to imagine. There were gators everywhere in Gainesville. One had just been spotted recently on our high school campus crossing an outdoor alleyway, traveling between a ditch and a water retention pond, one of the hazards of building a town in the middle of a swamp.

I'd overheard Mason's head was caught in the steering wheel. "Does Hartsfield think the gators tore the body from the head?"

"No, the head was severed cleanly." She made a chopping motion with her hand like an axe. "One fast, hard chop."

"With what?"

"We don't know yet, but it would take some strength to sever the spinal cord and vertebrae with just one blow."

"Is that how he died?" If that was the case, Mason must have been restrained. It was terrible to think Mason might have been alive for that final death blow.

"We'll have to wait for the medical examiner's report, though it's going to be harder without a body to examine." Mom glanced past me to my bedroom door. "In the meantime I don't want you involved in this case, on any level. Or with that young man."

"Dare's a friend, Mom. Boots likes him."

"Dare could be a murderer, Charlie, and Boots isn't the best judge of character."

We stared at each other. It was a standoff. Mom liked to joke that the only person she'd ever known more stubborn than herself was me. Except at times like these, neither of us was laughing.

"Remember, I'm still the parent," she said as her final reprimand. She kissed the top of my head and stood. "I'm beat. I want Dare Chalmers out of my house first thing in the morning."

I said good night and fell back into the couch, unable to fall asleep right away. I was still ruminating on the unusual circumstances of Mason Chalmers's murder and the peculiar relationship I'd had with the Chalmers twins over the years. Watching Mischief and Mayhem from a distance, being entertained by their antics, observing with a kind of vague envy at their brotherhood and the fun they created in a universe all their own. And now Dare Chalmers was sleeping in my bedroom, having lost his other half in a most gruesome and terrifying way. I wasn't a superstitious person, but Mason reaching out to me last Friday afternoon after months of no contact almost felt like an omen.

"Charlie?"

I shot up to a seated position on the couch. Dare was hanging back in the doorway to my bedroom. The moonlight from the window filtered in and cast a pale glow on his sharply featured face. The Phantom, I thought, only without the mask.

"Hey, Dare. Can't sleep?" I patted the couch next to me, and he shuffled over. His eyes were swollen from crying, which he must have done in the bedroom. I didn't turn on the light and expose him. I could see his pain well enough.

"I heard your mom come in." He slouched forward with his elbows on his knees and wouldn't meet my eyes. "She thinks I did it, doesn't she?"

Dare must have overheard our conversation. I kicked myself for not making sure my bedroom door was closed and that he was asleep.

"It's her job to suspect everyone, Dare. She doesn't know you like I do."

"Do you know me, Charlie?" His eyes searched mine, and I saw something flicker there, like a match burning in a sooty pan. Then his eyes softened and he glanced away miserably. "Do any of us really know anyone?"

I sensed he was asking a much larger question, one I couldn't answer. I thought of my father and all the secrets he'd kept from us, his own family. His depression and thoughts of suicide. His loneliness and feelings of despair. He hid all of that from us. You can never know what's in the heart and mind of another person. You can't know all the things they don't tell you.

"No, we don't."

His sigh had a note of sadness in it. "I agree with your mom that you shouldn't see me or be involved with this, but I need you, Charlie." That yearning in his voice, it was almost musical the way it struck me on a very basic level. "I know it's selfish of me to ask you this, but…. Mason was hiding things from me, from all of us, and my friends—" He glanced away, looking guilty. "I can't trust them to be honest with me. We all know each other too well… and not well enough." His brooding eyes met mine again. "You weren't fooled by us, Charlie."

"What do you mean, Dare?" He was speaking in riddles again, and I was having trouble keeping up.

"You saw Mason as he is when you busted him for cheating. You didn't let his charm or his money or his popularity at our school influence you. You saw something wrong going on, and you did something about it. That took a lot of guts."

In all the time since it had happened, no one—not even my mother— had seen it like that. No one *ever* took my side. Like when your favorite celebrity is exposed as a criminal and everyone jumps in to deny it, the student body didn't want to face the fact that Mason Chalmers lied and cheated, knowingly. Everyone wanted to maintain that illusion of the golden boy, and when I exposed him, I'd ruined that fantasy for everyone.

People really can't handle the truth.

"I need your help, Charlie. I need you to find whoever killed Mason, because I think it was someone close to us. And I can't be objective anymore."

"My mom is the best homicide detective on the force," I told him. And what if the murderer turned out to be one of his closest friends? Could Dare really handle it?

"But she doesn't know Mason. She doesn't know what it's like to be in high school—all the pressure and expectations. And she doesn't have access the way you do."

In crime solving you never go with your instincts, especially if the evidence doesn't support it. I'd be doing Mason a disservice if I eliminated Dare as a suspect.

"I can't rule you out, Dare. Not yet, at least."

He nodded. "Then investigate me too. You don't have to tell me anything you're not supposed to. I just want to know who did that to my brother." He closed his eyes and leaned back against the couch. His grief had utterly depleted him. Within seconds tears were spilling out the corners of his eyes and making trails past his temples.

I knew all the reasons why this was a bad idea, but Dare needed me, and so did Mason. I had a unique skill set, and it felt wrong not to at least ask a few questions. I glanced toward my mom's bedroom. Even though she couldn't hear us, I kept my voice low. "I'll see what I can find out."

He sniffed and wiped his eyes, then grabbed for my hand and shook it, sealing my commitment.

"Thanks, Charlie." He sat up and glanced around as if expecting my mother to pop in and find us scheming, or maybe that was just my guilty conscience. "I should go." He stood and headed for the door.

"Let me drive you home. Whoever killed Mason is still out there."

"Maybe they'll come for me next," he said, voicing my exact fear.

"Doesn't that scare you?"

He traced one elegant finger along the doorframe and said sinisterly, "I wish they would."

He left, shutting the door softly behind him. I watched his slanted walk through the window until he reached the end of our street. The deadbolt made a dull click as I engaged it.

Their relationship had always fascinated me, and even with my mother's warning and the full realization that Dare could be a murderer, I couldn't help but dissect everything I knew about the Chalmerses. I placed those threads into neat little boxes inside my mind, to be unraveled and examined later, along with the most critical questions: Who wanted Mason Chalmers dead, enough to murder him so viciously?

And why?

CHAPTER 7

AROUND HERE rumors spread faster than gonorrhea, both unfortunate side effects of living in a small town. The gossip mill could be hell on your love life, but it was great for sussing out the truth. Mom wanted me to stay home from school on Tuesday—take a day off to recover—but I wanted to see what stories were circulating in the halls of Eastview High. Some of it was sure to be garbage, but sometimes rumors had truthful origins. If the killer was someone we knew, then my first order of business was finding out who at Eastview wanted Mason dead.

Unfortunately, my three main sources of information were absent. Dare, Joey and Daniela all stayed home. The school's online Story was flooded with pictures and videos of Mason, most of which also had Dare in them. Students clustered in the hallways, crying on each other's shoulders, or slammed things with their fists. The teachers were out of sorts as well, consoling each other between classes and fighting to keep their composure while giving lessons. A few dirty looks were cast my way by those who still held a grudge from last year. Principal Thornton made an announcement in homeroom that anyone who wanted could come to the media center during lunch and talk to a guidance counselor. They even brought in therapy dogs, which was a nice thing to do. Of course I was sad, but I had a job to do, and focusing on that allowed me to keep my personal feelings in check.

I kept my ears open during classes but didn't pick up on anything I didn't already know. My peers knew Mason was dead and that his truck had been found in Newnans Lake under suspicious circumstances, but they didn't know the particulars of the crime, which meant the media didn't know either. That was a good thing for now; it made GPD's job a little easier.

I wanted to see if there were crimes similar to what happened to Mason that had been committed elsewhere, something to link his murder to the pattern of a serial killer. It wouldn't be the first time a killer had made Gainesville his hunting grounds. My mom was my age when Danny Rolling went on his killing spree and murdered five students not even two miles from our high school. Strangely enough, that was what made my mom want to go into homicide investigations, to bring killers like him to justice.

I also knew that statistically there were between twenty-five and fifty active serial killers in the United States at any given time, which, given the transient nature of our community and the plethora of young and somewhat naïve students at the university, meant Mason's death could be part of a very disturbing pattern.

During lunch I went to the media center and did a little searching online for decapitation cases where the murderer was still at large. I couldn't find anything recent, and most of the crimes were committed against people within the household, not strangers.

What I wouldn't give to have access to the FBI's database.

Then I remembered something I'd forgotten before. I erased my browser history from the school's computer and called my mom.

"Something I remembered from Saturday," I said into the phone after a brief greeting. "There was a lean to Mason's truck."

"Why aren't you in class?" she asked me.

"Mom, it's lunch. I have it the same time every day."

Her sigh went on for so long that I had to cut her off. "The truck. Was the axle broken?"

"No. The front passenger-side tire was flat."

"Had it been tampered with?"

"We're not discussing this case anymore, Charlie. I love you. Goodbye."

"Mom," I said testily, but she'd already hung up on me.

If Mason's tire had been tampered with, it would have had to happen in the school parking lot. The school had cameras. I had to get my hands on that footage. There was about ten minutes left of lunch, so I headed to the front office and asked to speak to Principal Thornton. I told her administrative assistant I was there on an errand from my mother, Detective Schiffer. I showed him my police ID even though he didn't ask to see it.

"Dr. Thornton," I said, ducking my head into her office once I'd gained permission.

"Hello, Charlie," she said and motioned to the chair across from her desk. Her face was drawn and tired-looking. Despite the ruckus I caused last year, Principal Thornton was still pretty nice to me. I think she was relieved the SAT cheating scandal was contained to Eastview High and never broke in the media.

"Is this about Mason Chalmers?" she asked.

"Yes, it is." I cleared my throat. I was never very good at the lying part. "My mom told me you had something for her?"

Her face scrunched up a little. "I don't believe so."

"Surveillance of the parking lot?" My pits were sweating like crazy, and I worried she could smell my lies from across the room.

"Oh yes." She nodded and glanced around as though looking for something. I couldn't believe it was so easy. Then she seemed to remember herself. "Wait. I turned that over already to GPD. Does she need another copy?"

"She must. She just asked me to come by and pick it up."

"Well, let me give her a quick call." Principal Thornton pulled out her cell phone. Apparently she had my mother stored in her contacts. Cripes.

"You know what? Never mind. I'm sure if she needs a second copy, she can just get it from the department." I stood quickly, more afraid of my mom finding out I was using her good name to get confidential evidence than I was of Principal Thornton discovering me.

I backed out of her office, kicking myself for my amateur hour. I'd never make it as an undercover agent.

Still, I had to figure out a way to get access to that footage.

I puzzled over it for the rest of the afternoon. Even though I could probably do it, I didn't want to hack into my mom's computer—that seemed like the ultimate betrayal, not to mention it was also a felony. I'd have to convince her somehow to show it to me.

Maybe GPD and my mom were already following promising leads and would have the killer in custody before nightfall. Then we could all rest a bit easier. I believed in my mom's ability—I'd seen her nail the bad guy (or gal) many times before. But in the meantime I had a few other people I wanted to question.

Tameka was my first stop. She had cheerleading practice after school in the multipurpose room, which was near the wrestling room. I caught her just before it was about to begin and asked for an update.

"We went over to Daniela's house last night after we got the news," she said.

"Who's *we*?"

"The cheerleading squad."

That's right, they traveled in a pack. "That was fast. How'd you hear about it?"

"Dare told Joey. Joey told Daniela. Daniela told the squad."

I reviewed her progression. "Dare didn't tell Joey." I was with Dare the entire time, and he didn't pick up his phone once.

"Well, that's what Daniela said. Anyway." She waited until she had my full attention. "She was a wreck. One of the girls baked cupcakes, and we brought them over. It looked like she hadn't left her room in days. Her nails were a mess. There were clothes everywhere, pictures of Mason, sad music playing. It was…." Tameka seemed to be choosing her words carefully. "It was a little disturbing."

I got a glimpse of Tameka's hands. Her green-and-white manicure had held up pretty well. "You said her nails were a mess?"

"Yeah. She'd pulled off all her acrylics. And you know manicures aren't cheap."

Perhaps it was Daniela's way of coping with Mason's disappearance, or maybe it was because she was hiding evidence—fake nails were likely to break and crack when performing activities such as decapitating your boyfriend and digging a hole for his dead body. Fingernails were also great reservoirs for skin cells and traces of blood—DNA evidence.

"Is she normally a nail-biter?"

Tameka shrugged. "I don't know. You want me to ask her?"

"No." I'd find out for myself. "Did she say anything about Mason or that night?"

"She said he was stupid and that he should have known better. She seemed really pissed at him. Sad too. She said she should have never let him go. Most of the time, she just cried, and we took turns hugging her."

"Did she know where he was going Friday night?"

"She didn't say. I heard his truck was found in the lake…." Tameka looked at me for confirmation. That much had already been reported on.

"Yeah, it was."

"He was murdered, wasn't he?"

I shrugged. "It's an ongoing investigation." That was as close to an affirmative as I could give.

She shivered. "It's so strange. I've never known someone my age who died before. Murdered." She whispered the last word like she was afraid to say it out loud.

"No, me neither."

"Who could have done that?"

"I don't know."

"It just doesn't seem real."

"It doesn't."

I kept expecting to see the two of them strolling down the hallway, Mischief and Mayhem. Dare, with his arm thrown casually over Mason's shoulder, leaned in to tell him a bit of gossip or tease him about something inappropriate. Mason shoving him off while laughing good-naturedly.

Theirs was a relationship that transcended family ties, as if their brotherhood belonged to the entire student body. If I hadn't seen what was left of Mason myself, I wouldn't believe it either. I thought back to Daniela and Mason's argument on Friday afternoon.

"You said you saw Daniela and Mason arguing on Friday. Could you show me where?"

Tameka nodded. "This way."

I followed her out of the multipurpose room and across the atrium to the door that led to the wrestling room. Daniela must have called Mason out of practice to confront him. On the other side of the door, I heard grunting and the shriek of Coach Gundry's whistle. It was possible that someone from inside the wrestling room might have overheard them.

"Thanks for your help on this, Tameka." Her practice was starting, and I didn't want to make her late.

"No problem, Dick. I'll talk to some of the other girls on the squad and keep you posted."

She walked away, shaking her shoulders as though a ghost had laid its cold fingers on her. If I wanted to talk to Coach Gundry and some of the other players, I'd have to wait until practice was over.

I was just settling in to do some more searching on my phone when I got a call from Dare.

"Charlie." He sounded out of breath. "Charlie, I found something."

"Where are you?" I hoped he wasn't back at the scene of the crime. That would look very bad for him.

"I'm in Mason's room. I found a baggie of pills. I think they're his."

Mason, an all-state athlete, using drugs?

"What do they look like?" I asked.

"White. Round."

"Are there any numbers or letters on them?"

"No. It looks like they've been… rubbed off or something."

Who would go through the trouble of sanding away the pills' identifiers? Someone afraid of getting caught.

"Send me a picture."

"Okay, hold on a minute."

I waited while Dare snapped a picture and texted it to me. He was right—they looked as nondescript as he'd said.

"You should give them to your parents so they can have the police compare them to the toxicology report."

"How long will that take?" Dare said. "The report, I mean."

"It might take a while." And without the body, the pathologists were limited to blood and hair samples. They might not be able to detect whatever drug Mason was taking.

"I thought so."

The way he said it made me worry.... Dare was known to be a little reckless and a lot impulsive. "You didn't take any of it, did you?"

There was a long pause.

"Dare?" I said in a voice of quiet authority, one my mom used on suspects, and me on occasion.

"Just one. Half, really. I wanted to know what it was. I thought it might be Xanax, but I'm pretty sure it's not."

I ran my hand through my hair, and it got stuck in my curls. I'd forgotten to comb it out this morning. "Dare, you don't know what the hell that is. It could be straight-up fentanyl or something."

"What's that?"

I growled into the phone. "Stay on the phone with me. I'm coming over."

"It doesn't feel like anything. Maybe I didn't take enough."

I was already jogging to my car. Talking to the wrestling team would have to wait. "Dare, if you take any more of it, I'm calling 911 and your parents."

"All right, I won't. But I don't need you to stay on the phone with me. I feel fine."

"Do it for me, then. I want to make sure you don't go into cardiac arrest or stop breathing."

"What should I do? This feels weird."

"I don't know. Recite your ABCs or count to a hundred. I just want to be able to hear your voice." The desperation in my own voice surprised me.

"Okay, let me see what I've got." I heard some shuffling around on the other end. "You like poetry?"

"Yeah, sure." I wondered if it was something he'd written.

"This one's called 'The Highwayman' by Alfred Noyes." He cleared his throat. "The wind was a torrent of darkness among the gusty trees. The moon was a ghostly galleon tossed upon cloudy seas. The road was a ribbon of moonlight over the purple moor, and the highwayman came riding— riding—riding—The highwayman came riding, up to the old inn-door...."

I'd never heard the poem before, but I began to get into the story of this outlawed highwayman and his clandestine affair with the innkeeper's black-eyed daughter. It ended horribly for both of them. She shot herself to warn him that the law was waiting for him inside her bedroom, and upon hearing of her death, he returned to the inn with a vengeance, only to be shot down in the street.

The story itself was sad enough, but the way Dare recited it nearly broke my heart. Even in his unhappiness, his voice spoke to me on a frequency all its own. I could listen to him recite terms and conditions and be utterly entranced.

I was about halfway to his house when he finished, and I asked him to read it again. It was no less moving the second time around. Dare greeted me at the door with a Bluetooth in his ear and a thick anthology of poetry balanced in both hands.

"One of my favorites." He snapped the book shut. "I don't feel much different. Dizzy and a little hyper, but it's hard to say if it's from the drugs."

I asked to see the pills in question, and Dare led me upstairs to Mason's room. He told me his parents were making arrangements for the service that was to take place in two days. Principal Thornton had said anyone who wanted to attend would receive an excused absence.

There were six and a half pills in an off-brand ziplock bag—the half was the remainder of the one Dare took—on Mason's bed. I spent a few minutes searching on my phone as to what they might be based on their shape and coloring but found too many options to be able to narrow it down.

"We should still take these to the police," I told him.

"Give them to your mom. She'll know what to do."

I took that as a note of confidence on his part. I glanced around Mason's room, taking it in. It still smelled like a teenage boy with the lingering scent of Mason's musk in the air. His clothes were scattered here and there, a belt thrown over his desk chair, textbooks stacked on the side of his desk, and an essay on springs pollution marked up for a rewrite in red pen. Mason's bed was still unmade, and I wondered if Dare had been sleeping there. I didn't ask.

"Where did you find them?"

Dare pulled back the curtain, where high up on the cloth a small pocket was sewn into the underside of it. I recalled the special pocket in Dare's jeans.

"You sew?" I asked.

Dare shrugged. "I had to learn to sew pockets or else wear this really embarrassing fanny pack to carry my EpiPen. I can make costumes too."

"Do you have a maid?" The room looked mostly untouched.

"A cleaning service. They come tomorrow."

"Didn't GPD search the room?"

"They searched both our rooms, but they don't know Mason's hiding spots, and I wasn't allowed in to show them."

GPD must have been careful in their search not to disturb anything unnecessarily. And it sounded like they were treating Dare as a suspect. Surely it must bother him, but he didn't comment any further on it.

"The pills could be something like ibuprofen or muscle relaxers." Though it was suspicious that Mason, presumably, would go through the trouble of concealing them and their identity. "Any euphoria?" I studied Dare's eyes to see if they were dilated. I was no doctor, but they looked fine to me.

"Not much, but it's kind of hard to tell. I don't know what's normal anymore."

I knew exactly what he meant. After my dad died, I was so full of emotions—anger, mostly. I dealt with the pain by picking fights with everyone I knew, including my mom. I smashed a kid's nose for saying my dad probably did it to get out of paying child support. That was when my mom made me go to counseling.

"How are you feeling now, Dare?" I asked, and I didn't mean as a result of the drugs.

He slumped down on the edge of Mason's bed and drew the comforter into his lap. He buried his face in it for a moment, then looked up at me with sorrowful eyes. "So many things. Right now, though, I feel stupid. Mason was doing drugs? For how long? Why didn't he tell me? I knew he'd been hiding things from me. And where was he even going Friday night? Why wouldn't he tell me on the phone when I asked?"

"You asked?"

"Yes, I was pissed. I told him I was sick of him blowing me off whenever he felt like it. It was our birthday, and didn't that mean anything to him? I laid it on thick, Charlie. I was a real asshole."

Dare didn't sound like an asshole to me, more like justifiably irritated, but I wasn't there to make the call on who was in the wrong. "And what did Mason say?"

"He told me not to get my panties twisted. That he'd only be a half hour or so. He gave me his order to put in for him at Waffle Kingdom so the food would be ready when he got there. He was always starving after practice."

"Did you put it in?"

"Yes, even though I was pissed, I didn't want him to go hungry."

Dare could put aside personal slights and still take care of his brother's needs. That wasn't something someone intent on murder would do, as far as I could tell.

"What did you order?" I'd check in on Waffle Kingdom to make sure Dare was telling the truth.

"Waffle fries with a side of bacon and sausage for Mason and a two-egg breakfast for me, eggs over easy, white toast, no butter."

"You watching your weight, Dare?" That question was more out of curiosity than anything else.

"Fatty food upsets my stomach. And if I ate waffles every time Mason and I went to Waffle Kingdom, I'd be big as a house."

So Waffle Kingdom was Mason's choice in restaurants, not Dare's. I turned over their conversation in my mind. Mason must have gotten a call toward the end of practice, and he pushed off plans with Dare to make an unexpected stop. Perhaps the drugs were part of it, and that's why Mason didn't want to tell Dare where he was going.

But that was impossible, because GPD had Mason's phone records. The only call came from Dare, and none of Mason's texts suggested a change in plans or a spontaneous meet-up.

Which meant if the murderer communicated with Mason that night, it had to be in person or through other channels.

"You think he might have been going to pick up drugs?" I asked Dare.

He shrugged. "An hour ago I would have said no, but now…." He stared out the window, and the light reflected as tiny squares in his eyes. "I drove by there, Charlie. Right at the time when…." He squeezed his eyes shut, perhaps trying to stave off the image of his brother's decapitated head. It had been assaulting me at random intervals as well. "I could have saved him. I could have…." He punched the pillow in his lap, then shook his head in frustration. There were no tears this time, just a shuddering, frustrated wail. I sat down and wrapped an arm around him. I didn't want to make this about myself, but I wanted to let him know I understood a little bit what he was going through.

"When my dad killed himself, I asked myself so many questions. Why would he do that to us? What was so awful about his life that he would end it? Did he think of me when he was putting the rope around his neck? Did he know the last time we saw each other that he was going to take his own life? I can't answer any of those questions, Dare. Even now. And it kills me." My whole body tensed up as an agitated feeling rose from the depths like ashes stirred in the wind. The sense of betrayal had taken root inside me, and it felt fresh, even after all this time.

"Does it ever get better?" he asked.

I wanted to give him hope, but I'd already resolved not to lie to him.

"Maybe. It hasn't for me."

He nodded and exhaled deeply.

"I'm probably not the best person to be giving advice." I started to stand, and Dare grabbed my arm to hold me there.

"You're the only person I can talk to about this. My parents are too devastated, and my friends...." He drifted off again and had a wild look about him. I wondered if it was the drugs finally kicking in. "I can't trust them." He shook his head. "Not even Joey. I feel like they're all lying to me. Hiding things from me to protect Mason. But it's too late. We failed him. *I* failed him."

What a terrible feeling that must be. Even though it wasn't true, I couldn't convince him otherwise. I knew from experience it was impossible. Dare couldn't be rational about this, but I could. I'd help him sort fact from fiction. "You can trust me, Dare."

He leaned his head on my shoulder and rubbed against me like a cat until I put an arm around him.

For comfort only.

I DIDN'T want to leave Dare alone in case whatever he'd taken started messing with him, but neither of us really wanted to stay cooped up in his house with all of Mason's half-finished projects, which only served to remind Dare of all the things he'd never get to do or experience with his brother. No wonder he'd had trouble sleeping.

I suggested we go back to the school so I could talk to Coach Gundry and Peter Orr. Wrestling practice should just be finishing up. I told Dare he could walk the track, but he wanted to come with me.

"I want to see their faces," he said. "That way I can tell if they're lying to me."

I thought about sharing with Dare how difficult it was to tell if people were lying, and often innocent people were thought to be guilty because of their nervous tics and profuse sweating under duress. But if Dare wanted to feel useful, I wasn't going to stop him.

I'd had Coach Gundry for Well-Fit (Wellness & Fitness) as a sophomore. He was in his early thirties and an Eastview alum himself.

Even though he was young as far as teachers go, he didn't talk much about himself or try to act "cool" like some of the other younger teachers. He was a no-nonsense kind of guy with a real mind for stats, not just sports stats but times and weights and conversions. He knew all the championships the school sports teams had won throughout his career at Eastview High, and he often knew the team's winning scores. It was kind of incredible, his level of recall.

After requesting a meeting with Coach, Dare and I waited for him in his classroom, where there were posters of human anatomy, including a diagram of a pregnant woman with a fetus. Those pictures always intrigued me, a body within a body, incubating there like a tiny alien before sliding out into the world.

Dare caught me looking at the poster and said, "When Mason and I were about to be birthed, he grabbed hold of my ankle." Dare hooked his hand to show me. "He actually pulled on it to keep me there in the womb with him. They had to cast my leg as a baby. And because of it, my right leg is a little shorter than the left. I wear special insoles in my shoes, so no one really notices."

I'd noticed Dare's gait was a little crooked that day he was walking down my street, but not all the time. It must be something he masked when he was around other people.

"Anyway." Dare knocked on the table with his knuckles and looked away, perhaps thinking my gaze was one of sympathy. It wasn't, though. I'd always studied Dare from a safe distance, and now he was giving me all these intimate details of his life. I felt a little guilty that it was under such horrible circumstances, but it didn't dim my fascination in the least.

To mask the awkward silence, I took stock of our surroundings. The wellness room was connected to the wrestling room but had access to the main hallway. I didn't know if it had always been the wrestling room, or if Coach had claimed it because of its proximity to his classroom. It meant he had a whole wing to himself, including access to the gym lockers through the wrestling room. Along the back of his classroom, there were locked closets and large padlocked trunks for storing his equipment. Same as in the wrestling room.

The other thing I knew about Coach Gundry was that he was obsessive in his inventory. Every playing ball, free weight, and penny was labeled and numbered, and he took great pains to make sure everything was returned to him at the end of class and stored in its proper compartment. I supposed it was shrinking budgets that made him so careful with his stuff, or maybe it was a counting thing. I'd always thought there was something just a little bit off about Coach Gundry, but I could never put my finger on it precisely.

"I'm terribly sorry about your brother, Dare," Coach Gundry said as he came into the room, his heavy footfalls announcing him. He turned one of the desks around so he could sit across from us. He removed his hat and wiped his forehead, which was shining with sweat. His eyes were puffy and bloodshot as well. "I loved Mason like a brother, watched him put in the time and effort to be a great wrestler and a good man. I hope they catch the bastard. Let him fry for what he did."

Dare was already withdrawing from the conversation, retreating into his mourning place. I saw it in his body language and his dejected expression. His eyes went unfocused as he stared blankly at the desktop. I quickly took over the conversation.

"Coach Gundry, we were hoping you could walk us through practice on Friday afternoon." I glanced over at Dare, hoping he wouldn't mind me using his need for closure as our reason for asking questions. "Dare would like to know more about Mason's last day."

Coach squinted and looked past me as he recalled it. "Well, like I told the officers who came by earlier, it was a match day for our tournament this coming weekend. I had the team pair off and spar to see who we'd enter in their weight class."

"Who was Mason's sparring partner?" I asked.

"Peter Orr," Coach said.

"Pete's in a different weight class," Dare said. His eyes were suddenly alert and focused, and he was sitting up in his seat.

"He was, but Mason gained some weight this summer. He's been weightlifting quite a bit too. Working hard at it. He moved into the 195 weight class."

"Who won the match?" Dare asked, fully engaged now.

"Mason won. Easily, I'd say. Surprised us all. Pete's no rookie."

"What was Peter's reaction?" I asked.

Coach shrugged. "You know Pete. He takes it on the chin. I told him he could try again next week, but he said he was going to drop down a weight class instead. Didn't want to fight Mason tooth and nail before every competition. He's hoping for a scholarship this year."

"That was Pete's idea? Pete was willing to give up his spot for Mason?" Dare sounded suspicious. I sensed there was some history there.

Coach Gundry shook his head. "I wouldn't say it was a sacrifice. Mason was in top form. Pete too, but we both thought he'd have a better shot dropping down. And it's better for the team's points overall."

"How much weight would Peter have to lose?" I made a note of it on my phone.

Coach Gundry squinted. "Well, he weighed in at 194 and change, and the weight class beneath him is 182. Twelve pounds? Thirteen to be safe."

"And he had a week to lose it?" I asked.

"Look, I don't encourage that type of thing." Coach held up his hands in a defensive posture. "I tell the boys they need to eat like athletes to keep up their strength. You can't win a match if you're weak and dehydrated. I don't want of any of them developing eating disorders."

"But losing thirteen pounds in a week," I persisted. "Can it even be done?"

Dare nodded. "Mason's done it before."

Coach Gundry shrugged like it wasn't his area of expertise, even though as the school's Well-Fit teacher, there was a whole unit devoted to nutrition.

"What's the school's policy on making weight?" I asked.

"There isn't one," Dare said sourly.

"Look, guys," Coach cut in. "We have a competitive program here at Eastview. We've made it to state almost every year that I've been coaching. Last year we had two state champions. Mason and Peter. This is their senior year, and they're hungry for another title. If they can make weight, it's not my place to stop them."

"Except Mason won't be making weight because somebody murdered him," Dare said, not even trying to hide his contempt.

Coach frowned, but he didn't seem all that sympathetic to me. There was something he was hiding. I felt sure of it. I put a hand on Dare's shoulder and went back to my timeline.

"Were there any interruptions during practice?" I was thinking of Mason and Daniela's argument.

"Mason got a call. I told him to take it outside. Then I heard him and his girlfriend arguing. She was not happy with him."

"Did you hear any of the argument?"

"No, but they were out there for a while. Don't think she let Mason get a word in."

"Did Mason say anything about it when he came back in?"

"He said it was going to take more than flowers this time."

"Those were his words exactly?"

Coach nodded. "Yep."

I jotted the expression down word for word. It seemed significant.

"What time did practice end?" I asked.

"Six o'clock, same as always. Everyone hit the showers then, except Pete. He suited up and started running the track."

"What did he suit up into?" I asked.

"A sauna suit. Helps cut weight."

"Did it belong to him or the school?"

"They're mine. I got a set of them here. The good ones are expensive, and this way I can get them properly laundered. Ringworm is a wrestler's worst nightmare. Haven't had a case of it in years." Coach knocked on the tabletop, for good luck, I assumed. He'd just lost a wrestler to homicide, but at least it wasn't ringworm.

"And what did you do after practice?" I asked him.

"Me?" Coach's eyebrows rose. His demeanor switched entirely, and his cocky attitude crumbled. I supposed whoever interviewed him from GPD didn't think to ask him that. They probably needed a motive to suspect a teacher, but to me everyone who had regular contact with Mason could be harboring ill will.

"Well, I... um. I waited for everyone to finish up. Then I... I went over to Gainesville High and checked out the meet they had going on there. To see how the competition was faring."

Was it just me, or had Coach Gundry broken out in a sweat?

"What time did you leave here?" I asked.

"Well, I guess... I don't really know."

That tipped me off. Coach Gundry wore a wristwatch *and* a stopwatch. If you were even a second late to his class, he sent you to the in-school suspension room. When we ran our timed miles, he told me to shave twenty-five seconds off my time if I wanted an A. He paid attention to clocks.

"Can you estimate?"

"Well, the meet started at seven."

"And what time did you leave here to go to it?"

"Around then, I guess. Meets like that usually last about two hours, so I must have gotten home around nine or nine thirty."

"And who won?"

Coach's eyebrows raised and his mouth opened, but no words came out.

"The meet?" I supplied.

"Columbia," Coach said. It sounded like a guess.

"By how much?"

He shook his head. "I don't remember. I've been in a bit of a shock since Mason's... death."

"He was murdered," Dare cut in, his eyes like knives.

"Yeah. Yes, he was." Coach swallowed tightly and looked down at his hands.

"Is there anything else you'd like to tell us?" I asked. "About Mason or the day he was murdered?"

Coach shook his head slowly and wouldn't meet our eyes. He seemed ashamed. But why?

I made a note to myself to check with GHS's wrestling coach to confirm Coach Gundry was there. It didn't sit right with me, but Coach had no motive as far as I knew. He clearly prided himself in his record of state championships, so why would he do anything to harm one of his most promising wrestlers?

Peter Orr, on the other hand....

I thanked Coach Gundry for his time, and then Dare and I waited outside the locker room, where the wrestling team was finishing up showering and changing. Dare wanted to march right in there and demand an audience with Peter straightaway, but I suggested we wait until he was clothed. I didn't enter the boys' locker room without good reason.

"Coach was lying about something," Dare said to me.

I nodded. "I got that feeling too." I didn't mention it to Dare, but I kind of always got the feeling Coach was hiding something.

"He's always tried to control Mason," Dare said, kneading his fist with his hand.

"What do you mean?"

"Our sophomore year, Mason had a growth spurt over the summer and moved up a weight class. Coach already had a senior in that weight class who was an all-state wrestler—Tyler Kim—so he put Mason on this eating plan that was superstrict so he could drop back down to his former weight. Mason was running the track every day too. I didn't like what it was doing to him. That deprivation, it was making him crazy. But he told me not to interfere."

"That must have hurt your feelings." I supposed there weren't many aspects of Mason's life that Dare wasn't involved in. I recalled my mom's theory of separation and individuation. How can you judge if a relationship, or more specifically a twinship, is normal?

"Yeah, well, it wasn't healthy. It's always been that way, though. Mason has his wrestling, and I have theater."

"Has he ever tried to interfere with theater?"

"I took up smoking for a while—everyone in drama smokes. I don't know why. It made my voice a little more sultry, you know? I thought it was sexy. Anyway, Mason hated it. It was a thing for a while. And then I quit. For him. Which is why this drug thing really pisses me off." He banged his closed fist against a locker, then doubled over and cradled it with his other hand.

"Any new sensations? Invincibility, perhaps?"

He snorted. "I'm angry, and I want to punch something, but I don't think it's the drugs."

Peter Orr exited the locker room and headed in our direction. We stood in the pathway to the parking lot, our hands clasped in front of us like two gangsters from a mafia movie.

"You want me to take this one solo?" I asked Dare.

"No, definitely not. I want to hear what Pete has to say."

Peter looked up from his phone and saw the two of us, shifted his duffel bag strap on his shoulder, and headed in our direction.

"Hey, Dare." He dropped the bag by his feet. It sounded heavy. "I still can't believe it. Mason, man. Jesus H. Christ."

I studied Peter's face. Even though he said the words, something about it felt wooden. Either he was especially stoic, or he didn't much care for Mason Chalmers. It looked like Peter was about to reach for Dare, but then thought better of it. Dare was glaring at him, nostrils already flaring. There was definite acrimony between them, and I wasn't sure if it was a jealousy thing, or if Dare had good reason to dislike Peter. I'd never had much cause to interact with Peter Orr myself. He always seemed like just another jock to me.

"We wanted to talk to you about practice on Friday," I said to Peter. "You got a minute?"

"Sure." He nodded to a couple of the other wrestlers who had stopped and were waiting for him at the door. "I'll catch up." Peter looked at me and waited. I had the distinct feeling he was sizing me up. He was powerfully built and had a lot of experience grappling 200-pound men. Mason would be a daunting opponent, but not indomitable, especially if he was caught off guard.

"Coach Gundry said you and Mason had a match on Friday to see who would enter into the tournament for the 195 weight class."

Peter rubbed a thick hand through his short hair. "Yeah, Mason came back from summer all beastly. Must have gained ten pounds, all muscle. He didn't just beat me in points; he pinned me."

"That must have been a blow to your ego," Dare said scornfully.

Peter either didn't notice Dare's insult or he ignored it. "Coach thought I'd have better luck dropping back down to 182."

"That's a big drop," I said. "Was it your idea or Coach's?"

Peter's head wobbled. "I suppose it was a meeting of the minds. I wasn't too excited about it, though. I had to start running that night."

"Where'd you run?"

"Outside, on the track."

I reviewed the layout of our high school in my mind. From the track you could see the student parking lot where Mason's truck was parked. "Did you see Mason leave?"

Peter shrugged. "I wasn't really paying attention."

"Did you see anyone mess with Mason's truck?" I asked.

Peter shook his head. "Like I said, I was focused on making weight."

I couldn't prove what Peter did or didn't see. I decided to switch tacks. "I heard Mason went to Café Risqué a few times this summer with someone from the wrestling team. Was that you?"

Peter stole a glance at Dare, then looked down as though he was ashamed. Color flared across his face and made his freckles more prominent. "Yeah, we went there a few times to burn off steam."

"Was Mason in a relationship with any of the dancers?"

Peter looked at me like he couldn't believe my suggestion. "Um, no. We got a couple of lap dances. We weren't making any proposals, though. They weren't exactly the kind of girls you wanted to take home to meet the family."

I really didn't like this kid.

"So you guys just went there for lap dances and left?"

"That and their tits and grits. The food's not bad, actually. Pretty cheap too."

Another stolen glance at Dare. For whatever reason Peter cared what Dare thought of him. Dare only glared at him with a stormy expression.

I didn't believe Peter and Mason went there for the cuisine. "There's a Denny's down the road if you're looking for a cheap, greasy breakfast. Why make the drive?"

"Because the waitresses at Café Risqué are buck naked? Mason thought I was wound too tight—hell, he was probably right. It started as a dare, and then we had fun, so we decided to go again. It wasn't anything, though."

"Mason never told me about it," Dare said bitterly.

Peter shot him a look. "Come on, Dare. Really?"

"What? He used to tell me *everything*."

"You both kept secrets. Don't act so innocent."

This time Dare was the one who looked ashamed. The two of them had an interesting dynamic, and I intended to pick it apart later.

"Do you know if Mason was taking any kind of drugs?" I asked Peter.

Peter leveled his gaze at me, then said very carefully, "I don't know anything about that."

He's lying.

"Did Mason have a fake ID?" I asked.

"Yeah, and I turned eighteen earlier this summer, so we were good to go."

"You were held back?" I didn't know that.

"I wasn't held back. I started kindergarten late. My parents thought I needed another year to mature." Peter, irritated now, glanced down at his watch. "Is there anything else? I have someplace I need to be."

"Where were you between seven and nine on Friday night?" Dare asked, still with the same defiant look on his face.

Peter narrowed his eyes at Dare. His expression quickly turned hostile, and I didn't like the menace rolling off him like a sour musk. "What, am I a suspect now, Dare?" he asked with condescension.

"Where were you, Pete?" Dare asked again, not backing down in the least.

"I was here." He motioned toward the track. "Sweating my ass off to make weight."

"With Mason gone, it looks like you won't have to make weight anymore," I said.

Peter looked at me, and I saw something dark and disturbing flicker in his eyes, and then, like a light winking out, it was gone. "I'd never hurt Mason or any of my other teammates. Cutting weight is a matter of pride for us. If you can't lose ten pounds in a week, then you aren't worth your salt as a wrestler. Besides, Mason was like a brother to me."

"Mason is *my* brother," Dare said. His lips curled in a vicious snarl. His fists were clenched at his sides. He looked like he wanted to deck him.

"How many laps did you run Friday night?" I asked Peter, trying to cut the tension between them.

Peter's head swiveled to mine. "A lot," he said, only I noticed a slight hesitation when he answered me.

"Don't you keep track of these sorts of things? Isn't that part of counting calories, knowing how far you ran?"

"I ran until I couldn't anymore. And here's a tip, Dick Tracy. Go ask Ms. Sparrow where she was Friday night. I saw her and Mason arguing during lunch last week, and it looked pretty heated to me."

Peter picked up his duffel bag and slung it over his shoulder. His bodily presence was intimidating, and it wasn't just his size. He blasted the door open with one hand and stalked across the track toward the parking lot. I made note of the make and model of his car. I'd look for it when I got my hands on those surveillance tapes.

"God, he pisses me off," Dare said, wiping his mouth viciously. His countenance was so completely different from the polite schoolboy vibe he usually gave off.

"I noticed." Something about Peter Orr was off, and he certainly wasn't going to win Mr. Congeniality in any beauty pageants, but that alone didn't make him a killer. "The two of you have history?" I asked Dare.

Dare's answers had always come easily, but now he hesitated.

"Not really."

Not really was somewhere between a "no" and a "yes," and not exactly easy to decipher. "It could help my investigation to know whatever grudge Peter might have had against you or Mason."

"It was nothing. Just a stupid prank Mason pulled last year, and Pete got over it. Look, I really don't want to talk about it, Charlie. I'm sorry."

He seemed really distressed by it. My sympathy for Dare's state of mind won out over my propensity to dig like a dachshund until the truth was exposed. I resolved to let it go… for now.

"Do you know anything about an argument with Ms. Sparrow?"

Dare shook his head. "No, but I'm not really that surprised. She's made it her personal quest to slander our family."

"I'll pay her a visit tomorrow during lunch. In the meantime there's someone else I want to talk to."

"Daniela?" Dare asked, and I nodded. "Then let's go to the mall."

CHAPTER 8

DANIELA WORKED at the BeautyCare makeup counter at Oaks Mall. As Dare described it to me on the way over, a BeautyCare consultant gives makeovers to mall customers and then tries to sell them the cosmetics that led to their transformation. Dare had bought coverup and eyeliner pencil after his makeover with Daniela—for the stage, he insisted, even though I didn't comment either way—and assorted cleansers and moisturizers since then. Dare spoke highly of her work. While I found Daniela's expertise interesting, what I was *more* interested in was her and Mason's relationship as Dare had observed it over the last eighteen months the two of them were together.

"We hated each other in the beginning," Dare said, speaking of his own relationship with Daniela. "I'm superpossessive of Mason, and she was the first serious girlfriend he's ever had."

"What changed your mind?"

"I mean, her devotion to him was just...." Dare gestured with one hand. "Have you ever been to a wrestling tournament, Charlie?" I shook my head. "Well, I've got to tell you, they're straight-up boring. I mean, even with music and a book and games... they take forever, and then it's only like, five minutes when Mason would actually be wrestling. Daniela went to all of his meets last year. All of them. And for the ones I went to, we got to talking. She comes off as this superbitchy femme fatale, but underneath her crusty exterior, she's actually very soft and gooey."

I recalled Coach Gundry's recollection of what Mason said after their fight, that it would take more than flowers to make up for whatever he'd done this time.

"Did Mason buy Daniela presents when they got into fights?"

"Yeah, it was kind of a cop-out if you ask me, but it seemed to work on her. Mason hates it when people are mad at him."

Dare was still speaking about his brother in the present tense, but I wasn't going to correct him.

"How did he make it up to you?" I asked.

Dare glanced over at me. Perhaps my question was too personal. "He'd mope around and act pitiful until I forgave him. Or he'd pester me to do something with him, like batting cages. God, he loved the batting cages." Dare bit down on his thumbnail. "What I wouldn't give to see his stupid puppy-dog face right now."

I let it rest there for a moment.

"Do you think it's strange that Daniela's missing school but still coming to work?" I asked Dare.

"Not really. Her mom lost her job last year and her dad has health issues, so they really need her paycheck. She almost had to quit cheerleading to work more hours, but Mason talked her out of it."

"Was Mason giving her money to subsidize her work?"

Dare considered it. "Maybe. That sounds like something he'd do."

If so, that meant a breakup would mean more than just hurt feelings— it meant a loss of income for Daniela.

"Didn't you both just come into some money?"

Dare slumped back into his seat. "Mason did, but not me. According to my parents, I still have some growing up to do."

A gloomy mood settled over the cabin of my car. Mason's death meant Dare was the only heir to the Chalmerses's land holdings along with the family's contract with Nestlé. With an uneasy feeling, I thought *People have killed for less.*

I parked the car, which roused Dare from his somber mood. "Follow me," he said.

Strolling through Oaks Mall with a tall, handsome man at my side made me wish we were there under different circumstances. Even in his current state of despair, Dare turned heads. Most women checked him out openly, and several men on the sly. His face was made for the movie screen. Or politics. Tall men had a real advantage.

We found Daniela in the center atrium, where the four quadrants of the mall intersected like a cross. BeautyCare had prime real estate with a circular shape that allowed for six makeover stations to be filled at any given time. Daniela herself was with a customer, a twentysomething woman who was getting wingtips on her eyelids with an eyelining pen. The work took a steady hand, and Daniela's attention didn't waver in the least. When she'd finished, the woman's eyes were perfectly symmetrical. Daniela handed her the mirror.

"Oooh, I love it," she said. Daniela managed a weak smile. The woman wanted to purchase the pen she'd been using. Daniela suggested a packaged set that included the mascara as well, along with BeautyCare's trademarked formula makeup remover. The woman agreed, and Daniela rang her up at the register. I admired Daniela's salesmanship. I'd always thought of her as just another social-climbing cheerleader, but finding out she was the sole income earner for her family made me feel bad for dismissing her so easily.

How many people had done the same to me over the years—written me off as just another egghead? It wasn't cool how we all let our reputations speak for us or relied on what other people said rather than take the time to meet a person and find out for ourselves what they're all about. I needed to get better at that. And quit assuming everybody hated me.

"I wish every sale was that easy," Daniela said when the woman was out of earshot. She wiped her hands on her green BeautyCare apron and held out her arms to Dare. "Come here, you." Her lower lip trembled and her eyes filled with tears. She looked very vulnerable and not at all like that brazen girl who less than a week ago claimed Mason as her own in the crowded high school gymnasium. Dare gave her a hug, stooping down to account for the height difference. Daniela squeezed him tightly and seemed to have a true affection for him. Her tears made smoky stains on his white T-shirt, and she apologized for it. She used a napkin to blot at her eyes in order to prevent her mascara from running even more.

I noticed her hands. The thick pads of her fingers were all pink and angry-looking, and her shale-like nails were bitten to the quick. Both were signs of a chronic nail-biter, but that didn't mean she was innocent. A guilty conscience could easily trigger bad habits.

"You bite your nails?" I asked, trying to sound only mildly interested.

"Only when I'm stressed," she practically hissed and clasped her hands together so I wouldn't stare. "What are you doing here, Dick?"

"Call him Charlie, Daniela," Dare said like he was trying to be gentle with the command. Daniela scowled at me but nodded.

"We have a few questions for you," I said, determined not to be swayed by her big Bambi eyes and quivering lips. Girls were crafty that way.

"I can't really talk right now, Dare." Her eyes flitted around to the shoppers walking past us. Something about her expression looked guilty to me. "If my boss sees me talking to you guys, he's going to deduct it from my commission."

"That seems extreme," I said.

"Do you know what it costs to rent this kiosk?" she asked.

I glanced around. Fair enough. "Do you have a break coming up?"

She shook her head. "I just used it. I saw this guy walking through the mall who looked like Mason from the back, and I followed him, but then I realized…."

Dare put a hand on her shoulder. "How about this? Charlie could use a facial, and I need something for the bags under my eyes. Why don't you fix him up while we ask you a few questions?"

"Dare," I warned. I definitely did *not* want a makeover.

Daniela's mouth quirked as she assessed me. "That's asking a lot, Dare. I'm no magician."

I glared at her. Dare nearly smiled. "I'm not asking for a miracle."

Before I had the chance to be incensed, Dare nudged me into the chair, and Daniela slung a silky black cape over my shoulders and kicked back the freestanding stool so I was reclined and at a definite disadvantage.

"Do you moisturize, Charlie?" Daniela asked, studying my pores way too closely.

"No."

She shook her head. "Well, that was your first mistake."

While Daniela prepared a warm towel for my face, I launched into my questions. The sooner this was over, the better.

"What was the fight between you and Mason about on Friday afternoon?"

Daniela's eyebrows pointed downward as she slapped the hot towel on my face and held it there.

"Ouch, that burns," I said, my voice muffled by her steady hand.

"That's the feeling of your pores opening up and expelling all the nastiness that's been accumulating over the years."

"They're screaming," I told her.

"For joy."

"So, the fight?"

"Couples fight all the time," she said evasively.

"Did you and Mason fight a lot?"

"Not that much. We had our ups and downs." She pressed on the edges of the towel, which intensified the heat and the burning sensation.

"What were some of the things you fought about?" I pressed.

"Mason wasn't always the most reliable person. He couldn't keep a calendar to save his life."

"That's true," Dare interjected.

"How long did your fights go on for?"

"I don't know. A day or two. Long enough for him to realize he was being a...." She stopped without finishing the thought.

"A what?" I asked, my voice still muffled by the towel.

"Nothing. I'm not going to say anything bad about him now. There's no sense in it."

There was if it meant I could get at why he was murdered.

Daniela removed the towel and started working a cream into my cheeks and forehead. It smelled minty and tingled a little. "This is a light moisturizing cream with an SPF base to protect your skin from sun damage." Daniela squinted at me. "You need to pluck these eyebrows, Charlie."

"Nope." I squirmed in my chair.

"She's a genius at it, Charlie. You should let her."

"Definitely not."

"Come on, Charlie, there's, like, five that really need to go. They're like distant planets to the rest of the solar system that is your eyebrows."

"Did you and Mason ever break up as a result of one of your fights?" I asked, growing impatient with her dodgy answers.

"I don't know. Maybe."

"Yes or no?"

"Close your eyes," she said, coming at me with a pair of tweezers.

"I said I don't want my eyebrows plucked." I started to get up, and she placed a firm hand on my chest.

"Don't be such a baby." Daniela looked to Dare imploringly.

Dare laid a hand on my arm. "Just shut your eyes, Charlie. It will only take a minute. It's a little pinch. That's it."

I groaned and squeezed my eyes shut.

"We broke up once over the summer," Daniela said. She yanked at one of my eyebrow hairs, and it stung so bad I thought I was going to start crying.

"Ow."

"Sorry, hon. That one was hanging on for dear life."

"Was it because of a trip to Café Risqué?" I asked while wincing in pain.

"That was part of it."

"What was the other part?"

"He was getting really jealous. We'd be out having fun and some guy would look at me wrong and he'd get all worked up about it. One time we were at the downtown market, picking up food for dinner, and this sweet little homeschooled kid asked me for my number. I didn't give it to him, but Mason overheard and threatened to beat the guy's ass. And then when I found out he'd been going to the strip club, I was like, oh hell no."

I could understand that. I was almost sympathizing with her when she plucked another one of my eyebrow hairs.

"Surely, with all the practice you've had, you could be a bit gentler," I huffed.

"Beauty is pain, Charlie. Don't let anyone tell you otherwise."

Back to the agenda. "So, this fight you had with Mason on Friday. Why didn't you tell my mom about it?"

I peered up at her, half-afraid of getting an eye stabbed out.

"Who's your mom?" she asked, bewildered.

"Detective Schiffer."

"That's *your* mom?" She seemed fearful and also a little impressed. Most everyone knew my mom was a cop, since I was often picked up in elementary and middle school in a police cruiser, but Daniela had gone to different schools from us until high school.

"Yes, and?"

Daniela sucked in her bottom lip and chewed on it. "I didn't think it would help them find Mason. I felt bad about it too." She stopped then and had to dab at her eyes again. Dare patted her shoulder sympathetically.

"Which brings me back to my original question," I continued. "What was the fight about?"

Daniela licked her lips and furrowed her pruned brow in concentration. I felt another pinch in my brow line. I was letting her torture me for answers.

"I overheard Mason on the phone with someone. I saw him come out of the wrestling room, and I was sneaking up behind him to surprise him when I heard him talking to…." She stopped and collected herself. I could see that she was trying to get her temper under control. I did something similar when I was mad. My therapist helped me come up with ways to calm down. Most of the time it worked.

"I don't know who he was talking to, but it sounded like a hookup."

"For that night?"

"That night or some other night. I know what I heard and I just… I went off on him."

I glanced over at Dare and wondered if he realized what this meant—Daniela had a motive. I decided to trust her with a bit of information in order to get a better answer. "Dare found a baggie of pills in Mason's room. Do you know if he'd been taking anything?"

Daniela's eyes went wide. "No, I don't know anything about that."

"The conversation he was having… do you think it could have been with a dealer?"

A look of horror passed over Daniela's face. "God, I hope not. I made him feel like complete shit."

"You're not the only one," Dare said, wiping his face with his hands.

"So, you had this argument with Mason. You gave him back his jacket and—"

"Wait, how do you know about the jacket?" she asked, looking surprised.

"Charlie's good at what he does," Dare said. "He didn't get the name Dick Tracy for nothing. That was my idea by the way." He turned to me. "I didn't intend for it to go viral, and I meant it as a compliment."

I couldn't find it in me to be sore at him now. Knowing it was Dare's idea actually made it a whole lot better.

"So, when did you leave school?" I said to Daniela. The two of them were really good at getting me off track.

"Around six forty-five."

"And where did you go?"

She looked from me to Dare. "I'd rather not say."

I was getting frustrated. If she had nothing to hide, then there was no reason for her to be so circuitous. "I'm trying to help establish your alibi, Daniela. Joey said you arrived to the party late, that your makeup was a mess, and you were still wearing your cheerleading uniform, which means you definitely didn't go home."

"No, I didn't." She thankfully put the tweezers away and pulled out a small jar of cream-colored liquid.

"No makeup," I told her.

"This is just a bit of concealer to blend. Your face is quite unevenly colored, Charlie. I'm doing you a favor."

Because I wanted more information, rather than argue with her, I let her continue her ministrations. "So where did you go?" I persisted.

She set her mouth in a determined line and focused all her attention on my face. It seemed she intended to ignore me altogether. Dare gently grabbed her arm, interrupting her, and gave her puppy-dog eyes. "Come on, Daniela, I know you'd never hurt Mason, but we need all the information so we can find out who did. You want to help us find the sicko who killed him, don't you?"

Her lower lip trembled again, and she nodded.

"Then just tell us where you went. We're not going to judge you. We're on the same side. Mason's side."

She set down the jar and sponge. "I drove out to Café Risqué. I thought I'd find Mason's truck there, but I didn't. Then I felt bad… really bad, so I went back to the high school to see if he was still there, but he wasn't. I tried calling him, but he didn't pick up…." She shook her head. "It's all my fault."

Dare hugged her. He looked over her shoulder at me, as if to say *Let me handle it*. I wondered if Dare had only been pretending to be her ally in order to get her to talk. Maybe he was a better actor than I thought.

"It's okay, Daniela," he said in soothing tones while petting her hair. "Whatever it is, you can tell us."

She shook her head, and I was certain there was going to be an abstract impression of her eye makeup on Darc's shirtfront when this was all over. "I did something bad, Dare," she snuffled.

"Whatever it is, you can tell me." His words were soft and soothing, but his eyes were hard as flint. I realized what a vulnerable position Daniela was in, her soft, supple neck cradled in his arms, his large hand cupping the base of her skull.

"You're going to hate me for it."

"I couldn't hate you, Daniela. I promise."

She pulled away, her face a mess, her breath coming out in hiccups. "I was so angry at him, Dare, and I thought he was going to meet another girl, so I…." She gulped and tried again. "I slashed his tires." She was full-on bawling now. "I did that to him on his birthday. And now because of it, he's dead."

DANIELA, UNFORTUNATELY, was in no shape to continue her shift. To make up for it, Dare bought an obscene amount of cosmetics and told the cashier to put it all on Daniela's commission. Then we took her to Swift Soup, and the three of us sat together over steaming bowls of soup and bread. Dare and Daniela talked about how Joey was handling it, which was not well. He'd not left his house since finding out about Mason's murder, and the only person he was answering his phone for was Dare. I got the impression that while Joey was a friend to both brothers, he was much closer to Mason. Perhaps he knew something about Mason's drug use or had a suspicion as to who Mason was going to meet Friday night. I had so many questions.

I drove Dare home through the gloom of twilight with the windows down, a cool breeze on our faces. The bats would be waking and setting out for their nightly feasts. My dad used to take me to the bat house on the UF campus at sunset to watch the bats come out—thousands of them. It was both terrifying and awe-inspiring to see them swooping overhead, so close it seemed you could reach out and grab one. I thought they were scary and gross until my dad explained to me their role in the ecosystem and how important they were as pollinators. My dad was always really good at getting me to slow down and observe things from different angles. Sometimes he'd bring up a topic for debate and convince me of his side, so that by the end we'd both taken opposite positions. The whole argument changed when you looked at it from another perspective.

I checked in with Dare to see how he was doing. He looked completely drained.

"I'm sad as hell, but at least it feels like we're getting somewhere."

I needed to get all my thoughts down on paper, because at that moment I felt a bit discombobulated. "We can't write Daniela off just yet," I told him. "She could be lying about her trip to Café Risqué, and since she didn't go inside, there's no way to prove she was there, which means she doesn't have an alibi."

"Neither do I," Dare said. He wasn't wrong. "And your mom thinks I did it."

I thought about how to frame it in a more positive light. "Not conclusively."

"That's good, though. If she didn't suspect me, she wouldn't be doing her job, right?"

"That's right. But if I thought you did it, I wouldn't be helping you."

"I have a motive." His luminous eyes searched mine. "We both know I do."

I nodded slowly, focusing back on the road while the weight of his admission settled in around us.

"Mason was good at being good," Dare said, studying his clasped hands. "Know what I mean?"

"Tell me."

"He played the game. He figured out the easiest way to do what people expected of him and he went with it, even if it was wrong. Mason realized early on that he could buy his way into or out of pretty much anything, like the SATs, and so he did. And my parents just… let him."

"Did that bother you?"

"Yeah, it did. But only because he didn't need to. He was smart enough to ace his SATs. He was strong enough to go up against that senior his sophomore year. He's always doubted his ability or thought he needed to cheat to get an edge, but he doesn't. He's just...." Dare shook his head, eyes shining. "And I keep thinking that's why this happened. He pissed off the wrong person or cheated the wrong dude and they came for him, and I...." Dare looked out the window. "I wasn't there to protect him. I failed him, Charlie. I wasn't there. And now he's dead."

I parked the car at the end of his winding driveway, pulled him into my arms, and let him rest there for a few minutes, until he felt strong enough to face the world outside my T-shirt again. Finally, he pulled away and scrabbled at his eyes with his knuckles.

"Anyway, I always respected you for that. For taking Mason down a notch. He needed that kind of lesson. Our parents and teachers, even me, we were always giving him a pass. But not you." He shook his head. "I only wish Mason would have learned his lesson then, instead of now."

I studied our hands clasped together, his slender fingers twined with my thick, sturdy ones. "I know you feel guilty, Dare, for what you think you should have done to prevent this, but the blame lies with just one person. That person is out there, and we're going to find them and bring them to justice."

Dare squeezed my hand, a hard, determined look in his eyes. "Yes, we are."

And in order to do that, there was someone I needed to talk to.

CHAPTER 9

WITH MY mother it was always best to take the honest approach.

"I'd like to review the case files," I told her later that evening. She was in her office, poring over the files in question when I made this request. The remnants of what looked to me like a sandwich and bowl of soup were on her desk, which meant I hadn't caught her on an empty stomach. That was good.

She took off her reading glasses and laid them on the desk.

"We talked about this already, Charlie. You're off the case."

"I've been asking around at school. I have some good information. If we joined forces, we could be that much stronger."

"Is that where you were all day? With Darren Chalmers?"

"You don't have to use his first and last name, Mom. That's weird. Just call him Dare."

"I'll call him Public Enemy #1 if it suits you better."

Boy, she could really get to sniping when she felt like it.

"No, it doesn't." I plopped down in the chair across from her. It had been a long day, and I wasn't in the mood to argue. She closed the manila folders so I wouldn't see anything *accidentally*. Boots waddled into her office and put his front paws on the edge of the chair. I lifted him the rest of the way into my lap, even though he was really too big for it.

"We need to put Boots on a diet," she said.

"Don't body shame him. Besides, it's just because his legs are so short that it makes his belly look big." I stroked the backs of his long, floppy ears, which he loved and showed me by licking my chin.

"You do realize that with Mason gone, Dare inherits the Chalmerses's fortune," Mom said. "All of it."

It was a weak reason because it had always been true. Unless something dramatic happened between the brothers to trigger some sort of fallout, I didn't see it as a motive. I told my mother as much. Then I pulled out the plastic baggie of pills and tossed them on the desk.

"What are those?" she asked.

I wanted the surveillance tapes, but I knew she wouldn't hand those over easily. Confidentiality, blah, blah, blah. That didn't mean I had to walk away with nothing.

"What was the murder weapon?"

"Where'd you get those pills, Charlie?"

"The murder weapon?"

She sighed with exasperation. It was lucky I was her only child because if not, I doubted I'd be her favorite.

"It was a flat-headed shovel. It was in the back of Mason's truck. It'd been scrubbed clean, but the handle was wood and absorbed some of Mason's blood, as did a pair of gardening gloves, which we assume were Mason's. There'd been some sort of tree planting with the Environmental Service Club the weekend before."

"It's Program. Environmental Service Program." And since when did Mason Chalmers hang out with do-good environmentalists? "What did the gloves look like?"

"They were green rubber-tipped."

"Any pattern on them?"

My mother pulled up a file and tilted it her way so only she could see it. "The pattern appears to be…." She squinted. "Pink peonies. Maybe carnations."

"I can't imagine Mason Chalmers picking out a pair of gardening gloves with that pattern."

"Maybe he'd borrowed them for the planting and forgot to return them?"

"Maybe. Any other DNA?"

"None that we've found so far. Now, how about the pills?"

"You find the body?"

She raised her eyebrows. I took that as a no.

"Dare found them in Mason's bedroom," I told her.

"We searched Mason's bedroom top to bottom."

"Not well enough, it would seem."

She tilted her head and studied me. I was deliberately provoking her to get her to reveal more, but this was a tactic she'd taught me, so of course she turned it around.

"Or Dare planted them," she said.

I nodded begrudgingly. She had a point, and I had no proof otherwise. "It just doesn't make sense, though."

"What's that?" she said.

"This had to be the luckiest murderer in the history of criminal activity to have a murder weapon, a stranded victim, and a lake nearby to dump the body. You find any footprints?"

She shook her head. "How do you know Mason was stranded?"

"The front tire. Mason was going to meet someone Friday night. Daniela overheard him making plans, and they fought about it. Somewhere along the way, he got a flat." Because Daniela slashed his tires, I'd only recently discovered. I figured my mom already knew that as well since she'd seen the footage of the school parking lot. "So either the killer was following him the whole time, or he just got really lucky. And why are there no other tire marks on the trail? Where did the other vehicle come from?" I needed to see that footage.

Mom rose slowly and stretched her arms. She quirked her neck to crack her back, which always gave me an ill feeling, like if she cracked it too hard her head might fall off. Then I thought of Mason's decapitated head and the nausea intensified.

"I blame myself for this obsession of yours," Mom said. "I'm afraid I've only fed your investigative nature over the years."

"Yeah, and also, I'm good at it." It sounded to me like she was taking all the credit.

She smiled. "Yes, Charlie, you *are* good at it, but I don't know what I have to do to convey to you how dangerous this is. If Dare is the killer, then you're exposing all of our evidence to him, and if he's not, then you're potentially putting his and your life in danger by asking these questions. What if you've tipped off the killer already? These private eye shenanigans have got to stop."

I swear she knew just what to say to get under my skin. "Private eye shenanigans? Really, Mom? It never stopped us before. It's a little late to pull the Mom card now."

"Firstly, it's never too late to pull the Mom card, and secondly, I pull it so infrequently that I'm a little surprised you're not taking me more seriously."

"I'm practically an adult, legally, and this is what we do. You don't need to sugarcoat it for me, and if you really wanted us to be successful and solve this case, you'd share what you know instead of playing spy vs. spy. The only reason for it that I can guess is you've hit a dead end."

Her mouth fell open. She didn't like that at all. I felt a little bad for the dig, but this was my best shot at getting information from her. I knew it was killing her not to prove me wrong.

"But I could help you," I insisted. "I just need to see the surveillance tapes from the high school parking lot to—"

"This discussion is over, young man," she snapped, cutting me off. "And, I've changed all my passwords just in case you thought you'd get in the backend."

I frowned. I should have had this discussion *after* I'd accessed the files. Grrr. I hated it when she won a battle of wits.

"And another thing," she said as I turned to go. "I spoke with Principal Thornton today, and she's been made aware that the school is not to hand over any information about the case unless it's to me *directly*."

I turned back long enough to see the beginnings of a triumphant smile on her face.

"What are you going to do next, ground me?" I asked petulantly.

Mom crossed her arms. "There's a first time for everything, Charles Scott Schiffer. Stay away from Dare Chalmers, or I swear, I will ground you."

I grumbled. Having a mom who's also a cop could be a real pain in the rear sometimes.

I HADN'T had a class with Ms. Sparrow since AP Environmental Science my sophomore year. Her lectures were engaging and informative and led me to the singular conclusion—we humans were doomed.

Like the fire-and-brimstone sermons of some preachers, Ms. Sparrow had a similar approach when it came to teaching climate change and mass extinction. Still, she hadn't given up all hope for our species. She talked a lot in class about how to decrease our carbon footprint and encouraged us all to eat less meat and bike or walk to school whenever we could.

But Ms. Sparrow's most ardent cause, and the one she crusaded relentlessly outside of the classroom, was to Save Our Springs by putting pressure on local landowners to terminate their contracts with Nestlé in order to relieve the springs of chronic overpumping. Ms. Sparrow had a long-standing feud with the Chalmerses over who owned the aquifer that fed Sweetwater Springs. The Chalmerses maintained that as landowners, the spring and everything contained within belonged to them. Ms. Sparrow contended the waters belonged to the citizens of Florida, who deserved clean, unpolluted water bodies. A few charges had been leveled against the Chalmerses, but the environmentalists' lawsuit money always dried up, excuse the pun.

To discover Mason helping his family's archnemesis with a tree planting was alarming, to say the least. The only conclusion I could draw was that Mason was working off some debt he owed to Ms. Sparrow. I had to wonder if that was what the fight between her and Mason was about.

During my lunch hour, I headed for Ms. Sparrow's classroom, where she was holding an Environmental Service Program meeting. I slipped inside and took a seat in the back. They were discussing logistics for a cleanup they were hosting that weekend at Rainbow Springs. Ms. Sparrow paused what she was saying to ask, "Thinking of joining ESP, Charlie?"

"I was actually hoping to talk to you after the meeting, Ms. Sparrow."

I didn't mention Mason or even hint at the investigation, but still she had a look of unease about her. And sorrow too. All the teachers appeared to be trying to put on a brave face for us students, and underneath Ms. Sparrow's forced cheer, I detected a similar sadness.

After everyone was dismissed, I approached Ms. Sparrow's desk. I didn't know how to justify the questions I had for her, so I decided to try honesty.

"I'm investigating the murder of Mason Chalmers," I told her. "I have a couple of questions for you."

Ms. Sparrow studied me with a calculating look, which made me think she had something to hide. "Shouldn't you leave the detective work to the authorities?" she asked with more than a little condescension.

I ignored the implication that I was out of my league. It was a classic gambit adults pulled, using their position of authority to avoid answering tough questions. "I didn't realize Mason Chalmers was a budding environmentalist," I said.

"There's no litmus test for caring about the environment, Charlie."

"He participated in ESP's tree planting last weekend?"

"Yes, I offered it to all of my classes as extra credit."

I glanced down at the stack of papers on her desk: student essays on springs degradation. I recognized the topic from the marked-up essay I saw in Mason's room, bleeding with corrections from her red pen. I never would have guessed Mason to choose an AP elective over something like weightlifting or shop.

"Did Mason need the extra credit?"

"Not really. He was doing quite well in my class."

"And at the tree planting, did he use your gloves?"

"Maybe. I keep several pairs on hand for those types of events."

That was true. I'd once attended a similar ESP activity, and Ms. Sparrow offered her gloves and yard tools readily. And she didn't keep inventory like Coach Gundry. It was possible the shovel belonged to her too. "What were you and Mason arguing about last week?"

She took her time reordering the papers on her desk into two tidy stacks. Stalling for an answer, I presumed.

"Was he upset about a grade you'd given him?" I prompted.

She huffed audibly. "We were having an academic discussion about the essay I'd assigned. Mason refused to acknowledge the overgrowth of algae in the springs as the result of reduced flows from overpumping. He blamed, among other things—" At this she shook her head so her brunette bob bounced a little. "—manatees deciding to go on a diet."

"Was he serious?" Mason was no idiot. Maybe it was his way of jabbing at her for all her campaigning against his family over the years.

She tilted her head and gave a wry smile that seemed touched with true affection. "I don't think so. He knew the initial draft wasn't for a grade and that I'd have to comment on it for revision. He was always saying things like that in class to get me excited."

Her eyes pooled with tears, and she grabbed for a tissue. There was already a pile of crumpled ones on her desk, and her nose was red and swollen. I took another look at Ms. Sparrow through the eyes of a male heterosexual high school teenager. She was pretty young, and there were times in class when she could even be funny with a biting, sarcastic kind of humor. A lot of guys joked about taking her class because they were "hot for teacher," though most of them regretted it when they realized it was no easy A. I wondered if Mason might have felt similarly.

"What kind of student was Mason?" I asked, a little gentler now, since she was clearly upset.

"Exasperating." She smiled again, a private little grin. "He was so contrary, and he loved a good debate, even if his points were ridiculous. You know, he actually started looking for false narratives about climate and the environment so he could present them to me in class?"

"Sounds like he went the extra mile." Obviously Mason was getting something out of their exchange as well. Was it only in the spirit of healthy debate, or was this Mason's way of flirting with Ms. Sparrow?

"He really did." She got quiet then, almost wistful. I studied her as she reflected on some fond memory they'd shared. I never would have expected Mason Chalmers to be a teachers' pet, but then, with his charms and good looks, I probably shouldn't be too surprised.

Ms. Sparrow glanced up as though just remembering I was there. She blew her nose and nodded. "The bell's about to ring, and I don't give late passes freely."

"One more question." I wanted to eliminate Ms. Sparrow as a suspect entirely and so I had to ask, "Where were you Friday night between 7:00 p.m. and 9:00 p.m.?"

She looked at me as though I'd slapped her. Her fingers fiddled with the pendant around her neck, some item from the natural world preserved in resin. "That's really none of your business, Charlie," she said indignantly.

"I know it isn't, Ms. Sparrow, but I'd really like to write you off as a suspect, and if you have an alibi, it makes it so much easier."

"A suspect?" Her features turned stony and the warmth in her eyes receded. Her posture became stiffer, and her words were cool and unaffected when she said, "Like I said before, you should leave the detective work to the professionals." She raised a finger and pointed to the door. Her intent was clear. She wanted me to leave.

As I threaded through throngs of people in the hallway, searching for Tameka, I suddenly didn't believe Ms. Sparrow was completely innocent. Perhaps it was rude of me to ask, but I'd told her why I was there. Her defensive reaction seemed altogether... guilty.

I found Tameka in a cluster of cheerleaders. I held my breath and entered the gaggle of high ponytails and short skirts as one wades through a den of vipers.

"Tameka?"

She caught my eye and nodded, told the others she had to copy my homework before class, and walked off with me.

"Like my cover?" she asked conspiratorially.

"I like the effort, but we don't share any classes, so what homework would you be copying?"

She rolled her eyes. "That's why you're the detective, Dick. So, what's the 411?"

I told Tameka about my interaction with Ms. Sparrow. To which she replied, "Is that the teacher whose classroom smells like dirty hippies?"

"Patchouli oil," I told her, though I couldn't argue with her assessment. "You're friends with the jocks. Can you see if there are any rumors circulating about Mason having a crush on Ms. Sparrow?"

Her eyebrows lifted. "You think she's the other woman?"

"I wouldn't want to start that rumor, but I think she's lying about something. There's something else too." I texted her a list of all the people involved so far in this investigation. "I need you to scour the social media accounts of these people for anything negative having to do with Mason—in particular, anything that sounds like revenge for pranks Mason or Dare might have pulled in the past. We're looking for motive."

Tameka scanned the names. Dare's was one of them. "That's a pretty long list. Why can't you do it? Oh, that's right, you have no friends."

She actually sounded like she felt bad for me, which made it worse. My phone rang, and I pulled it out of my pocket. Dare Chalmers. I stopped walking to answer it. I expected Tameka to continue on, but instead she ducked into the alcove with me to listen to our conversation. She was an expert at eavesdropping.

"Charlie," Dare said. "Mason's funeral is tomorrow. You coming?"

I thought he'd be calling me for an update on the case. "Yeah, Dare. Of course I'll be there."

"Good. That's good." There was a long pause and then, "That's what I was hoping… that you'd be there. I'm sorry to disturb you. I know you're at school."

"Don't worry about it. You want me to call you later?"

"No, no. I'm fine. I'll see you tomorrow."

We said goodbye, and Tameka's raised eyebrow suggested at a scandal. "We're friends," I said defensively.

"Mmm-hmm," she said, unconvinced. "Sounds like you're mixing business with pleasure, Dick."

"That's ludicrous."

"Whatever you say, player. Just remember, the boy is in a world of hurt, so don't go messing with his emotions."

"I wouldn't," I protested.

Dare and I had a strictly business arrangement. Of course, I'd offered him my shoulder to lean on, but there was nothing romantic or starry-eyed about it. I was about to explain that to Tameka when she held up her hand and said, "Save it."

I may have succeeded in fooling myself, but I wasn't fooling her.

CHAPTER 10

THE LAST time I went to a funeral was five years ago for my father's burial. This time I stood in front of the mirror wearing one of his old suits. Black coat, black slacks, and a black silk tie. Did Dad ever imagine me one day reaching his height and weight? Could he have known my shoulders would span the same exact width? Did he ever wish to see that day?

Sometimes I went through my father's things and pulled out an old T-shirt or flannel. It always surprised my mom to see me wearing his clothing, but it was one of the ways I felt close to him without being bitter.

"You look nice, Charlie," Mom said when I joined her in the kitchen.

Mom wore her standard black pantsuit with a lavender shirt underneath and pearls. The color of her shirt complemented her green eyes. "You too, Mom." On her hip were her badge and gun as well. I supposed this was more than just a social call for her.

I wasn't sure if I was attending as Dare's friend or private investigator. Both, I supposed.

Our car ride to the Methodist church where the visitation was being held was quiet. Mom tried to engage me on the topic of school, how my grades were, how my senior portfolio for IB was coming along, and whether I'd finished the essay for my UF application, but after a few one-word answers, she got the hint and gave up. Memories of my father's death hovered around us like a fog. I knew Mom would talk to me about it if I brought it up, but I was already feeling a little raw. I wanted to be strong for Dare and focus on honoring Mason, not feeling sorry about my own loss.

Mom liked to remind me from time to time my father had a mental illness, like cancer or any other debilitating disease, and we couldn't blame him for what he did, but I was still angry he didn't get help. And rather than answer our appeals to see him and be with him, he retreated into his own world, turtle-like. One thing my therapist taught me was that I had a right to my feelings and denying them, however shameful, wouldn't make them go away. Still, it was one thing to know it and an entirely other thing to believe it.

I pushed those thoughts aside as I entered the church.

Mason's visitation was a closed casket, and staring at the coffin placed in front of the altar reminded me of what was left of his body and the fact that GPD had never found his remains. Mom must be feeling pretty bad about that. I'd overheard some conversations between her and Hartsfield indicating that the Chalmerses were deeply unhappy with GPD's handling of the case. Whether it was GPD's or my own, today I'd be praying for a breakthrough.

The Chalmerses stood at the head of the aisle, greeting people as they came up to pay their respects. Dare sat in the front pew, head bowed, with Daniela and Joey on either side, propping him up like an old pylon. I told my mom I was going to say hello, and she shot me a warning look. I nodded in acknowledgment but didn't deviate in my path.

Dare's head lifted as I approached, and he stood to greet me. As we embraced, it felt as though he collapsed into me. I was happy to support him for as long as he needed. Joey shifted over a seat so that I could sit next to Dare. It seemed significant that Joey was willing to give up his seat for me and include me in their circle.

"How you holding up?" I asked.

Dare shook his head slowly. I offered my hand, and he took it. In between greeting friends and family members, Dare always sought my hand. It felt like an important job. I wanted to be useful in whatever way I could.

The visitation seemed to stretch on for hours, with friends and relatives in an endless train that only seemed to suck more and more energy from Dare. His life in the theater hadn't prepared him for the amount of effort it took to sustain this kind of event. Afterward my mom and I, along with Mason's relations, followed in a solemn line of cars with police escorts to the cemetery, where the actual service would be held. It seemed our entire high school had gathered in the cutting winter light of early afternoon. There wasn't room enough in the tent for all the bodies. The crowd's collective grief was sharp and frequently punctuated with mournful sobs.

Despite the somber atmosphere and my own feelings of sorrow at Dare's profound loss, I found myself searching for the faces of my suspects. All were present. Ms. Sparrow and Coach Gundry stood in a group of Eastview High staff, each of them clutching a program in their hands, tears in their eyes. Peter Orr was with the rest of the wrestling team, wearing their green letterman jackets in a show of solidarity. Mason's jacket was laid over the casket, having been recovered from the cabin of Mason's truck with no traces of blood or any DNA evidence other than Mason's and

Daniela's, which wasn't unusual since she was more often the wearer of the jacket.

Peter had a hard look on his face, but so did many of the wrestlers, as though they were afraid the slightest show of sadness might lead to an embarrassing emotional outburst. The code of man was rigid indeed. Joey had his arm around Daniela, who hadn't stopped crying since the service began. Joey had tears in his eyes too. Only Dare seemed removed from the scene, with a distant, vacant expression on his face. I remembered when he'd gone into shock after seeing his brother dead. I suspected he might be disassociating from the situation altogether.

The adults said what needed to be said, painting a version of Mason that was rosy and good and utterly boring. They listed a few of his and Dare's pranks over the years, but even that didn't do him justice. I sat dutifully at Dare's side and offered up my presence as a comfort. Finally, the pastor officiating the service invited Dare to speak. He took the microphone and glanced out at the crowd. Even in his grief, his stage presence was commanding, and it seemed as if this was what we had all been waiting for. No one, not even his parents by our estimation, loved Mason as fervently as his brother.

"There is nothing I wouldn't give or do to have Mason back for even a day." Dare's lashes dewed with tears, and he closed his eyes for a moment to gather himself. "And there's nothing I could say that would capture the kind of person he was and what he meant to me." His eyes scanned the crowd for a moment, before landing on Joey. "What he meant to us."

Joey gave him a wan smile.

"So, instead, I'll relate to you all a plan the two of us made when we were sixteen. It was around the time he started dating Daniela." Dare gazed down at her before continuing. "I was jealous Mason wasn't spending all of his free time with me, so he made me a promise that when we got our inheritance, we'd start up our own ice cream business, like Ben & Jerry's, but instead of clever names that referenced pop culture, we'd come up with flavors to capture all the feelings that were difficult to put into words... 'Christmas morning' and 'Scoring the lead in the school musical,' but sad feelings too, like 'Instagram envy' and 'Making weight,' which was going to be a really terrible flavor of nonfat frozen yogurt." Dare shook his head, and a small smile appeared on his face as if remembering.

"And one of the flavors was 'Missing Mason,' and I was supposed to eat it whenever I was lonely because he was away at sports camp or off with Daniela…." He pressed his lips together as if trying to hold back a sob.

"But there is no flavor for a world without Mason. And the saddest thing is knowing I'm all alone in remembering, and all of my thoughts of my brother will forever be looking backward and never forward." At this Dare started breaking down.

"We'll never be able to make our stupid flop of an ice cream business or take secret video of each other and post it online or make each other laugh over something stupid. We won't wear tuxes at each other's weddings and make really bad toasts. I'll never be Uncle Dare and he'll never be a father. So what is the flavor for that? Huh, brother?" Dare laid his hand on the shiny wood casket. He seemed for a moment to be communicating with Mason's ghost. Then he tore his eyes away and shook his head remorsefully. "It's absolutely nothing."

Dare passed off the microphone. His shoulders shuddered as he tried to contain his sobs. I expected him to go to his parents for comfort, but instead he headed for Joey, who pulled him into his arms and gripped the back of his head possessively while whispering words of comfort into his ear. Then, instead of resuming his seat in the chair next to mine, Dare strode out of the tent and continued along a path between two rows of headstones. I glanced over at Joey and Daniela to see if someone should follow him.

"You go, Charlie," Daniela said.

I gave Dare a bit of a head start, then left the ceremony in pursuit, allowing him a few minutes to himself. The cemetery lawns were lushly green, the weather having just turned but not yet cold enough to kill the grass. The sky was blindingly blue. It was far too colorful a day for such a bleak occasion.

I caught up with Dare where he sat in a bed of pine needles at the base of two trees that had grown so close together they'd fused at the bottom. Dare was smoking a cigarette and flicking a Zippo lighter. I watched him for a moment, his eyes focused on the flame before snuffing it out, the metallic clink like a tomb being shut. Over and over he did it, in a rhythm that suggested it was a regular kind of ritual for him. Finally he glanced up and saw me.

"Hey there, Charlie-bo-barley," he said sadly.

"I don't want to disturb you."

"You're not. I could do that for hours—stare at an open flame. Did it a lot growing up." He picked up the lighter but didn't summon the flame. "Mason gave this to me last year for our birthday."

He flashed the side toward me. DLC was engraved into it in an ornate script. *Darren Lee Chalmers.* "He told me not to start any fires bigger than me with it." Dare's fist closed around the lighter, and he tucked it back inside his coat. "So far, I haven't."

I took that as an invitation and sat down next to him with my forearms on my knees. The hem of my slacks tugged up to show off my dress socks, which were decorated with the sequence of pi in an unending spiral.

"You are such a geek, Charlie," he said with a weak laugh and pointed to my socks. "Don't ever change." I was glad I'd chosen these socks to wear; anything to bring a moment of levity to this sorrowful day.

"You did a good job back there." I didn't know what it meant to do a "good job" giving a loved one's eulogy, but Dare's speech felt honest, and that seemed like the most important thing to me.

"Thanks," he said glumly. He squinted at the blinding sun. "Mason and I were supposed to go to Europe this summer. Just the two of us. And Joey if we could convince him. Mason wanted to spit off the side of the Eiffel Tower."

"Sounds like Mason."

"Yeah, he couldn't admit that he actually wanted to see it without making it into a joke. Not even to me."

"We're all trying to be something, I guess." I cringed inwardly at my psychobabble. I sounded like a cheap imitation of Dr. Rangala.

"You believe in heaven, Charlie?"

I cleared my throat. He sure didn't ask easy questions. "No."

"Hell?"

"Nope."

He exhaled a cloud of smoke. When it cleared, his gray eyes were staring at me. "So, where is he, then?"

Judaism was pretty ambiguous about the afterlife. My mom tended to focus on the complexities of the observable world. She said humans have the capacity to create their own hell on earth for themselves and others. And she'd seen a lot of nastiness in her line of work, which caused her to doubt that humans—even the best of us—had any right to eternal life.

My dad was a little less cynical, though he too had no answers on the subject. Something he always told me: people will try to tell you they know what happens after we die, but the truth is, no one knows. So you'd better make the most of what you got. I supposed that was the question that kept some of us awake late into the night.

Looking at Dare's forlorn face, I wished I had a better answer for him. "I don't know, Dare."

"It's like he's just... gone. Forever." His shoulders slumped, and he stared at the ground while flicking the ash out of habit. "I can't watch them lower the coffin. I don't want to see my brother being put into the ground."

He seemed to be looking for permission to miss the rest of the service. "You don't have to go back."

Dare nodded. He smoked, and I stared out at the rows upon rows of headstones. My father's body was interred at my mother's family burial plot in a cemetery not far from here. At the end of shivah, we floated down the Itchetucknee River, where we'd spent some of our happiest times as a family. Mom and I made a yearly trip during the summer and allowed ourselves to grieve. I wondered if the Chalmerses would do something similar to honor Mason.

Nearby a chickadee made its call, *cheeseburger, cheeseburger, cheeseburger*, reminding me how strange it was that even with your loved ones gone, the world continues on.

"It's all my fault," Dare said, biting down on his lower lip.

"It's not."

"It is. It absolutely is. Here's something you should know about my brother. Mason hated scary movies, and the only way he'd watch one was if I'd already seen it and could tell him when bad things were about to happen." He took a terse drag from his cigarette and blew out the smoke aggressively. "And I keep thinking about what he must have experienced the night he died—how scared he must have been—and I wasn't there to protect him."

I placed a hand on his back to reassure him. I understood what he felt.

"He needed me, Charlie, and I bailed on him."

"If you had known, you would have fought his attacker with everything you have."

"Yes, I would have." His regret was threaded with menace. "And I will." He blew out a deep smoke-fumed sigh and crushed his spent cigarette on the sole of his shoe. "How's the investigation going?"

I sensed this was his attempt to switch topics, though the subject certainly wasn't light-hearted. I didn't want to tell him I'd reached a dead end, but I owed him the truth. "I still need to check on a few alibis, but right now, everyone acts suspicious but no one seems to have a strong enough motive. My mom also hasn't been too cooperative with sharing evidence."

"Didn't Daniela say my brother had been going to Café Risqué this summer?"

I nodded. "You think there's something there?"

"He never told me about it. Just like the drugs. Mason was hiding things from everyone, including me. I feel like the key to finding his murderer is figuring out what the hell he was up to."

"I can check it out," I told him. "But I won't be able to get inside. I don't turn eighteen until April, and I don't have a fake ID."

"I can get around that. What are you doing this afternoon?"

"Isn't there a reception happening at your house?" I asked.

Dare grunted. "Yeah, I have to be there for that. My mother will kill me if I miss it. How about after then?"

I'd have to make up an excuse to tell my mom. Not an excuse, I'd have to flat-out lie to her, but maybe she'd be busy following up on her own leads. "Sure, I'll hang out until you're finished and we'll go together."

Dare stood and offered me his hand. He looked a bit brighter than when I'd found him. Searching for his brother's killer gave him purpose. I understood that. Part of what was so maddening with my father was there was no one to direct all my anger and frustration at, except for him and in a roundabout way, myself.

I worried, though, when Mason's killer was found, if Dare might not be worse off for it.

CHAPTER 11

THE RECEPTION at Dare's house lasted for a few hours, and then some of Mason and Dare's friends hung out by the pool and reminisced. I was on the outside of their shared experiences, which allowed me to listen for any clues that might be nested in their conversation, but most of the stories I'd heard already, and none of them hinted at any undiscovered scandal. Dare seemed to delight in their stories, though all were tinged with a pallor of melancholy. I kept thinking about what Dare had said about looking backward and never forward. Like that pendant Ms. Sparrow wore, a life forever trapped in resin.

While waiting for the bathroom, I heard a snuffling noise coming from inside. It sounded like someone was crying. I drew back into the shadows of the hallway and waited for the mourner to emerge. I was shocked to see Peter Orr with a splotchy, tear-stained face, and instead of rejoining the group of friends out back, he skirted around the remaining members of the Chalmerses's party and headed for the front door. I felt as though this was my chance, if ever there was one, to get Peter to open up.

"Hey, Peter, wait up." He swiveled around with a savage expression, upset that I'd caught him emoting, as if it weren't a natural and healthy expression to be sad over a friend's death.

"What do you want?" he growled. His eyes were red and his freckles stood out more prominently on his brick-like face.

"I just wanted to thank you and the team for coming out. I'm sure Dare appreciated it."

Peter shook his head, a rueful twist to his lips. "It's all about Dare, isn't it? Even now. Mason is dead and Dare's still on stage getting all the applause."

That seemed like a pretty harsh assessment, but I was curious to follow that trail to see where we might end up.

"You don't like Dare," I said.

"It's not that." Peter plugged his eyes with his fists. "They just… they get whatever they want, you know? Everything's been handed to them, their whole lives. They don't even have to work for it. Makes me mad, is all."

I could argue that none of it mattered now because Mason was dead and Dare was missing his other half desperately, but I decided to take a more sympathetic route. "Like in wrestling? It just came easy to Mason."

"Yeah, it did. God, they're so stupid, the both of them. I just wish...."

I waited for him to finish the thought.

And waited.

"What do you wish, Peter?"

Peter looked at me as though trying to determine whether or not I could be trusted. "I wish Mason had more common sense, is all. Maybe if the two of them weren't always trying to one-up each other, this might have never happened."

He shook his head again and stalked out the front door. A moment later I heard tires squealing as I puzzled over how a competitive streak between the brothers and a penchant for pranks could lead to Mason's murder. And what Peter might know about Mason's death that he wasn't revealing.

"Anger issues," said a voice beside me. Joey had snuck up on us in the hallway and caught the tail end of our interaction. He still wore his black funeral suit, along with his UF ball cap. Still, it wasn't enough to hide his swollen eyes.

"You know Peter well?" I asked Joey.

"Well enough. I don't care to know him any better."

Interesting.

"Were Mason and Peter close?"

"Mason tolerated Peter. That's about the extent of their friendship."

"Why's that?"

"Peter's a dick, but Mason said Peter made him better. More competitive, I mean. If Mason could beat Peter in a match, he could beat anyone."

"Did Mason ever throw that in his face?"

Joey shrugged. "The usual trash talk. Nothing out of the ordinary, though."

I recalled then a rumor from last year, some kind of falling-out between Joey and Peter. "Didn't you and Peter get in a fight last year?"

Joey wiped his mouth with his knuckles. "Yeah."

"What was that about?"

He frowned and shook his head. "Nothing."

I stared at him, and he stared back. His eyebrows lifted like he was waiting for me to say something. Beating me at my own game. Something had gone down between the three of them last year, and I suspected Dare was involved too. None of them wanted to talk about it, though. I'd need Tameka's help to get to the bottom of this.

Joey's alibi was airtight—if the killer was working alone. But if Joey knew where Mason was headed the night he was murdered, he could have alerted the killer to his whereabouts.

"You were pretty close to Mason, weren't you?"

"Best friends since kindergarten," Joey said with a sigh.

"Your friendship must have had its ups and downs."

"Ups, mostly." He swallowed and closed his eyes. It looked as if he was trying to stop himself from crying. Sorrow or guilt?

Joey was the one to determine whether a new member was allowed into their circle. It was something less stated and more understood. But what if Joey felt threatened that Mason might gain a new best friend?

"Mason was pretty popular. It must have been hard to keep his attention, huh?"

Joey looked up, perhaps realizing the nature of my questions had taken a turn.

"If you're trying to say I was jealous of Peter Orr, I wasn't. Peter's a tool."

"What about Dare's relationship with Mason?"

"Dare's my friend too. The three of us are like brothers."

"But they're not your actual brothers. Did you ever feel left out?"

"Sure, but that's the way it goes, right?" He glanced past me to the rapidly thinning crowd of guests. "Looks like the party's over. I'd better go check on Dare." He patted my shoulder on his way past me. "Keep up the good work, Dick."

I couldn't tell if Joey was mocking me or encouraging me. I was still ruminating about a possible motive while he and Dare said their goodbyes.

"You still want to make the trip to Micanopy?" I asked Dare after all his guests had left. It was late. He must be exhausted by the day.

"Absolutely. It's the only thing getting me through this."

The fight was still on my mind, though, and even though Dare had stonewalled me last time I asked him about it, it couldn't hurt to try again. "Joey and Peter Orr got into a fight last year, didn't they?" I studied Dare closely as I said it.

"Yeah," he admitted after a long pause.

"What was that about?"

He shook his head. "It was stupid. Not important."

"It might be important to the case. You have to trust me, Dare."

He placed a hand on my shoulder, his eyes crinkling at the corners. He really knew how to gain my sympathies. "I do trust you, Charlie, and I want to be honest with you, but some secrets aren't mine to tell. This is one of them."

I narrowed my eyes, wishing again for the superpower of mindreading, so I could know exactly what was going on inside that beautiful head of his. Instead I opened his front door to guide him out into the eerily quiet night.

So many secrets.

WE HEADED out into the inky, starless night, southbound on I-75. All along the stretch of interstate between Gainesville and Ocala, Café Risqué billboards promised great food in a welcoming venue where "We bare all." The billboards used to have a picture of this blonde woman from the eighties with feathered hair, which could have easily been mistaken for a teen pregnancy hotline or a missing persons advertisement. But in recent years, the business rebranded to feature silhouettes of busty women in provocative poses, and one in particular of a woman gripping a pole in ecstasy.

It seemed we were all chasing some ridiculous fantasy.

A trip to Café Risqué was something like a rite of passage for central Florida teens on the cusp of manhood, and one I'd always assumed I'd happily forgo due to my sexual orientation, and yet, there I was, racing to the famed truck stop with Dare in his sleek silver Jaguar, intent on looking for clues to the identity of Mason's killer.

We arrived at about 10:00 p.m. Dare gave me Mason's ID, which could pass for my own if the lighting was dim and the bouncer didn't look too closely. Still, I was nervous about potentially breaking the law. The first place they'd call was the local police, who would contact my mom. She'd probably send someone to arrest me just to scare me straight.

The bouncer in question roved his flashlight over Dare's ID and then over his person. Dare's height made him look older, along with the scruff of a few days without shaving that had accumulated on his jaw. It was pretty sexy, actually, and I scolded myself for even looking at him in that way.

When it was my turn, the bouncer inspected me a little closer.

"You're twins?" he asked while side-eyeing the both of us. "You don't look alike."

"Fraternal," Dare clarified. He made a motion to move past the bouncer, who held out his hand to block him. The man turned to me.

"What's up with your hair?"

"It grew out."

"What's your sign...." He squinted at the ID. "Mason?"

"Scorpio," I said easily. I'd memorized that a long time ago.

"Where do you live?"

I recited the Chalmerses's address. I had a knack for memorization. And riding past their house on my bike when I was at the height of my stalking phase didn't hurt my recall either.

"You been drinking?" he flashed his light in my eyes, blinding me.

"No, sir," I answered.

"All right, then." He passed the ID back to me. "No funny business, and make sure you tip the ladies. They aren't here for their health."

I wasn't sure what to expect when I entered into the surprisingly well-lit Café Risqué. It was kind of like when you built something up in your mind so much that the reality couldn't possibly match up to your expectations. I wasn't disappointed by the interior, not exactly, but it seemed so much smaller than I'd imagined. Other than the poles, it really did resemble a Denny's or some other greasy spoon. There were booths along one side of the dining area and a bar that butted up to a small empty stage, where I assumed the main event would take place. There was also a side shop that sold ladies' lingerie and pornographic DVDs, but overall, it was pretty underwhelming.

There were a few truckers in the booths, being served by women in revealing outfits, something like a costume you might pick up on a discount rack after Halloween—naughty nurse or curious co-ed. So far, nothing that lived up to the motto of "We bare all."

Dare suggested we sit at the bar and soon after, a waitress approached us. She appeared to be in her late thirties, dyed red hair, heavy on the makeup, with her ample, freckled bosom squeezed into a cropped leather bustier. "What would you handsome fellas like to drink?" she asked with a salacious grin.

I knew from the signs out front they didn't serve alcohol, which seemed a little strange to me, but if this venue really catered to truckers, then I supposed it wouldn't do to get them liquored up while pulling an all-nighter. In fact, the idea of a place where truckers could get a square meal while also admiring naked women to help pass their long and lonely rides had an almost wholesome appeal.

"Cherry coke?" Dare asked, looking at me. He seemed perfectly comfortable with our situation and not at all put off by the strange mix of fry grease and sex pheromones circulating in the air.

"Coke's good. Regular for me," I said as I steered my eyes away from our server's chest. I'd kind of zoned out there for a minute. She left us with two menus, and Dare scanned his dutifully.

"This is not what I was expecting," he said in a low voice.

"No, me neither," I admitted.

"I really can't believe this." He studied his menu with a look of deep concentration.

"What is it?" I thought perhaps he'd stumbled across a clue.

"The food's actually very reasonably priced."

I laughed out loud at Dare's practicality. He glanced over with a small smile that acknowledged the sheer oddity of our situation. Our waitress, Cherry, returned soon after and took our order. Mine was a hamburger and curly fries. Dare's was soup and salad, and I remembered what he'd told me before about how greasy food upset his stomach. As she was leaving, Dare grabbed her arm. "Wait a minute, if you would."

"No touching, sweetie," she said in an almost motherly fashion.

Dare released her immediately and apologized. "I was wondering if you've ever seen this man." Dare pulled up a photo of him and Mason on his phone, the one taken from the pep rally with Mason in his singlet.

"You a cop?" she asked with dismay.

"No, ma'am. It's my brother. He's gone missing, and he used to come here from time to time, over the summer, I believe. I was wondering when he might have been here last. If you might have seen him?"

His sincere desperation came through in his appeal and Cherry took another hard look. "I don't recognize him, but one of the late-night girls might." She pointed to the stage, which was really just an extension of the bar and less than two feet in front of us. "They come on in about a half an hour, if you want to ask them."

The place had a definite between-shift vibe. Cherry herself said she'd close out our order when she brought us our food. "It's past my bedtime," she said, yawning unapologetically as she collected the money for the food and her tip. Dare insisted on paying for my meal, but it wasn't like we were on a date. More like he was paying my expenses.

We were just finishing our meal when the jukebox kicked on. I hadn't noticed it before, but it stood in a dim corner of the room. There were a couple of burly men going over the choices with an almost academic fastidiousness.

I recognized the song after the first couple intro bars of a searing guitar riff: "Sweet Child of Mine" by Guns N' Roses. Dare grabbed my arm. "Charlie, look."

I turned. Onstage, among a cloud of fog and strobe lights, five women of varying ages, ethnicities, and statures entered the spotlights, wearing stilettos and nothing else.

"We bare all," Dare said with wonder. As it turned out, Café Risqué's motto was absolutely true. Dare handed me a stack of bills. "Time to splash some cash, Charlie."

And then with a look of childlike glee, Dare made it rain.

I DIDN'T realize until after their performance, Dare was baiting the dancers. When they finished their set, the women circulated through the bar, offering up private dances to the patrons. All of them had their eyes on Dare. The first two women he slipped a twenty and showed them his phone, asked them if they'd seen Mason. They hadn't but were happy to take his cash nonetheless. One of the women told Dare she'd give him a deep discount on a private dance on account of him being so easy on the eyes. It actually took quite a bit of the Chalmers's charm to let her off easy.

The third woman, who was blonde, or perhaps wearing a blonde wig, was the closest to our age. She looked from the picture to Dare and said, "Private dances are forty bucks."

I thought she was only angling for an upsale, but Dare seemed on board with it. "My friend Charlie here wants a dance. And I want to watch."

"Each dance is forty. No freebies," she studied me with a peculiar expression. I wiped my mouth, thinking there might be ketchup on my face.

"Lucky for me, I'm a rich bastard," Dare replied.

The woman introduced herself as Crystal and led us to a back room where there were booths covered in red vinyl, kind of like a Pizza Hut. Easy to wipe clean, I thought and then shivered with disgust. About five feet away was a video camera recording everything that happened in the room. I prayed my mother never saw this footage.

"Don't worry," Crystal said, perhaps noticing my unease. "It doesn't record sound." She then gave us a list of rules, which included, among other things, no touching.

"You don't have to worry about that," I assured her, sweating profusely. I'd never seen a naked woman this close before, and even after watching Crystal grind and gyrate on the pole, having her practically on top of me felt criminal. Her boobs were everywhere. I didn't know where to put my hands so I wouldn't accidentally touch her, so I shoved them between my legs.

"Are you sure this is legal?" I asked Dare.

He gave me an amused look. "You'll have to excuse my friend, Crystal. Charlie has a girlfriend, but like I told him, so long as there's no touching, it's not cheating. Am I right?"

"That's right, baby," she said, winking at Dare. A rap song came on, something fast with a deep bass line. Crystal straddled my knees, which were pressed tightly together. "Just relax now, baby. Crystal will make you feel all right," she cooed in my ear. Her hair tickled my neck, and her heavy bosoms nearly brushed up against me.

"Maybe you should take this one," I said to Dare, who sat to the side of us, watching with complete rapture. His arms stretched out along the top of the booth like this was an everyday occurrence. Funny thing was, his attention seemed more focused on me than the naked woman on my lap.

Dare shook his head with a huge smile on his face. He was really getting a kick out of this. "It's your birthday, Bud. Just sit back and enjoy it. Let's see what turns up."

I gulped and pressed back as far as I could into the slightly reclined seat. It felt a little bit like being at the dentist's office when you're trying really hard not to get any of your bodily juices on the dental hygienist. But the more I retreated, the more Crystal advanced. She gyrated in lazy circles, cupping her boobs and pinching her nipples to perhaps add to the excitement. She moaned a little, trying to sell it. I wanted to squeeze my eyes shut and count in my head until it was over, but I didn't want to be rude.

"Did you recognize my brother Mason?" Dare finally asked, studying her critically. He didn't seem aroused in the least by her performance, just deadly focused on getting answers.

"I saw him in the news," she said. "Is he... dead?"

"Yes, he is." Dare ducked his head so that she wouldn't see his face. Still, Crystal seemed sympathetic to his pain.

"I'm sorry. He seemed like a nice guy."

"He was," Dare said quietly. "So, you met him?"

"He came in here a couple times while I was on shift." She reached down to spread my knees open, as though she could force me to relax. She grabbed my hands as if we were dance partners. I probably resembled a very stiff puppet.

"I thought there was no touching," I said, feeling a little panicked.

"You can't touch me, but I can touch you," she said with a teasing smile. It made absolutely no sense to me. Touching was touching, but I didn't want to argue the point with her.

"Did you see him with anyone else?" Dare asked.

"Yeah, a beefy red-headed kid. Bad attitude. He complained about the girls being fat. He was kind of an asshole, if I'm honest. Not your brother, though. He was a good tipper, just like you." She dabbed Dare's nose with the tip of her finger. He went cross-eyed for a moment and then drew his finger along the end of his nose where she'd touched him.

"Did it seem like my brother was just here to enjoy the entertainment, or was he meeting someone?" Dare asked.

Crystal turned around so I could get a full view of her bulbous butt, jumping up and down to the beat with practiced efficiency. At least now she couldn't see me cower.

"There was another man here with them. Older. White hair and a fake tan. Looks like he works out a lot. He's a regular."

Dare leaned in closer. "When was the last time you saw him?"

"He's here tonight," she said. "He was sitting next to you at the bar."

My mind flashed back to the guy she was describing. He was wearing a sleeveless shirt and a red bandana and his arms were grossly huge, like a Hulk Hogan wannabe. I suddenly knew what pills Mason had been taking.

"Steroids," I said aloud.

Dare slumped back into his seat, realizing my meaning. A speaker piped up in the room. "Crystal, finish up. The cops are here."

I glanced over at Dare. "It might be GPD." As I was indisposed, Dare poked his head out of the room to take a look down the hallway. He turned back to the two of us, both of us having given up this charade and awaiting his word.

"One more favor, Crystal. You've got to get us out the back." Dare laid a stack of bills on the red vinyl booth.

"Is it your girlfriend?" she asked with exasperation, as though that sort of thing happened frequently.

"Nope," Dare said. "It's Charlie's mother."

CRYSTAL LED us out through the kitchen. Thankfully the kitchen staff wore *all* their clothing and bared nothing. Crystal didn't go any farther than the back door because she was nude and it was a bit nippy outside. Before she shut the door, Dare said to her, "We're going to hang out in the woods over there until the cops leave. If you can get me the name of that muscle-bound guy, I've got another hundred-dollar bill with your name on it."

She smiled. "Sure thing, baby. I owe you a free DVD too. What are you boys into?"

We glanced at each other, and for once Dare was as tongue-tied as me. Crystal rolled her eyes. She really had no patience for our naivety. "Forget it. I'll pick you out something good."

We jogged across the parking lot and into the woods behind the dumpster, just in case the police did a sweep of the perimeter. I wondered if my mother was here checking out a lead, or if GPD was making a routine stop to make sure no one was underage. I didn't think it was the latter because Micanopy was outside GPD's jurisdiction, and my mom typically wasn't sent on those runs anyway. She must know something of Mason's visits to Café Risqué.

If only we teamed up, we'd be that much stronger.

"Did you enjoy your private dance?" Dare's eyes were full of mirth as he looked me over.

I shook my head. "Why is it that I seem to be the one making all the sacrifices for this investigation? First a makeover, then a lap dance. What's next?"

Dare laughed. I'd almost forgotten what it sounded like, so much like Mason's.

"I thought you might enjoy it," he said, "but you looked the same way you did that time in eighth grade when Aaron Ramirez was passing around his girlfriend's panties in the boys' bathroom."

I recoiled from the memory. I'd somehow managed to block that out. "If I didn't already know I was gay, I'm pretty sure that experience just proved it."

Dare stopped laughing and looked at me with a serious expression. "Wait a minute, you're gay?"

I studied him to see if he was teasing me. "Are you messing with me?"

"I swear I'm not." He crossed himself, loosely. "I seriously didn't know that."

"How could you *not* know that?" I asked with incredulity.

"I mean, I've heard rumors, but you never said anything to me about it."

"I thought the rule of the drama department is you're gay until proven otherwise." For the record, that wasn't a rule I made up. It was already in existence when I started hanging out backstage with the Phantom and his cast and crew.

"Yeah, but you're not exactly a drama kid." Dare studied me as though seeing me again for the first time. I felt like a frog being pinned down for dissection.

"Are *you* gay?" I asked to take the attention off me.

"Probably," he said with a shrug, which kind of frustrated me that he couldn't even commit to that. "Well, this changes everything," Dare said. I was about to ask him what he meant by it when he turned on me again, advancing in my direction. "Have you ever had a boyfriend before?"

"No," I admitted.

"Have you ever kissed someone?"

I swallowed tightly, feeling a little embarrassed by my answer. "No."

"Well, that's just ridiculous." He sounded almost angry about it.

I didn't want Dare's pity. Surely there was at least one person out there who thought me desirable. Maybe not at Eastview High, but the world was far bigger than our high school or even the town of Gainesville. I could be patient.

I turned away, unable to stand the judgment in his stare, and surveyed the building, wondering how much longer we'd need to hide in the trees before we could collect Dare's car and get the heck out of there.

Dare grabbed my hand and turned me around to face him. I still wore my funeral slacks and a white button-down shirt, though I'd left my coat and tie in Dare's car. The smell of sex was upon me, even if it wasn't my own. That and Crystal's residual perfume. Dare seized my shirtfront and pulled me to him.

"Can I kiss you, Charlie?" he asked in a deep baritone that made my balls hum like a tuning fork.

Did I hear him correctly? Dare Chalmers just asked to kiss me? Me, of all people? Dare looked at me with a curious tilt to his head, a small smile curving his lips. Almost like… anticipation.

"Ummm, yesss," I slurred in a stupor.

In my mind the opening notes of "All I Ask of You" started playing, and as our lips met, all those feelings of elation and joy I'd experienced in listening to Dare sing as the Phantom rushed back at me, lifting me a little onto the balls of my feet. I expected Dare to pull away after the initial sweep of our lips, but he gripped my shirtfront and pulled me in closer, breaching my mouth with his tongue. I welcomed him inside. I'd never had someone else's tongue touching mine before, but Dare's mouth was so soft, his lips as sweet and pliable as saltwater taffy. His stubble tickled my cheek, and the contrast of his soft mouth and rough beard made my head spin. I was glad for Dare's grip because I felt a little light-headed, like I was falling backward in some kind of trust fall, perhaps because my blood was rushing elsewhere. My fists wrinkled the silky material at Dare's waist and without thinking, I pressed my groin against his to discover both of us aroused, and me immediately and intensely hard. I ground my hips to cause a little friction, and he gasped into my mouth. His sweet cherry-cola breath put me in a trancelike state of arousal as my thigh nudged between his legs. I didn't know what I was initiating, only that I wanted his long, lithe body pressed up against mine. Like two live wires coiled together, that's how close I wanted him to me.

"Char-lie," he whispered provocatively. My mind flashed back to Boots showering Dare with affection, and I told my body to show some restraint. Before I could summon the self-control to break away, the sound of someone clearing their throat interrupted us.

"Yeah, that's what I thought."

Crystal was back, wearing a fleece robe and flip-flops this time. She handed Dare a business card.

"What's this?" he asked, looking disheveled and disoriented. His lips were puffy and his green-gray eyes were blown out with desire, his irises like twin eclipses. Could I possibly have had that effect on Dare Chalmers?

"That's your man." She held out her hand for payment. Dare studied the card as if memorizing it, then tucked it carefully into his wallet. He pulled out a crisp hundred-dollar bill and laid it on Crystal's open palm.

"Pleasure doing business with you." Her fist closed around the money, and she took another critical look at the two of us. "Why are the nice ones always gay?" She handed me a DVD wrapped in a black plastic bag and sauntered back toward the building. Over her shoulder she said, "Oh yeah, and the cops are gone."

I'd forgotten why we'd even come out here in the first place. Dare's kiss scrambled my brain, but in the best possible way.

"You're a good kisser, Charlie," Dare said with a shy smile. His voice had a husky, dreamlike quality to it.

"Back at ya, Dare."

We stared at each other for a long moment and then Dare broke the silence with, "So, what titillating DVD did Crystal pick for us?"

I'd forgotten I was even holding anything. "It looks like, *dum, dum, dum*...." I pulled it out of the bag. "*Jocks on Cocks*?"

Dare laughed and took the DVD to inspect it closer. It was definitely gay porn, and the men appeared to be well versed in athletic pursuits as well. "Sounds like a Dr. Seuss title," he remarked.

I smirked. "Maybe it rhymes."

Dare handed me the DVD. "Promise me this, Charlie, when you're ready to experience *Jocks on Cocks*, please call me, and we'll watch it together."

It could either be really good or really bad. "I would, Dare, but I don't even have a DVD player."

"I got you covered. I have one hooked up with surround sound." He threw his arm around my shoulders as we walked back to his car under the neon lights of Café Risqué.

I'd always assumed that, like my door-holding duties, once my sleuthing services concluded, Dare and I would retreat back into our separate circles on opposite poles of the social strata, but Dare made it seem like there might be a friendship for us at the end of all this.

I hoped so.

CHAPTER 12

ON OUR way back to Gainesville, Dare wanted to pull over at a rest stop and make a call to the tip line from one of the pay phones so they couldn't identify his cell phone number. I was on board with his idea. It meant my mom never had to know I'd visited Café Risqué.

On the phone, Dare disguised his voice by making it slow and southern with an exaggerated drawl. He really was a better actor than I gave him credit for. The dispatcher asked for his name, but he wouldn't give it.

"Ain't this supposed to be anonymous?" he said like a cantankerous old man. "I'm not trying to give my name and number to the law, ma'am." She said something conciliatory in response, and Dare continued. "Yeah, well, I was over at the Café Risqué, and I saw a man selling pills to this young man you got listed here. Uh, Mason Chalmers?"

The dispatcher asked some questions, and Dare described the muscle-bound man. "I got his name too." Dare read it from the card. "Clayton Benson. Works out of Dunnellon. Mainstream Freight is the name of his outfit—that's his day job, I guess. Selling drugs to kids must be his side business."

Dare answered a few more of the dispatcher's questions without once breaking character and then hung up. "I hope that guy gets busted." Dare glared at the phone, his long fingers still splayed along the spine of the receiver.

"Me too." But while Dare had been making his anonymous tip, I'd been thinking about Mason's steroid use. "I don't think Clayton Benson is the murderer, Dare."

"Why not?"

I laid out my theory for him. "Mason made trips to Café Risqué this summer, but once school started, he stopped going, and you found the remaining pills in his bedroom, which meant he'd also stopped using."

"Because he didn't want them to show up on a drug test," Dare concluded for me.

"Which means Mason wasn't going to meet his drug dealer on Friday night."

"So who the hell was he meeting?" Dare asked, his brow wrinkled in frustration.

"I don't know," I admitted. There was nothing at the end of that road but a ghost town. "I'm going to search the property appraisers' website and see who lives in the town of Rochelle."

"That's a good idea. You want me to come over?"

My mother wouldn't want me having Dare over after midnight. Or at all.

"No, it's all right. I'll do some research tonight, and I'll call you in the morning with what I find."

For the rest of the drive home, I wondered if Dare was going to bring up the kiss we shared, but he seemed lost in thought, no doubt about Mason. His parting words when he dropped me off at my house were "Today sucked, but having you by my side made it a little more bearable. I appreciate everything you're doing for me, Charlie. And Mason too."

We said goodbye, and I spent the next few hours online. Boots snuggled up to me in bed and snuffled a complaint whenever I switched positions. I was a night owl and he was a morning person, but somehow we made it work. I came up with a long list of names—none of which I recognized—and fell asleep with my computer in my lap, my homework far from finished. Dare called me in the morning to see if I'd made any progress.

"Not really," I told him, "but I have an idea."

"I'm listening."

"Stakeout."

"I'm *so* there," Dare said with a hint of excitement.

Dare had told me he wouldn't be coming back to school until Monday, and I couldn't afford to skip school this close to our end-of-semester exams. If I let my grades slip, my mom really would ground me.

"I'll pick you up after school," I told Dare. "We'll take my car. It's a little less conspicuous."

"I'll bring snacks," Dare said. I smiled on my end, thinking he'd probably picked that up from watching television. Though snacks were never a bad idea.

I struggled through the school day, barely able to focus on classwork or what my teachers were saying. Luckily it was a Friday, and since most of the student body and teaching staff had attended Mason's funeral the day before, no one was really intent on learning anything. We were all looking forward to the weekend.

I did manage to catch up with Tameka during lunch. "Do you remember a fight between Peter Orr and Joey Pikramenos last year?" I asked. We were sitting on the brick wall outside the cafeteria, away from her curious clutch of eavesdropping cheerleaders.

"Yeah, I was there when it happened. In the hallway of the Kelso building. The two of them just exploded. It was over so fast, I don't think teachers even knew."

"Do you know what it was about?"

She shook her head. "I didn't even realize it was a fight at first. I thought they were just messing around."

"Was Mason or Dare there?"

She tilted her head. "Don't think so."

Even still, something told me one or both of the twins was involved. "You think you can ask around? See what might have started it?"

She glanced sideways at me. "You get that Amazon wish list I sent you?"

"Real subtle." I nodded. "Your items have shipped."

She smiled smugly and squeezed my shoulder. "Then yes, I would be happy to ask around."

I thanked her, then hopped up and crossed the courtyard to where Peter stood with a mishmash of football, wrestling, and baseball players. My mind flashed back to the cover of *Jocks on Cocks*, and I had to shake myself to clear my mental palate.

"Hey, Peter, got a minute?"

He gave me a wary look. "Make it quick," he said and motioned for me to follow him away from his friends. I didn't want to spread rumors about Mason, especially now, but some reveal was essential to the investigation.

"Did you know Mason was using steroids?" I asked Peter with a note of incredulity.

"No, but it makes sense," Peter said without much reaction. The kid was really hard to read, and I didn't know if it was because he had a thick skin or if he was just really good at hiding his emotions.

"How does it make sense?"

"You don't get stacked like that so quickly just from working out." He glanced around to make sure no one was nearby to overhear us. "Coach probably suggested it."

"Coach Gundry?" I asked with astonishment. Peter looked bored. "Isn't that... illegal?"

"Whatever it takes to win, right?" he said flatly.

This was certainly a surprising discovery. I'd never played sports competitively, so I didn't know if this was an isolated incident or a systemic problem. "Is that normal?" I asked Peter. He only shrugged, so I pursued it further. "Did Coach ever encourage you to take steroids?"

Peter glared at me. "This isn't about me."

If what Peter said was true, then Mason had leverage; if Mason told the school about Coach's methods, he could get fired, possibly even face charges, especially considering how sue-happy the Chalmerses were.

"Is that why you were the one who had to cut weight? Because Mason threatened to tell on Coach?"

Peter grunted and spat on the ground. "I don't ask questions. I just follow orders."

He said it so dispassionately, but I found it hard to believe that Peter would go along with that plan so willingly.

"Doesn't that make you mad? Having to drop down an entire weight class? I mean, Mason was basically cheating, and Coach was helping him."

Peter stared at me like I was being dramatic. "It might make me mad if we were still competing, but we're not, so...." He glanced around as though he had someplace better to be.

I wanted to needle him more, if only to see what he might reveal. "You must have been using too, then, huh?"

Peter's eyes cut back to mine. They had a reptilian coldness about them, especially with his shovel-like face. I wasn't sure if this was just his standard response to a challenge or if it was something special for me.

"Are you accusing me of something, Dick?"

He was using the nickname, which told me I was finally getting under his skin. Good. That was when I got my best information. "Mason was buying the drugs from a guy at Café Risqué, and you were there, Peter. Seems like steroid use is grounds for suspension from the team. You could miss out on your entire senior year."

Peter crossed his arms, perhaps to better contain his fists, which I'd noticed were tense. "Mason paid for me to get a private dance. He probably made the deal then. I don't do drugs, because I'm not a cheater. And if you're planning on putting your nose in *my* business, then you and I are going to have problems."

He jammed one meaty finger against my chest, then stalked back toward his friends with his head ducked low and his broad shoulders swinging. One thing was for certain, I wouldn't want to be alone in a dark alley with him.

Still, talking with Peter hadn't been a waste of time, because I now knew that Coach Gundry had a motive after all. If Mason had threatened Coach with going public, he might have taken drastic measures to silence him.

After school, I picked up Dare from his house and we drove out of town along Hawthorne Road, then turned off where Mason was most likely headed Friday night before his tire went flat. County Road 2082 was rough and full of potholes, a further deterrent, especially for someone like Mason who, according to Dare, didn't especially like long car rides. I pulled in at the parking area for cyclists who wished to travel the paved trail that ran alongside the road. My car was angled so we'd face the sparse afternoon traffic.

The murderer could have been on a bicycle, I reasoned. That would explain why there was no second set of tire tracks between the road and the lake. It struck me as weird, though. How many serial killers have stalked their victims by bicycle, and how many cyclists have spontaneously decided to murder?

Once I parked, Dare opened up his backpack to show me his stash of granola bars, fresh fruit, and potato chips. "See anything you like?" he asked suggestively.

My face flushed with embarrassment as lustful memories of last night's kiss flooded my senses. Dare's mouth on mine, our bodies pressed together, the flare of desire he ignited in me that throbbed in my nether regions like a dull, persistent ache. I cleared my throat.

"I'll take one of these." I grabbed an apple. I needed something to sink my teeth into.

We made a plan. Every time a car approached from either direction, Dare would grab the binoculars, and I'd get my phone ready to punch in the license plate numbers as he recited them. My mom had access to a program where she could look them up later. Maybe she'd even let me do it, since the work was so tedious. It wasn't "rush hour," so there wasn't a lot of traffic on the road, which meant long stretches of time where we sat in companionable silence.

"Are we going to talk about last night?" Dare said during one of those occasions.

"I haven't heard anything from my mom about why GPD was there." She wasn't home when I got in last night and I didn't see her that morning either, which meant she must have stayed the night at the station. She did send me a text in the morning reminding me to put the trash cans by the road, which I did.

"Not that, Charlie." Dare rolled his head and picked at a piece of flaking vinyl on the center console. "You know…."

"Oh." He meant our kiss. I hadn't expected him to bring it up at all. "It was… a surprise. A nice one, though. Really nice." I stared at the steering wheel, worried he might see the raw desire right there on my face. Stake out or make out?

"It *was* nice." He smiled faintly. "You know the only reason I asked you to hold that door in *Phantom* was because I had a crush on you?"

My head swiveled in his direction; the boy was full of surprises. He glanced up and seemed a little embarrassed by it. "I mean, we probably could have rigged something up."

My jaw dropped. Literally. "I thought I was providing a valuable service to the theater."

Dare laughed. "You were, Charlie. Most definitely. You probably don't know this, but I tasked the entire drama department with finding out if you were straight or not, but no one could pin you down."

I recalled some of the pointed conversations I'd had with Dare's friends, and more than a couple of the female cast members who'd tried to make a move on me. I thought their flirtations were just part of their love-in culture. "You could have just asked me. Since when are you so shy, Dare?"

He hid his smile behind his hand. "I mean, I'm not shy, but I'm not an idiot either."

"You should have made a move." I smiled at him. What a nice surprise that would have been.

"I was going to ask you out at the cast party at Aaron's, but you never showed."

"I was there." I took a deep breath. A bit of honesty was in order. "I was too nervous to talk to you, so I basically hid in a closet all night."

"You what?" He looked shocked *and* dismayed.

"Yeah, then I went out and bought the *Phantom* soundtrack because I had this huge crush on you too." I paused and then figured, why not? "And if we're being honest, it didn't start last spring."

His eyebrows rose into another stratosphere.

"And then the SAT thing with Mason happened," I continued. After that, Dare would say hello to me in the halls, but not much else. "That kind of derailed everything."

He looked down at his hands. "I wasn't mad at you, but I had to take Mason's side."

I nodded. "I understand."

He sighed and glanced up at the empty road before us. "So these feelings of yours…." He licked his lips, then bit down on the lower one. So tempting. "Are they past or present tense?"

I reached for his hand. "Both."

He smiled and pressed my knuckles to his lips. Then he dropped it back into his lap with a deep sigh. "I like you, Charlie. A lot. And that kiss last night was amazing. But I'm pretty messed up right now."

People did strange things when they were in mourning. I punched a classmate in the face. Dare kissed me on the mouth, with tongue. "You're grieving."

"That doesn't mean I don't want to do it again."

"Okay." This was getting confusing.

"What I mean is, maybe we could take it slow?" There was that shy smile again, one that revealed Dare to have a bashful tenderness hidden beneath all that center-stage swagger.

Here was the simple truth. When Dare approached me months ago and sold me on the idea of holding a door shut for the spring musical, I didn't need much convincing. When Dare asked me earlier that week to help find his brother's killer, I didn't hesitate. Now Dare was asking me to be patient so we could see if there might be something between us on the other end of this horror show, and of course, I would honor his request. Gladly.

I squeezed his hand. "It was a really nice kiss, and I'm glad you did it. Now I can at least say I've made it to first base. But we don't need to stress about that right now. We have to stay focused."

Dare nodded, still looking conflicted. "I just didn't want you to think—"

I glanced up as a car came into view. I hadn't even heard it coming. Dare missed the license plate, but I recognized the car immediately. A blue Prius with a collage of activist bumper stickers, one of which said *Save Our Springs* in a retro seventies font.

"Ms. Sparrow," I muttered.

As Dare tried to glimpse the driver through the rear window with his binoculars, I started the engine, intent on following Ms. Sparrow to whatever destination she was headed.

"What's she doing out here?" Dare asked, his eyes focused on the back of her car as he recorded the license plate number. We followed at a safe distance until we saw her turn off onto a dirt road with pines crowding in on either side.

"That must be her house." Sparrow wasn't one of the names that came up on the property appraiser's search, so either she rented or owned property under a different name or she was living with someone else. "What should we do?" I asked Dare. We were idling at the end of her driveway.

"Let's talk to her," Dare said severely.

"Maybe we should wait until Monday. It feels weird going to a teacher's home."

"We can't wait, Charlie. Besides, I'll bet you anything Mason's been here."

I didn't know what he was basing his assumption on, but I agreed we couldn't afford to wait until Monday. "What if she has a big angry boyfriend? Or a big angry dog. Or a gun."

"I'm not scared of any of those things," he said. "Just let me do the talking."

I drove farther up the driveway, where there was another car parked—a battered old Nissan pickup truck. Jealous boyfriend, perhaps? I turned the car around so we were facing the road in case we needed to make a speedy exit. Without waiting for me to catch up, Dare marched up to the screen door and rapped hard on the flimsy aluminum. No one came to the door, so he shouted, "We know you're in there, Ms. Sparrow, and we know what you've been doing with my brother."

Not the approach I would have taken. Dare was bluffing—we had no idea what, if anything, she might have been doing with Mason—but it must've spooked her, because Ms. Sparrow opened the door soon after.

"What are you boys doing here?" she asked with a big, fake smile. I'd never in my life seen Ms. Sparrow grin with so much ferocity.

I glanced around at our surroundings. The place was pretty secluded, with the nearest neighbors a couple of forested acres away. It was possible Mason's murder could have been committed at the lake and his body brought here, though if that was the case, I doubted Ms. Sparrow had the physical strength to do it alone.

Unless she dismembered his body first.

I spotted a pile of firewood stacked at the other end of the front porch. I remembered my mother making the motion with her hand of one fast, hard chop. Like an axe or a shovel, both of which Ms. Sparrow would have experience using.

"We have some questions to ask you," I said to her. "Perhaps we could take this inside?"

Ms. Sparrow hesitated, then held open the door and showed us to a couch and matching love seat the color of mud. Dare perched on the edge of the love seat, and I took the spot next to him. I wanted to keep him close. Ms. Sparrow's house had a similar smell as her classroom—an earthy, incense-infused aroma—and it was decorated with a lot of artifacts from the natural world—sticks and crystals and hand-woven art. I bet if I looked hard enough I'd find a bong or hookah somewhere around here. Also known as the Berkley of Florida, Gainesville had a reputation for its proliferation of pot smoking. My mom had worked for a while in food service before joining GPD, and people would often try to pay for their meals with marijuana. It usually worked too, because Gainesville green was pretty widely accepted as currency. Of course, once Mom became a cop, those offers dropped off significantly.

But even though Ms. Sparrow was pretty young and fairly hip, it was still weird being in a teacher's house. I didn't really care to think about them having lives outside of Eastview High, and I didn't want to imagine Ms. Sparrow smoking pot or dancing naked around a fire, which was another ritual you'd often stumble across at a Gainesville party, especially when dealing with the kids from the massage school, according to my mother.

"Can I get you something to drink?" she asked pleasantly, playing hostess—or more likely, getting her lies in order. "Lemonade? Water?"

"I'll take a Dr Pepper," Dare said. Ms. Sparrow squinted at him and seemed thrown off by that request.

"I'm afraid I don't keep soda in the house," she said slowly, measuring her words. "Processed sugar is bad for your health."

"Are you sure?" Dare asked with a sneer. "That's Mason's favorite."

Ms. Sparrow sat down on the edge of the couch and pressed her lips together in a tight seam. "I know you're upset about your brother's death, Dare, but I'm not sure what I can do for you."

Dare stood suddenly and stalked through the small living room as if looking for proof of his brother's presence. His crooked gait was more pronounced in his agitated state, and I debated on whether to take over this interrogation. I didn't think Dare could be level-headed about it.

"Mason's truck was found not far from here," I told Ms. Sparrow. "So was his… body. He had no reason to come out this way unless it was to visit someone."

"Visit you," Dare accused.

"I'm sorry, but there seems to be a misunderstanding." Ms. Sparrow collected her courage as she stood. "I think you boys should leave."

Dare studied Ms. Sparrow a little closer. I didn't understand what he was looking at so intently until he whipped out his phone and snapped a picture.

"My brother gave you that." He pointed to the pendant around her neck.

"What?" Her hand fluttered to her amber-colored necklace. "That's ridiculous. I bought this myself."

"Where'd you buy it?" Dare asked.

"I…." She trailed off.

"My cousin works at the herbarium. She takes samples from plant cuttings and encases them in resin. I recognize that necklace because my mother has one just like it, and if you don't tell us what the hell is going on, my next stop is GPD to tell them you murdered my brother."

Ms. Sparrow collapsed into the couch. Her lower lip quivered, and even though she didn't cry, her face had a melty look about it. She was obviously lying to us, but I still felt a little bad for her. Dare seemed entirely unmoved.

"Speak," he commanded and gestured forcefully with his hand as though he could summon her confession by his will alone.

She glanced at me as though I could help her out of this situation. I only shrugged. As my mom was fond of saying, Ms. Sparrow had made her bed; now she had to lie in it.

"He was supposed to come over Friday night, but he never made it here. I swear I'd never hurt him."

"You were having an affair?" I asked.

She nodded. "Stupid. It was so *stupid* of me."

"Did you kill him?" Dare asked. "Because you were worried he'd tell someone?"

"No, of course not. He didn't want anyone to know about it either. It was just…." She shook her head miserably and wouldn't look at us. "It was a mistake."

"You have no alibi," Dare said. It sounded like a threat. His demeanor completely shifted when he thought someone had wronged Mason. He was cold and precise. Like a scalpel.

"I was here all night watching television," Ms. Sparrow said, wide-eyed. "There's a camera aimed at my front gate. Its footage is kept off-site. I'm sure they have it."

I asked her the name of the security company and made a note on my phone to follow up. Still, there was a hole in her story. "When did you and Mason make plans to meet?"

"Around 5:30 in the afternoon? I was…." She looked away. "It was Friday night. I was lonely."

"You called him out of wrestling practice?" I asked.

"No, of course not. We spoke by phone."

"What phone?"

"His cell."

I studied her. She didn't seem to be lying, and it fit with the timeline Daniela had given me, which meant Mason must have had a second phone. "Give me the number." She went to her purse, pulled out her phone, and scrolled through her contacts until she found the one labeled MC. Mason Chalmers. I took down the number.

"You won't tell anyone about this, will you?" She was asking Dare, not me.

Dare glared at her with no compassion whatsoever. "If you hadn't called my brother out here Friday night, he would have met me at Waffle Kingdom like he promised. And if he'd done that, he might still be alive right now. So I wouldn't be asking me for any favors."

"I'm so sorry, Dare," she said, sniffling. "He was a very special young man."

"You don't know anything about him," Dare snapped and stormed out of her house, slamming the screen door behind him. I mumbled a hurried goodbye to Ms. Sparrow and followed him out. Dare strode over to a pine tree and kicked it, chipping away at the flaky bark. I waited by the car to give him a minute to cool off. Even though he was furious, I considered it a breakthrough.

This information was the leverage I needed to make a deal with my mother.

Chapter 13

I GOT home that afternoon before my mom and cooked burgers on the charcoal grill outside. I gave one of the cooked patties to Boots because he was a very good boy. Then I threw a stick with him so he could work off the extra calories. Mom was right; he was getting a bit pudgy around the middle.

Mom arrived home when I was toasting the buns.

"What's this?" she asked. "You cooked dinner without being asked?"

"We haven't seen much of each other lately, and I wanted to catch up." That was true, even if it also meant catching up on the investigation.

"What a wonderful son you are." She kissed my cheek.

Mom asked me about my classes and upcoming tests, and I answered her questions adequately. When we were deep into a case, it was hard to focus on school. Priorities, I supposed.

After we ate, Mom helped clear the table and even offered to wash dishes. I told her I'd do it, but first I wanted to talk to her about something. We sat across from each other at the kitchen table. Her eyebrows lifted a little. She knew something was up.

"I've been doing a little digging," I began.

"Charlie," she groaned. "I don't want to hear anymore. You are *not* working on this case."

Her saying it didn't make it true. She started to stand, and I didn't want her to dismiss me so easily, so I went ahead and dropped a bomb.

"Mason was having an affair with a teacher."

She sat back down with a deep sigh of resignation and studied me. "How on earth do you know this?"

"Like I said, I've been doing some digging."

"You have proof?"

"The teacher confessed it to me." I didn't mention Dare was also with me when that confession occurred.

My mother was working it over in her mind, debating as to how relevant this was to her investigation and whether she could use this information she'd told me not to get. I decided to sweeten the pot. "They were communicating on a second phone."

Mom placed her palms flat on the table as though willing herself to be calm.

"Are you going to tell me who it is?" she asked. "Or are you going to make me guess?"

"I want to see the surveillance tapes of the high school parking lot from the night Mason went missing."

Her mouth dropped open in dismay. "That's not fair, Charlie. Do you realize I could lose my job if I showed those to you? And compromise the entire investigation?"

"I want to solve this case just as much as you, Mom. My intentions are pure."

She blew out her breath. "If that was true, you wouldn't be blackmailing me."

"This is a bribe, not blackmail." That word got thrown around way too liberally, and she of all people should recognize the difference.

She walked over to the kitchen sink and stared out the window. "You clearly have no regard for my feelings anymore," she said, laying on the guilt thicker than peanut butter on a dog treat.

"Of course I care about your feelings. I told you I had an inside track, and now it's proven useful. I know you're trying to protect me, but I'm committed to solving this case."

"And what if something happens to you? I can't lose you both, Charlie. Have you thought about what that would do to me?"

Even though I knew she wasn't lying, it didn't seem fair to bring my dad into it and make me feel guilty for doing something I'd been trained by her to do. It was like throwing a stick and telling Boots not to fetch it.

"I just want to look at the tapes. I'm not about to make a citizen's arrest or anything. And if there's anything I discover from watching them, I'll tell you. Like I always do."

She glared at me for another second, then strode out of the room, her low heels clicking on the linoleum like an insect's wings. I thought perhaps she was going to ground me, but a minute later she returned with her laptop, already open to the video. She used her remote to push Play and stood behind me while we watched the footage together.

There were two cameras set up at our school, one for the student parking lot and one for the faculty. The footage played side by side on her screen. The student parking lot camera only offered a clear shot of the front passenger side of Mason's truck, which was parked next to Daniela's Kia, and closer to the camera were Dare's Jag and Peter's Impala. In the faculty parking lot, I identified Coach Gundry's champagne-colored LeBaron convertible and Ms. Sparrow's blue Prius. My car was parked in BFE where no one cared enough to monitor with a camera. I recalled seeing Joey's Jeep there as well from time to time. He often arrived to school late, when all the other spots were filled.

Mom fast-forwarded the footage through the dismissal bell when several students and faculty left, including Ms. Sparrow and Dare. She resumed it right around 5:35 p.m. "This is where it gets interesting," she said.

Daniela came out first, holding a pair of metal scissors—she must have gotten them from the art room. She stabbed the front tire on the passenger side of Mason's truck. The footage showed her heading toward the tailgate, but because of the bad angle, we couldn't be certain of what happened on the back end or the driver's side. After completing the task, Daniela climbed into her car and left. The direction she turned out of the parking lot was toward the interstate, not Hawthorne Road.

"Why was there only one flat tire?" I asked Mom. "It looks like she slashed all of them."

"There were marks on all four tires, but only one was fully punctured, the first one she slashed. She didn't use enough force on the others. Perhaps her arm grew tired or she lacked the physical strength to finish the job."

"Or her desire for vengeance was waning."

Mom gave me a look that was part skepticism, part pride. "Just watch the video, Shakespeare."

The next person to come out to the parking lot was Peter Orr, already wearing a sauna suit that resembled puffy black trash bags. He stuffed a duffel bag into the back seat of his car and then jogged past Mason's truck on his way to the track. Coach Gundry came soon after, squinted in the direction of the setting sun as if trying to determine the time, glanced at his watch to confirm it, and then got into his car and drove away.

"When I talked to him, he acted like he didn't know what time it was when he left," I told my mom. "Coach keeps track of time. Always."

While it was suspicious, it wasn't proof of any wrongdoing, and I understood the difference. I thought about telling Mom that Coach Gundry was also the one to encourage Mason to use steroids, according to Peter Orr, but that would invite more questions, which might lead to me having to admit we'd gone to Café Risqué. I'd check on Coach's alibi before going down that road.

Finally Mason appeared. I recognized his jaunty, carefree walk. Despite just arguing with Daniela, he looked pretty optimistic. It was his birthday, after all. He was heading to an illicit rendezvous with Ms. Sparrow and then meeting up with Dare to eat waffles at his favorite breakfast dive. He looked happy and completely unaware that someone with malicious intent was about to take *everything* from him. It was hard to believe this footage was taken only a little more than a week ago. It felt like a lifetime already. Mason could have been or done anything. What a shame.

I couldn't see Mason get into his truck, but I did see him toss his duffel bag and letterman jacket into the passenger seat, which meant he was alone in the cab. He started up his engine with no problem and headed out of the parking lot. As he drove past the camera, I spotted the shovel in the bed of the truck, along with several other yard tools, a couple of five-gallon buckets, and a full black trash bag.

"What was in the bag?" I asked Mom.

"I don't know. It wasn't there when we pulled Mason's truck out of the lake."

"Must have been a slow leak," I commented, for him not to realize he had a flat tire until he was two miles away from school. If he'd realized sooner, he might still be alive.

Mom fast-forwarded to about 9:00 p.m. when Peter finally came into frame, sweating profusely with a washed-out, waxy complexion. He'd been running the track for more than two hours. He must have been drop-dead exhausted as he leaned heavily against the driver's-side door of his Impala. His sauna suit was gone, and he was back down to wearing only his practice singlet. He fumbled with the door and collapsed inside. His was the last car to leave the lot.

"That's all there is," Mom said.

"That's it?" I sat back and crossed my arms, frustrated that the video didn't tell me anything I didn't already know. "I expected someone to get in the truck with him," I said. "Or follow him out." Peter's car was there the whole time, which meant he was running the track, just like he said.

"I've reviewed this footage at least a dozen times, and other than Daniela slashing Mason's tires, nothing seems amiss," she said.

A deep frustration settled over me. I'd bargained my only bit of evidence for this?

"Maybe Daniela followed him, waited until his tire went flat, lured him into the woods and… you know," I posited.

She tilted her head thoughtfully. "It's possible. Without the body it's difficult to determine the exact cause of death, but we think Mason must have been laid out on a flat surface for the perpetrator to achieve that kind of complete amputation, which means someone had to drag the body to the lake or bury it, both of which take a bit of strength. Mason weighed quite a lot."

"He weighed 195 pounds." I knew because Coach Gundry had weighed him that same day in the wrestling room. "The killer could have dismembered the body first."

She nodded. "If that were the case, it would have been messy. There would be blood everywhere. And the killer still would have had to seduce him into a compliant state or medicate him heavily."

Which meant any one of them could have been the killer. And Dare....

Dare was a mystery.

"Have you gotten back the toxicology report?"

"Not yet."

"You have any other leads?" I asked.

"The lab results came back from those pills you gave me. Anabolic steroids. And we got a tip from the line saying they'd seen Mason buying pills from a man at Café Risqué. We questioned him today. He has an alibi with video footage to prove it. He may be a drug dealer, but he didn't kill Mason."

Just as I suspected. I figured it was safe to tell her what I knew, so long as it was couched as common knowledge. "I heard a rumor at school that Coach Gundry encourages steroid use among his wrestlers."

"Who told you that?" she asked, making a note of it on her phone.

"Peter Orr."

She nodded. "I'll be sure to follow up on that."

"Does this mean we're working together now?" I asked hopefully.

"No, this means you give me the name of the teacher who was having an affair with Mason. And you keep your nose out of this nasty business."

I'd give her the name, but I wasn't agreeing to anything else.

"The teacher's name is Eliza Sparrow. She teaches biology and AP Environmental Science. She's also the sponsor of the Environmental Service Program. Mason was taking her class and planted trees the weekend prior for extra credit. The shovel and gloves were probably hers. She says there's video footage of her driveway showing she never left Friday night. And here's the number to the phone they were communicating on."

I wrote down the number Ms. Sparrow had listed in her phone under MC. Hopefully Mom could pull the phone records and find something useful.

"Didn't you take that class your sophomore year?"

"Yeah, and I got an A too." I waggled my eyebrows suggestively, and she shook her head.

"I can take it from here, Charlie," she said.

"Of course you can," I said to appease her.

But until Mason's killer was found, I was not giving up.

I SPENT my weekend like most teens in the midst of a homicide investigation: I made a murder board. At the center of the web was Mason Chalmers and surrounding him were his closest friends and lovers. I put an X by those whose alibis checked out: Peter Orr, Joey Pikramenos, Clayton Benson. Presumably Ms. Sparrow and Coach Gundry's alibis would check out as well, which left me with only Daniela and Dare. Both of them had argued with Mason just hours before his death. Both of them claimed to be driving alone between 7:00 and 9:00 p.m., but neither could prove it.

I certainly didn't like what my murder board was telling me.

I also created a narrative of what I believed happened on the night Mason was murdered, along with the stories of everyone involved. And the newest question: did his killer know he'd be stranded on the side of 2082, and if so, how?

When I wasn't scrapbooking Mason's murder, I caught up on homework and wrote a paper for AP Government about the role of open primaries in moderating the policies of candidates campaigning for office. Boots wasn't too interested in my work, academic or otherwise, but he did appreciate the extra attention and the snacks I provided during breaks.

I texted with Dare throughout the weekend too. He still had family in town because of the funeral and was, as he termed it, performing his familial duties. We didn't discuss the investigation, but I did send him encouraging texts where I could.

On Monday morning Tameka met me in the misfit parking lot before I'd even gotten out of my car. She must have been waiting there for me.

"Have you heard?" she asked impatiently as we walked together toward the main building.

"No, what?"

"Ms. Sparrow's been arrested."

My mom must have followed up on the info I gave her. "Do you know why?"

"No, but I heard it has something to do with Mason Chalmers. Do you think she killed him?" Tameka's eyes were wide, and she looked a little frightened. I didn't think Ms. Sparrow was Mason's killer, but I hadn't ruled it out. "I mean, why else would they arrest her?" Tameka continued. "Unless…." Her eyes narrowed shrewdly. "They were knocking boots! Were they, Charlie?"

Tameka was on my team. I had to trust her with this information, even if it meant spreading gossip. A scandal like this one was simply too juicy. "I think they were. Did you find out anything about the fight last year?" She'd told me over the weekend she was going to ask Daniela about it.

"I tried, but Daniela wouldn't talk. She said Mason had sworn her to secrecy and I had to ask Dare about it."

Another dead end. This line of questioning was like a snake eating its own tail.

"Did you find anything online?"

"Nothing but a whole lot of white people problems." She rolled her eyes. "Trifling."

"Too bad we can't get into Mason's accounts."

"Dare probably has the passwords," she said.

"Yeah, maybe." It also meant Dare could erase anything potentially incriminating from Mason's social media.

"Speak of the devil." Tameka glanced past me. I turned to find Dare approaching, looking slightly more rested but certainly not well. This would be his first day back at school since finding out his brother had been murdered.

"He looks like he could kill someone," she muttered with a whole lot of side-eye.

"Tameka," I said reproachfully.

"Sorry to trash-talk your boy, but he looks… ill."

"He's just lost his brother," I reminded her. But even on a good day, Dare did have a slightly miscreant look to him. Not all good, not all bad. It was what made him such a good Phantom. Dare was complex, and I liked that about him. Perhaps I had a thing for bad boys.

"Yeah, well. I'll leave the suspecting up to you. Catch ya later, Dick." She gave me a quick pat and nodded curtly at Dare as she passed by him, like she didn't want to get too close. Dare responded in kind.

"Hey, Charlie," Dare said with a weak smile. We hadn't seen each other since Friday. Two days felt like two weeks.

"Hey, Dare. You hear about Ms. Sparrow?"

He glanced away and seemed to be studying the brick side of the auditorium. I sensed there was something he didn't want to tell me. "What is it?"

"I told my parents. I couldn't let her get away with it."

I told my mom, too, but it was to make sure she had all the evidence. That was twice now Dare had turned in the people who'd preyed on Mason. He had every right to, of course. I only wondered if Dare's goal was justice or revenge. What would he do when he found out Coach Gundry's role in all this?

"Do you know what the charge is?" I asked.

"No, but I don't think we should give up on the investigation."

"I agree. I actually need to make a call to Gainesville High today and see if Coach Gundry's alibi checks out."

"We should do it in person," Dare said. "Let's drive over during lunch." The warning bell rang, which meant I wouldn't have time to go to my locker before class. I'd just have to borrow a book from a classmate.

"Meet me back here," I told Dare and jogged off to the IB building.

I didn't want to admit it, but this case was definitely beginning to wear on my GPA.

WE ARRIVED at Gainesville High during their lunch hour. Rather than go to the front office and check in, Dare thought we'd have better luck pretending we were GHS students and circulating among the student body. After asking around, we discovered their wrestling coach was also a math teacher. We headed for his classroom.

We introduced ourselves to Coach Dimmit as reporters from Eastview High doing a write-up about our wrestling team's countywide competition. Coach Dimmit was happy to give the highlights from their last meet along with some stats of his starting wrestlers. He directed us to their website for the spelling of the wrestlers' names. Then we launched into the real reason we were there.

"Coach Gundry often checks out our competition's meets ahead of tournaments," I said. "Was he here last Friday when GHS faced off against Columbia?"

Coach Dimmit had to think about that for a moment. "Well, I do sometimes see him when Eastview isn't wrestling, but I don't recall him at that meet. Usually he'll at least come up and say hello."

"Are you sure about that?" Dare asked, leaning in. "Because we have him on record saying he was there."

"Well, if he says he was, then I suppose it's true, but I myself didn't see him," Coach Dimmit said with a matter-of-fact nod.

We asked a couple more inconsequential questions and then bid him goodbye. Back in the car, we compared notes. "We could drive up to Lake City and see if the Columbia coach saw him," I suggested.

Dare shook his head. "I don't think we need to. Coach Gundry was lying."

"Yeah, there's something else you should know." He glanced over at me expectantly. "Peter Orr said the steroids were Coach's idea."

Dare slammed his fist against his steering wheel. I winced on behalf of the Jag. Dare apologized for his outburst.

"It's okay," I said. "I know it's hard to hear, but it does give Coach Gundry a motive, if Mason threatened to tell."

"Everyone in this town is a goddamn liar," Dare seethed.

I nodded sympathetically. I had more or less the same assessment, which included Dare, because whatever it was he wasn't telling me was almost as bad as a lie. I didn't tell him that, though. I knew how to read the room.

Dare drove us back to Eastview. We got back in the middle of fifth period and hung out in the hallways outside the wrestling room to wait for the change in classes. Dare intended to pry the truth out of Coach Gundry, and I wasn't about to let him do it alone.

While we were waiting, I got a strange text from my mom: *Don't be alarmed. We're headed to Eastview High to make an arrest.*

I showed it to Dare. It couldn't be Ms. Sparrow because she'd already been arrested over the weekend. Eastview teachers were dropping like flies. A minute later we saw a half dozen police cars pull up in the athletics parking lot, and a bunch of uniformed officers filed out, my mom among them. I expected her to head to the front office, but instead they stalked to the building where we were waiting.

"What's going on?" I asked her as officers lined up in formation outside the wrestling room. They made us back away and stand on the other side of the atrium. Their guns weren't drawn, but their hands rested on their grips.

"When does the period end?" Mom asked me.

"In about two minutes."

"Why aren't you in class?" She shook her head. "Never mind."

Mom spoke to her team of officers. "Stand down until then. We don't know how he's going to react, and we don't want any students harmed. We need to get in there and do a sweep before he can destroy any evidence."

"Mom?"

She crossed the hall and pulled me aside. "We found the phone." She nodded toward Gundry's room. "We think it's in that classroom."

I told her what we'd recently discovered from our trip to Gainesville High.

"What were you doing checking up on his alibi?" she said testily, aiming some of her ire at Dare, who couldn't hear her terse words but cringed nonetheless. "I thought we had an agreement."

"The good news is, it looks like you've got your man, right?" I said to distract her from my own transgressions.

"Yes," she said with a look of concern.

"What is it?"

"Nothing. You and Dare get going. I don't want you around for this."

I nodded but still we lingered, not wanting to miss the arrest. The bell rang, and students filed out of Coach Gundry's classroom. The police officers all smiled and nodded at the students walking by, who then immediately got on their phones to spread the news that cops were on campus and standing outside the wrestling room. Ten seconds later, I received a text from Tameka: *I heard the cops are here. What's going on?*

I replied back with: *Don't tell anyone, but they think Mason's second phone is in Coach Gundry's classroom.*

She replied with several openmouthed emojis.

Meanwhile, Dare stood frozen right beside me. His whole body appeared stiff with rage as my mom and Hartsfield led Coach Gundry out of his classroom with his head bowed. Hartsfield was reciting him his Miranda rights.

"Your mom thinks he did it?" Dare asked.

"They think Mason's phone is in that classroom. The second one."

Dare's eyes tracked Coach's retreating form with menace. "I've always hated Coach Gundry for putting so much pressure on Mason to make weight, but now…." He crushed his fist into his open palm. "God, I could kill him myself."

I laid a hand on his shoulder. "He'll pay for what he did to Mason."

"Not enough," Dare seethed.

"Why don't we cut the rest of school?" I suggested. "My mom's going to be at the station for the rest of the day. We could go to my house and chill."

"I'd like to see Boots," Dare said, and I wasn't even that surprised. Boots was good company. I glanced out the glass door to see Hartsfield loading Coach Gundry in the back of a police cruiser, guiding his head with his hand in an almost holy gesture.

I was glad GPD caught their man, and if the evidence supported it, then this investigation was officially over.

"They'll find out if he did it," I assured Dare, but Dare didn't seem worried about it in the least.

"Of course he did it."

Dare already considered Coach Gundry to be guilty.

I wasn't so sure.

CHAPTER 14

WITH COACH Gundry in custody, Dare's parents had taken off for the night to a nearby spa and golf resort so they could de-stress. I thought it pretty selfish of them to leave Dare all alone in that big, empty house with all those memories of Mason, but Dare made it seem like that type of behavior was the norm. I took Dare back to my house, where Boots promptly set to worshipping him. Then the two of them lounged together on the couch in their now regular positions—Dare stretched out with his long legs up, and Boots sidled up next to him with his head on his chest. If it weren't so weird, I'd take a picture of their easy bliss. I liked seeing Dare draped over my furniture.

"I like your house, Charlie. It's so cozy." Boots snuffled and licked his chin. "I like you too, buddy. Obviously."

"Thanks, Dare."

A lot of kids our age wanted material things—fancy cars, trendy clothes, beach homes… but I liked what we had. My mom was good to me, and we had stimulating conversations. My dog was awesome, and even though our house was small, it felt like home. My life was pretty simple, but I had a place to belong. I wanted that for Dare too.

We watched another episode of the Vietnam War documentary—I'd kind of gotten into it since the first one—and then we took Boots for a walk in the woods behind my house. I'd always known Dare to be exciting in a crowd, but as it turned out, I also liked him in our quiet moments. He asked me where I wanted to go to college and I told him.

"Are you applying anywhere else?" he asked.

"Nope."

"Wow. You sound so certain. What a relief that must be."

I thought about his observation. "I don't know if it's certainty or fear of taking a risk."

"You think things through, don't you?" he asked and I nodded.

"I don't just think things through. I go over every possible outcome. I treat life like a logic puzzle."

"I've never been very good at that," Dare admitted.

"That's not necessarily a bad thing. I can get obsessive about it, which isn't good. I probably need to work on letting things go. Do you have plans for after graduation?"

He shook his head. "Mason and I were going to take a year off. Bum around Europe and spend down our trust funds. Live it up like rock stars...." Dare gazed off into the trees as if remembering. "But now... I have no idea. My grades are decent, but nothing special. I don't know if I'm good enough to get into a theater program."

"You are," I assured him.

"Seems like acting is something you learn by doing, you know? I don't know if college is for me, especially now that I'm alone."

I squeezed his hand. "You're not alone."

He nodded and dragged his arm across his eyes. We fell into a comfortable silence, just listening to the sounds of our footfalls on the forest floor. When we got back to my house, I suggested we go downtown and get something to eat.

"Let's go clubbing tonight," Dare said.

"Like, dancing in bars with all the sweaty college kids?"

"Yeah, I need to blow off some steam, and dancing is my release."

Dancing was not my anything. Other than being forced to dance at weddings and bar and bat mitzvahs, I didn't do much of it at all. "Maybe you should go out with some of your drama friends."

"No, Charlie, I want to go with *you*." He gave me the pouty lips and sad, crinkled eyes. His hound-dog face was better than Boots's.

"Okay. Sure." I'd never denied Dare before. Why start now?

"Awesome. Let me message the squad. They're the best dancers, and the bouncers always let them in."

I made us both sandwiches, and Dare helped himself to my closet, sifting through racks of clothing. I didn't throw much away, so I'd built up quite a collection over the years. For me he pulled out a fitted blue short-sleeved shirt. "I want to see you in this," Dare said and pushed it at me.

I smiled at his insistence. "And for you?"

"You pick."

I surveyed my clothing as I hadn't in a while. Everything seemed so utterly tame compared to Dare's style and personality, but there was one article of clothing I'd saved of my dad's that I was never brave enough to wear. An authentic muscle shirt from the eighties with a black mesh that was silky and formfitting. I'd never seen my dad wear it, but I thought it was cool, so I'd saved it. Perhaps I'd been saving it for Dare.

"What do you think?" I presented it to him.

"I love it." Dare shed his shirt easily, and I couldn't help but admire his lean, athletic build. Even though he didn't play sports, he had the grace of an athlete, with surprisingly toned muscle definition.

"You work out?" I asked as he slipped the shirt over his head.

Dare chuckled. "It's a 'Move Your Body' web workout with the choreographers for Beyoncé's videos."

"It's working for you," I told him with admiration.

His eyes centered on me with intent, and a sudden heat flamed my cheeks. Warm lust pooled in my stomach and channeled its way south. I felt that familiar tug at my crotch that I'd savored during many nights alone in my bed, thinking about Dare and what it might be like to touch him. It was just the two of us in my bedroom in an empty house. My mom wouldn't be back for hours. Of course I wanted to make out with him, but it seemed wrong on multiple levels.

"I'd better get changed," I stuttered, backing slowly out of the room.

Once dressed, Dare went through my mom's collection of hair products and found something to slick back his hair. Instead of taming my curls, he teased them up a bit so they were even wilder. Dare rimmed his eyes with liner and offered to do mine. I declined. "I'm not a good enough dancer to own that just yet."

Dare shook his head. "You're too modest, Charlie." With his eyeliner, muscle shirt, and androgynous starlet appeal, he looked like every gay man's erotic fantasy, and I suddenly felt unworthy. Dare could have *anyone* he wanted. There was no way he'd ever settle for me.

"What is it?" he asked, concern threaded through his voice.

"Nothing," I said, making my face blank. "I'm more of a backstage person, you know?"

"Well, tonight you're with me. Center stage, baby." He made jazz hands. I laughed.

Dare drove us downtown where we met Daniela, Tameka, and three other girls from the squad. With all the hair product and polyester, we were a flammable group indeed. Dare knew a place where we could all get in, even though technically we were supposed to be eighteen. The name of the place was Hickey's, this campy nightclub that was something out of a *Grease* musical number where the male bartenders wore tight jeans, white shirts, and slicked-back hair, and the female staff had tattoos and pink T-shirts that said *Pink Ladies*. Other than the costumes, the décor was pretty standard for a nightclub—two rows of long bars, a tiered balcony surrounding the dance floor, a slightly elevated stage where the DJ was mixing, and a patio outside where smokers went to get their fix. The night was cool, but the crowd provided enough body heat to keep it from being too chilly.

We hung out at a high top for a little while, just checking out the scenery. It was hard for me to keep my eyes off Dare. I wasn't alone in that regard. Several of the club's patrons threw a sly eye in his direction. I tried to shrug it off. Dare didn't belong to me, and I wasn't there as his boyfriend. At one point he caught me looking, gave a small smile, and bit down on his lower lip as if to tempt me. Tempt me it did.

A Beyoncé remix came on, and Dare's eyes lit up. "I think they're playing our song," he crowed, and the girls all flocked around him like backup dancers onto the floor.

"Charlie, you coming?" he asked when he saw me hesitating.

"I'm still getting my bearings. I'll be out there in a minute."

It didn't take long for the rhythm to move them. Dare and Daniela formed the nucleus, their lithe bodies writhing in time to the beat. The squad fanned out around them and attracted more dancers to their huddle. Dare and Daniela brought the party, and I was content to simply watch him move in the flickering lights of the strobe. Now you see him, now you don't. An ill feeling overcame me, and I had to look away. It must be all the blinking lights.

A new song by Taylor Swift came on the speakers, and Tameka exited the floor.

"Me and Taylor don't get down," she said by way of explanation. "What's up with you, Dick? You look like you're chewing on some gristle over here."

I shook my head, trying to rid myself of the eerie feeling creeping up my spine along with my own thoughts of inadequacy. "I'm still thinking about the case," I admitted to her. "Whoever killed Mason must have had a lot of pent-up rage inside them. Mason's murder was brutal and physical. Coach is a hardass, but he never seemed dangerous or mean-spirited to me. Seems like a big leap for him with no escalation."

"Maybe because he didn't do it," she said.

"They found Mason's phone in his classroom."

"Have you ever taken Coach Gundry's class?"

"Yeah, I had him sophomore year."

"Then you know he takes your cell phone if he hears it ringing. Someone probably just dropped it into that drawer where he keeps all the phones."

Cell phone cemetery, where devices go to die. I'd completely forgotten about that. And it would be so easy to accomplish, because Coach was always going back and forth between his classroom and the wrestling room to get props and equipment for his class. Tameka was absolutely right. I told her so.

"Mason had keys to the classroom too," Tameka said. "Sometimes he was the first one to practice, and he'd unlock the door before Coach was back from break."

"Anyone could have taken that key off his ring if they knew which one it was."

Tameka nodded. "So, I wouldn't get too cozy with your man piece just yet." She eyed Dare with purpose.

"Dare didn't do it," I reminded her.

She only gave me her classic *mmm-hmmm* response. I was about to argue further when a Cardi B song came on and Tameka pointed to the air. "Now that's my jam."

Out on the floor, Dare and Daniela had by now attracted quite a crowd. The air in the club had grown hotter and moister, the collective breath of more than a hundred revelers. A thin sheen of sweat covered Dare's arms and face, giving him a glossy glow. Club angel. Or demon. I supposed it was a matter of lighting and perspective.

"Hey there, what's your name?"

I glanced up to find a college-aged guy had joined me at my high-top island. He was blond and tanned, with a few streaks of color in his hair in a rainbow pattern.

"Charlie Schiffer," I said, offering my hand to shake.

"I'm Nathan," he said with smile. "You must not come downtown very often. I've never seen you here before."

"No, actually, I'm not much of a dancer." I pointed to his hair. "How'd you do that?"

He smiled and combed one hand through it as if to adjust it. "My mom owns a beauty parlor in Gretna. I've been doing color since I was in middle school."

"I like it. Very colorful."

"I could do yours sometime. You have great hair." He reached over and tugged at one of my curls.

"It's probably a little too wild for me as it is." I reached up to tame it down a bit.

"No, that style looks great on you." He smiled again, this time with dimples. He was actually pretty cute, and not *too* much older than me.

"Hi, Charlie." Dare was beside me with his hand on my shoulder. "Who's your friend?" Dare gave Nathan a tight smile that seemed a bit competitive. The Phantom wasn't used to having to share the spotlight.

"I'm Nathan," he said, as pleasant as could be, but I sensed there was tension between them. "Are you two together?"

I glanced over at Dare with a questioning look and was relieved when he answered, "We're together for the night. Come on, Charlie, let's get you out on the dance floor."

Dare threaded his arm around mine and led me gently to the dance floor. I waved a weak goodbye to Nathan, who watched us leaving with disappointment. Only when Dare and I were standing across from each other with his forearms slung over my shoulders possessively did I realize Nathan had been flirting with me, and Dare didn't like it.

"What are you smiling about?" Dare asked with a teasing grin.

"Nothing." I shook my head. "I don't know where to put my hands." I felt awkward and stiff. Thankfully the club was dark and loud enough that we were more an anonymous mass of bodies than anything else.

"Put them wherever you want," Dare said in a sultry rumble.

Not needing to be told twice, I gripped his hips to get a feel for his rhythm. Dare stepped a bit closer, and my hands slid around to the base of his spine, where his tight shirt had ridden up and exposed his skin, now slick with sweat. He seemed to quiver in my hands.

"Just feel the beat," he whispered into my ear. I didn't know if I was feeling the beat, but I was definitely feeling the growing mass in my pants, which made it difficult to focus on anything but the insatiable desire to be naked and alone with him. Dare noticed when he brushed up against me. He smiled seductively.

"Can I kiss you again, Charlie?"

"Here?" I asked incredulously. He nodded.

I licked my lips as he reached for the back of my neck to draw me in closer. I probably stopped moving altogether when Dare's mouth met mine. All around us the cheerleaders whoop-whooped at our kissing, but their presence faded away completely and all I could feel were Dare's warm lips, his tongue sliding deliciously against my own, and the sound of my heartbeat drumming in my throat. For the moment I didn't feel plain or forgettable. When Dare kissed me, I felt extraordinary.

"That was nice," I told him when we broke apart at last. "I like that a lot."

He smiled. "Me too."

We danced a while longer, stopping to hydrate when the songs weren't any good. I couldn't tell the difference, but I gathered the good songs were fast and grinding and the bad songs were more poppy and sentimental. Dare excused himself to go to the bathroom, and I must have had a completely dazed expression on my face. Daniela was drinking a coke with about a dozen cherries in it—Dare's specialty—and she offered a cherry to me. The sickly sweetness of the fruit tasted good on my sandpapery tongue.

"You like Dare?" she asked me.

Even though Daniela was a prime suspect just yesterday, I'd made my feelings for Dare pretty obvious on the dance floor, and confirming it to her shouldn't jeopardize the investigation too much.

"Yeah, I do. I have for a while, actually."

She nodded. "I could tell, even before that very hot kiss."

Who did I think I was fooling? When Dare was around, my eyes gravitated toward him like metal shavings to a magnet. He made my crusty exterior fade away completely so that I was positively squishy.

"I don't know what this is," I told her. "For him, I mean. He's going through something, and I'm letting him take the lead. I hope you don't think I'm taking advantage of the situation."

She patted my shoulder reassuringly. "I don't think that at all. You're the only thing keeping him afloat right now. Even before Mason…." She drifted off and took a moment to collect herself before continuing. "Dare is flighty and easily discouraged. He doesn't have the best self-esteem, thanks to their shitty-ass parents. He needs someone to anchor him."

I knew she meant well, but I didn't like thinking of myself as an anchor, and I wasn't sure that was even what Dare needed. His enthusiasm and vivacity were what made him so special. To think I might dampen his spirit made me question what I was bringing to the table.

"Another go-round?" Dare asked, suddenly at my side again. He pulled a cherry out of Daniela's glass and popped it into his mouth. His bright white teeth tore the fruit from its stem. I found myself staring at his lips and flushed face. Dare bumped me with his hip.

"Come on, Charlie," he said. "I want to make you sweat."

HOURS LATER, after we'd walked Daniela and the squad to their cars and were climbing into Dare's Jag, he turned to me.

"You want to come home with me?" he asked. I glanced over at him, wide-eyed. That seemed the exact opposite of taking it slow. Perhaps because I didn't answer right away, he added, "I don't want to be alone tonight."

To spend the night with Dare Chalmers was definitely the basis for being grounded, but the thought of Dare being all alone in that big house bothered me. Not to mention this was the opportunity of a lifetime and one more item to cross off my bucket list. Not that I was expecting anything. Anticipating but not expecting.

"Yeah, sure," I said, trying to sound casual about it and not like it was a literal fantasy of mine come true.

I texted my mom to tell her I was staying the night at a friend's. Hopefully she would be too occupied with nailing Coach Gundry's ass to the wall to ask me questions, and if not, it was something to be dealt with tomorrow.

Dare pulled his car into the garage, closing the door behind us. It was a five-car garage, but only Dare's Jag and his mom's Mercedes were inside. Mason's truck was probably still impounded for evidence. Our footsteps echoed hollowly as we crossed the concrete floor.

Inside, the Chalmers house felt a little haunted, and it wasn't just because of all the antiques and fancy furniture. When we walked past Mason's room, Dare turned his head as if it was habit to see if Mason was there, but of course, he wasn't. At Dare's bedroom, I stood just inside his doorway, wondering if this was a friendly sleepover or if Dare had something else in mind. Without the cover of dim lighting and loud music, I felt very shy and nervous.

Dare reached for my hand and drew me inside. He shut the door behind us, which seemed significant to me in a way I couldn't describe.

"That boy with the rainbow hair was hitting on you." Dare stared at me intently, perhaps to gauge my reaction.

"Was he?" I said with a slow smile. If he was jealous, that must mean he cared.

"I leave you alone for one minute...." He shook his head, then leaned closer so I could see the delicate hollow where his stubbled jaw met his neck and smell his cherry-cola breath. My eyes fluttered a little, and my head tilted forward, falling under his spell.

"Did I mention my parents aren't home?" He swallowed, his Adam's apple dipping a little in his elegant throat.

I touched the tip of his pointed chin with my finger. "You did."

He bowed his head and looked up at me under his thick, dark lashes. His lips curved into a teasing grin. "I think we should take advantage of the situation."

I could feel the heat of his body and smell his sweat and cologne, a heady cocktail that thrilled my senses and made my body ache for him, even while my mind was telling me to be careful.

With the exception of solving crimes, I was cautious to a fault. Never in my wildest dreams did I think I'd actually end up in Dare Chalmers's bedroom, being invited to make out with him so sweetly and tenderly. I didn't want to take advantage of Dare's shaky emotional state. Still, I couldn't resist the needy, vulnerable look in his eyes.

"Whatever you want, Dare."

I placed my hand on his waist as though we were dancing, a slow one this time. Starting at my wrist, he ran his fingertips up the inside of my forearm and traced the hill of my bicep.

He drifted closer, as if by accident, and nudged the tip of my nose with his own. I inhaled him, letting his scent wash over me and flavor my mounting brew of desire. I went for the underside of his jaw, leaving a constellation of kisses until I reached his neck, still with the subtle spice from his cologne. His stubble scratched my lips where I brushed up against him.

"Mmmmm…," he murmured, leaning back and rolling his shoulders. He reached for my buckle and unfastened it, slowly pulling the belt from around my waist one loop at a time while watching my expression. Slowly, as if building the suspense. I tugged at the elastic collar of his shirt and kissed him from his collarbone to his shoulder and back, becoming better acquainted with the taste of his skin. Dare slipped his thigh between my legs and pressed against me. I answered the call, my hard-on surging against the fly of my pants, stretched tight to contain it.

"Thanks for coming out with me tonight," Dare whispered. His hand trailed down to the outside of my pants, and he gave me a proprietary squeeze. "Did you have fun?"

I moaned in assent. My hands found the angles of his shoulder blades, and I pulled him closer, so there was nothing between us except the thin, swishy fabric of our shirts. "You're a good dancer. And kisser. And you're so, so hot, Dare." I panted on his neck. His skin was like fire, or maybe it was my own. Even when my mouth wasn't on him, I felt like I couldn't get a full breath.

"Is this for me?" He rubbed me with slow, rhythmic strokes. I leaned on him for support, my forearms resting on his shoulders, unable to think about anything outside the sensations he was coaxing from me. Peaks and valleys of pleasure, electric tremors, he put me in a throbbing torpor.

"It's for you." I was breathless, each word coming out in a rasp. "All… for… you."

I ran my hands up under his shirt, over the hard planes of his chest, then around to his smooth, muscled back. Unsatisfied with that barrier, I tugged at it, and like magic, his shirt came off. His chest was smooth with hardly any hair, and I wondered if he shaved. His nipples pebbled from the cold, and I touched one of them with my fingertip experimentally. I wanted to taste it, but there was so much bare skin, I was a little overwhelmed by where to begin.

Meanwhile his nimble fingers unbuttoned my shirt, and I shrugged it off my shoulders. Our chests pressed together, and it felt like metal being forged by fire where our skin touched. My fingers scaled up his back while his hands fisted the curls atop my head and his tongue drove deeper into my mouth. Then he pulled me back by my hair and latched on to my neck. Sucked hard.

"Dare," I groaned, the vibrations rumbling in my chest like an idling engine.

He pushed me back so that I was sitting on his bed. I scooted backward, and in my utter inexperience, prepared for him as a catcher might for a curve ball. Dare's eyes went from soft and dewy to sharp and catlike as he crawled toward me. He saddled my lap with his ropey thighs digging in on either side of my hips and pressed his warm mouth against mine. His kiss was aggressive this time, his teeth scraping against my lower lip with urgency.

"I am so here for this," I murmured, trying to match his tempo. How many times had I fantasized some variation of this scene with only my hand to inspire me? This was a whole new dimension for me, like a color never before seen by my naked eye. Dare's skin-lips-muscles-moans-scents… so much to process all at once. "I can't believe this is happening."

"Believe it…," Dare murmured, nibbling at my earlobe.

He slowed it down a little as I kissed his neck and chest, making my way down to taste one nipple and then the other. I hoped I wasn't being too slobbery, but his skin tasted so good, and I liked leaving a bit of myself behind. I tried not to think about what came next and to just enjoy these sensations as they built within me. Dare ground against me in a languid motion, both of us still constrained by our pants. *Damn these clothes.* As if knowing my thoughts, Dare reached down and unfastened the button of my jeans, yanked open the zippered fly, and caught me squarely in his fist.

"Oh shit, Dare." I gasped as he squeezed with just the right amount of pressure. I didn't know what to expect in all this, but I trusted Dare to know what to do. He'd take care of me.

"Like that?" he whispered, his hot breath tickling my ear, followed soon after by his tongue.

"Yesssss," I hissed as his hand slid over me a few more times. I curled inward while trying to maintain some semblance of control, but Dare was swiftly undoing me. Somewhere in the back of my mind I thought I should be doing something for him in return, but my need for him to keep going was louder than my reason.

Then he stood above me on the bed, peeled back his pants—no underwear—shoved them down to his ankles, and kicked them off.

"We bare all," I quipped, and he smiled devilishly before dropping back down to my lap and grinding against me once more. I leaned up to close the gap between us as he dug his knees into my sides.

"Tell me what I can do for you." I didn't want to be selfish.

"I got this one, Charlie. Just sit back and enjoy the ride."

Still smiling, Dare reached over to his top drawer, pulled out a plastic container, and pumped some gel into his fist. He rubbed his hands together to warm them, then grabbed on to both of us. His slick hand rolled up and over the tip of my straining cock with practiced skill while his hips echoed the motion. My heart galloped in my chest, and I gasped like we were in the last sprint of a marathon, trying to ride out this sensation before I climaxed and proved to him just how enthusiastically new to this I was.

"Kiss me," I begged. I wanted every part of him attached to me.

His mouth found mine again, and I grabbed ahold of his smooth asscheeks. We locked on to each other like two pistons, grinding hotter and faster. His motions were so in sync with what I wanted. I squeezed the globes of his ass and urged him on. He bucked against me, getting us both off with a mounting friction, and I gripped him hard enough to leave bruises, loving his weight and the pressure of his pounding. I imagined impaling him from that angle, driving right up into him, and that's when I exploded into Dare's fist. Stars danced behind my eyes and my vision went fuzzy as Dare groaned, a deep guttural utterance that sounded as old as time—for as long as humankind has been satiating their carnal lust with the flesh of another. Dare lifted up to his knees and arched back, letting go of his cock completely. It twitched twice, then spurted hot ribbons of cum that cascaded over my chest like paint splashed across a canvas. Dare howled a deep, thundering war cry that reverberated in my chest.

"Whoa," I said in response to his stellar performance, almost theatric in nature. Dare shuddered once from the aftershocks, then smiled triumphantly and pushed me back against the decorative pillows with his now messy hand. He spread his palm across my chest and mixed our juices together. What a delightful mess.

He kissed me softly, then sat back on his heels and finger painted symbols around my nipples.

"I'm marking you," he explained.

"Consider me marked," I said with a grin.

"It's going to be a bitch getting all that jizz out of your chest hair," he said, rubbing it in even more.

"Not even worried about it."

He smiled and shook his head. "Well, I am. That's my pillow. I'll be right back."

He walked over to the bathroom, and I watched his naked form—long legs, tight, twitching ass—still shocked that this was my life. I heard the water running, and he returned with a warm towel and carefully wiped up the traces of our mutual orgasms. It reminded me of Daniela's hot towel when she gave me my first facial. His tenderness disarmed me.

"Hop up," he said when he'd finished cleaning me. He turned down the comforter and threw the fancy pillows on the floor so only the sleeping ones remained. He gestured for me to climb in. I wasn't sure if I should dress or not, but he was still buck naked, so I left just my boxers on, still too shy to sleep completely naked. At any point I expected Dare to pull away, but once under the covers, he sidled up next to me again. "You a cuddler?" he asked.

His question put me in a tailspin. *Was I a cuddler? Shouldn't I already know that about myself?* There was so much about my sensuality I had yet to discover. I lived most of my days in the land of logic while observing from a safe distance. Perhaps part of me knew, in watching Dare onstage, that I needed someone like him to come along and shake me up. Draw me out of my own head and poke me in the best possible way. "I think I am," I said with more confidence than I felt. I wrapped him up in my arms and nuzzled my nose in his hair, feeling content and fully satiated. For once, my mind was completely empty.

I was suddenly very tired and didn't want to think about the fact that we both had to wake up early for school the next day. My eyelids drooped, and I felt myself slipping off into dreamland.

"Did you think that guy was attractive?" Dare said, rousing me.

"What guy?" I asked, playing dumb.

"Gay pride."

I smiled into my pillow. "Nathan? Yeah, he was cute."

"But I'm cuter."

I couldn't believe he'd make the comparison. "There's a lot more to a person than what they look like, Dare. Obviously, or you wouldn't be interested in me."

That set him off. He sat up and climbed on top of me, straddling my hips again. "You don't think you're hot?" he asked with a dismayed look.

I glanced away, feeling bashful. "I don't know. I may be cute to my mother and little old ladies."

He planted his palms on my chest. "Charlie, you've got a definite hot dork vibe going on. You're the guy who never dated because you were too focused on your studies and kept so much to yourself that no one knew you were available. Lucky me for figuring it out. I am just getting started with you."

I laughed. Did that mean we were together? Or that I might have the opportunity to do that with him again? I didn't ask. I'd already promised not to force him into anything he wasn't ready for.

"I'm the lucky one, Dare."

He leaned down and kissed me again, nuzzling my cheek a little. "Don't ever let me hear you doubt your sex appeal again. I find it personally offensive."

"Yes, sir." I dug my fingertips into his skin, liking the way our scents mingled and formed something new. Dare Chalmers naked on top of me? This was something I could get used to.

"Charlie?" Dare asked when he was sidled up next to me and I was once again skirting the edges of sleep.

"Hmmm?"

"Do you think Coach Gundry did it?"

I pulled him closer to me, so my mouth was resting comfortably by the shell of his ear. His brother must be on his mind every waking second. I wanted to guarantee him that GPD had gotten their man, but I wasn't so sure.

"I don't know, Dare. But I swear to you, we will find whoever did it. Mason's death won't go unanswered."

"That's what I thought," he murmured. I couldn't see his face, but I heard the disappointment in his voice, and even though he was right there in my arms, I felt him drifting away.

"Get some sleep now, Dare. We'll know more in the morning."

He scooted backward against me so we were two concave circles, overlapping. I kissed his shoulder, hoping that even if my words couldn't reassure him, my body would.

CHAPTER 15

I AWOKE the next morning to the door to Dare's bedroom being flung open. Standing in the doorway was none other than my mother and Lieutenant Hartsfield, both with guns drawn. I pulled up the covers to hide my near-nakedness and glanced around for Dare. He was gone and I was alone with the early morning light streaming in through the edges of the window blinds like a bald accusation.

"Mom?" I sat up on the side of the bed and reached for my jeans to tug them on. "What the hell's going on?"

"Where's Darren Chalmers?" Hartsfield barked.

"I don't know." I searched the room again. No Dare. "Maybe in the bathroom?"

My mother stalked over to the en suite bath and threw open the door. "Clear."

Meanwhile, I heard heavy footfalls tromping throughout the house and orders being given. They were searching the entire house. For Dare?

"Is he okay?" Did something bad happen to him? Is that why they were here? Hartsfield looked at me like I was a criminal. "Did I do something wrong?" I asked Mom, who looked only slightly less wary.

"Dare is missing, Charlie," Mom said.

"Missing?" I ran to the window, looking outside as if they might have walked right past him.

"Is his car still in the garage?" I asked.

"No," Mom said.

"Where could he be?" My panic was escalating by the second. If the police were here already, that meant he was in trouble, and how could I have let this happen on my watch?

"Finish getting dressed," Hartsfield said. "We're bringing you down to the station. We've got a few questions for you."

I glanced to my mom to see if what he was saying could possibly be true. She only nodded slightly. "Am I in trouble?" I asked her.

Before she could answer, Hartsfield cut in. "You know your Miranda rights, don't you, son?" It sounded like he was giving me fair warning, that anything I said could and would be used against me in a court of law. Sure sounded like they thought I was guilty. I pulled on my shirt, the one Dare had picked out for me just yesterday and buttoned it up. My mother avoided making eye contact, and I could only surmise the investigation had taken a horrible turn.

Dare was missing, and I was now their number one suspect.

WHEN I was little, as my parents and I were going over the Sunshine Skyway, a very large and high bridge that spans Tampa Bay, they told me a very horrid story. In its former iteration, the bridge was the site of several tragedies, including an accident in 1980 where a freighter collided with a support column during a blinding thunderstorm and broke the bridge. The drivers, not realizing the bridge had collapsed, continued to plummet, one after another, over the edge of the broken bridge and into Tampa Bay, where most of them died on impact or drowned inside their cars.

As a result, there was a nightmare that has plagued me most of my life. In it, I'm driving up a bridge that closely resembles the Skyway, but when I reach the apex, the bridge curves up and around, so that inevitably I will get caught in the curled arm of the bridge and fall off. In my dream I try to accelerate fast enough so that my vehicle will mimic a roller coaster, but I can never reach the centrifugal force necessary to hold me to the bridge, and so, like those drivers of old, I too plummet.

I thought about this dream as I waited to be questioned in the interrogation room of the Gainesville Police Department. The room was a gray cinder block box, cold and impersonal. The metal chairs were bolted to the floor, as was the table, and every surface was smooth, hard, and reflective. The room was designed to make suspects want to get out of there as quickly as possible, and even though I knew the psychology behind it, I found myself having the same compulsion to leave.

They made me wait. For some reason I thought my loyalty to GPD and my service over the years might afford me some special treatment, but either they were purposely making me sweat or they were busy following up on some other lead. Even though I presumed myself to be in a world of trouble, the main reason I wanted to get the hell out of that interrogation room was to help them find Dare.

Somebody took him, right from under me, and I might never get him back. The thought of it nearly brought me to tears. How could this have even happened? I was with him—he was literally in my arms when we fell asleep last night, so either he left on his own, or someone snuck in and stole him away.

How could I have slept through that?

Hours later it seemed, Lieutenant Hartsfield and my mother entered the room, only instead of taking the chair across from me, my mother came and sat beside me. "I'm off the investigation," she told me dispassionately. I could tell she was steeling her nerves for what was to come. "I'm here as your guardian. I want you to be honest and answer all of Lieutenant Hartsfield's questions to the best of your ability." Then she turned to Hartsfield. "If at any point, I determine we need a lawyer, this interrogation is over."

I gulped. For my mother to say that must mean there was some shred of doubt in her heart at my innocence.

"Mom, I didn't do anything, I swear." Nothing criminal, at least.

She laid a comforting hand on mine. "I know, sweetheart. Just be calm and answer the questions."

At that point Hartsfield took over. I could tell he was torn up a little about the task at hand, but he didn't offer me any warmth or encouraging words, just started right in on the interrogation.

"Start with yesterday when we saw you at the high school," Hartsfield began. "Tell us everything about your day with Darren Chalmers. Everything—phone calls, times, what you ate, where you went. Don't leave out any details."

I went through our day in painstaking detail, knowing this would not only prove my innocence, but it was also what they needed to find Dare. I was so close to the investigation now that I couldn't be objective, especially when my mind was spinning like a centrifuge worrying that Dare might be in danger. I needed GPD to do their job, find Dare, and bring him home safely.

Hartsfield kept making me repeat parts of my story and interrupting me to ask the same questions in a different way in an attempt to catch me in a lie. But there was nothing for me to hide.

"And this club?" Harsfield asked, looking at his notes. "Hickey's. How did the six of you get in when not all of you are eighteen?"

"Dare and Daniela had been there before. The bouncer waved us in. We didn't drink, though," I assured him. "Just cherry cola and bottled water." Dare wasn't drugged. Not on my watch.

Hartsfield asked me more questions—who we spoke to, what songs were played, when we left. Then it became time to tell Hartsfield about what happened in Dare's bedroom, and that's where I started messing up.

"You said the two of you hooked up. What does that mean?"

I concentrated on the smooth, reflective metal and the pressure of my fingertip where it pressed against it. "It means kissing and stuff."

"Stuff?" Hartsfield asked, unsatisfied with my ambiguity. "What's 'stuff'?"

I looked at him intently. "Do we have to do this in front of my mom?"

Hartsfield shot a questioning look at my mother, who crossed her arms and sat back a little in her chair. "I'm not leaving," she said flatly.

"I'm afraid you have no other choice, Charlie." Hartsfield said stiffly.

I narrated the scene—taking off our clothes, getting each other off, cleaning up, going to bed. I snuck a look at my mom just once, but her face was a fortress. If I didn't know better, I'd think she was playing bad cop. Hartsfield asked a few pointed questions—who climaxed first, was it consensual, did Dare seemed pleased by my performance? It helped a little to know why he was asking those questions. It wasn't some voyeuristic perversion; he wanted to make sure I hadn't coerced Dare into anything.

"And what was the tone of this sexual encounter?"

"Tone?"

"Was it tender or rough?"

"It was both," I said, flummoxed. I knew how bad that sounded. "Parts of it were tender and parts were more...." I remembered the way I'd gripped his hips and ass to match his athletic humping. "It was a little bit aggressive," I admitted.

"Did you leave marks on his body?"

"No—well... maybe a couple bruises."

Hartsfield eyed me like he was getting fed up with having to hear about my sexual exploits. He pulled a sheet of paper from his notes. On it was a diagram of a man, his front and back outlines side-by-side. "Mark on here where you might have bruised him."

If there was a hell, this had to be one version of it.

With a pen I circled the areas where my fingers had dug into Dare's flesh. If he came back to us injured, or—I didn't even want to think about it—dead, they'd compare the marks on his body to this sheet of paper. It would look bad to any investigator and worse for a jury. I tried not to think about it. We had to find Dare.

"Anything else I should know?" Hartsfield asked gruffly. "What's that on your neck?"

"Umm... I haven't looked in a mirror since last night, so...."

My mom peeled back my collar to reveal what I assumed was a hickey. Hartsfield called in a forensic photographer to snap a few pictures. I focused my gaze on the metal table so I wouldn't have to look at my mother. I could feel the tension like taut ropes between us. I didn't want to imagine the car ride home. If they let me go. I prayed they would.

When that particular nightmare was over, Hartsfield continued with his questions.

"And what were you wearing at the time you fell asleep?" he asked.

"I was wearing my underwear. Boxers. Blue ones."

"And Dare?"

"Nothing. He was naked." I started to visualize it, then stopped.

Hartsfield cleared his throat. "And what did the two of you talk about prior to falling asleep?"

I went over our conversation again about Nathan. I told him Dare seemed a little jealous, but not seriously so. "I don't even know that we're together," I told him. "Dare's still grieving."

I felt like a real asshole then. On top of everything else, I'd taken advantage of Dare in his hour of need to satisfy a lusting desire I'd been harboring toward him for years. I knew he was feeling vulnerable and confused. Did I make it worse for him? Was that the reason he was now missing?

I waited for Hartsfield's judgment to follow, but he didn't comment on my character. He did ask if Dare had received or made any calls.

"I never saw him pick up his phone." I tried to recall if I heard any bumps in the night, but I slept soundly. I couldn't even recall dreaming.

"I'd like to turn now to the incident that happened last year between you and Mason Chalmers."

My mother held up one hand. "That has no bearing on this interrogation."

Hartsfield gave her a patient but stern look. "Rebekah, your son is now a person of interest. I wouldn't be doing my job if I didn't try to establish a motive."

"He's not a murderer, Jim," she snapped.

"It's fine, Mom," I assured her. "I have nothing to hide."

So I answered all of Hartsfield's questions about the SAT sting and my role in bringing it down.

"And why did you target Mason Chalmers?" Hartsfield asked.

That word, "target," was a loaded one, but I didn't challenge it. "There was the obvious. He was one of the only jocks I resembled."

"But that's not all?" he said.

I shook my head. "Mason was, like, king of Eastview High, and I knew if he came forward, the whole scheme would implode. Even though Mason wasn't the only person responsible, I wanted to take down the kingpin. That's how he seemed in my eyes."

"To make a statement?" Hartsfield asked.

"I suppose."

"Did you hold a grudge against Mason?"

That was a question that took some reflection on my part, because I wanted to say no. Like I was somehow above that jealous pettiness, but if I was being completely honest…. "Yeah, I guess I did. He got a lot of passes in life."

Hartsfield's silence at that said more than words. "When's the last time you saw Mason Chalmers alive?"

"The afternoon of his death."

"At the pep rally?"

"No…." This sounded terrible. "It was in my car. After school."

"Mason Chalmers was in your car." He looked surprised, as did my mother. I'd never told her about that. It seemed irrelevant at the time. Would they swab my car looking for Mason's DNA? Shit, was I going to get charged with Mason's murder? I took a deep breath and forced myself to stay calm. I focused on the smooth reflective metal table.

"Yeah, he climbed in without asking. I think he wanted to talk to me alone."

"What did the two of you talk about?"

I shook my head. My pits started sweating something fierce. I felt a little dizzy too.

"Mason wanted to know if I was interested in Dare."

"And were you?"

"Yes."

"What else?"

I shook my head. "Nothing, really."

Hartsfield blew out a bullish sigh, meant to convey that his patience with me was wearing thin. "This is a murder investigation, Charlie, and you are skating on very thin ice, so if there's something that happened in that car—something Mason said to you, something you did to him—you'd better spit it out now, because it's going to be much worse for you later."

I raked my fingernails through my hair. "He warned me not to hurt Dare. And I promised him I wouldn't. That's it."

Hartsfield sat back, crossed his arms and squinted at me. It was meant to intimidate me and it worked. "Why would he do that, Charlie?"

"I don't know. I guess he thought I was setting Dare up or something."

My mom opened her mouth to speak, but I cut her off before she could defend me.

"Here's the truth, Lieutenant Hartsfield. Even though the Geek Squad and the jocks deserved to be taken down for that operation, I always felt bad for going after Mason. Truthfully, I liked him. I'd never hurt him or anyone else. I'm not that kind of person, but I'd especially never do anything to hurt Dare."

Hartsfield sat back and studied me. I sounded like every other suspect pleading his case. One word flashed above his forehead in neon lights like a Broadway marquis: GUILTY.

"Where were you the night of November 5?"

And this was where I had to admit I had no alibi. My innocence was looking more dubious by the second. "I was at home with my dog, Boots."

He asked me if I watched any television, and I told him I was reading a book.

"For school?"

"No, for pleasure. *Life of Pi.* I wanted to watch the movie, but I wanted to read the book first."

"When did you finish reading it?" he asked.

I shook my head. "I haven't. When Mason was murdered, everything else was put on the back burner."

"You've been spending a lot of time with Darren Chalmers," he commented.

I nodded.

"Weren't you worried, given your history with Mason, that you might be considered a suspect?" he asked.

I shrugged. "We've been going to school together, some of us since kindergarten. I'm not the only one who has history with Mason Chalmers." Hartsfield scribbled something on his notepad while I went over the events of last night in my head, trying to look for the clue hidden there as to who might have taken Dare.

"There was one more thing he said before we fell asleep," I told Hartsfield. I'd forgotten it altogether until that moment. "I was half-asleep at the time, but he asked me if I thought Coach Gundry had done it—killed Mason—and I told him, I didn't know."

"Why would you say that?" Hartsfield asked.

Why indeed? Because it was my gut instinct. "Coach Gundry is a hardass, but I don't think he's a killer."

Hartsfield shot my mother an uneasy look, and something like agreement passed between them. Or maybe that was just what I wanted to see.

"Under no circumstance are you to be involved in this case," Hartsfield said sternly. "You leave this investigation to me and my team."

"Yes, sir," I replied automatically.

Hartsfield asked a few more questions, but I sensed the interrogation was winding down. He read over his notes and asked me to clarify a few sequences in my timeline. Again, probably trying to catch me in a lie, but my story was legit.

"You're free to go, Charlie, but know that you are now a person of interest. I'd suggest sticking close to home for the time being."

"I certainly will, Lieutenant."

In leaving the interrogation room and heading toward the exit, we had to pass by Dare's parents. They stood when they saw us. Both of them looked utterly distressed, and I felt really bad for them. I'd failed Dare and fucked up royally, and now Dare was in trouble because of my incompetence. I deserved the withering glare Mrs. Chalmers gave me. I wanted to apologize and maybe even find out what had tipped them off that Dare was in trouble, but my mother only gripped my arm tighter and dragged me along. Once in her car, I apologized profusely for disobeying her and getting her thrown off the case. In response she gave me the silent treatment. The whole way home. It was rare for her to do that. And unbearable.

Finally I couldn't repress my questions any longer. "Mom, what do they think happened to Dare?"

"It's none of your concern, Charlie."

"Mom, please. I care about him a lot." And then I started crying. Partly it was the stress of the day, but also if anything happened to him, I'd never forgive myself.

She glanced over at me, looking tired and overwhelmed. No mother ever wants their child in the interrogation room under any circumstance. "The Chalmerses received a concerning text from Dare. They sent us to check on him. We found you."

"What did the text say?"

"None of your business."

"Where was Dare's car?"

"We don't know."

"He's in trouble."

"You don't know that."

But I did know it. There was no doubt in my mind something terrible had happened to him.

"Where's Coach Gundry?"

"Released."

"What? Why?"

She gave me a look that told me not to ask any more questions.

For the remainder of the car ride home, I wracked my brain on what piece of the puzzle I was missing while Mom listed the new rules of my punishment. I was not to leave the house except to go to school. I'd lost my car and cell phone, and I wasn't allowed online unless it was for schoolwork.

"I've taken off the next week to make sure you follow these rules."

"I'm sorry, Mom. I really am."

"You should have told me about the conversation between you and Mason. I can't protect you if I don't have all the facts."

"I didn't do anything to hurt Mason or Dare. I swear."

She turned off the car and continued to grip the steering wheel with both hands. "I know you didn't, Charlie, but my biggest concern right now is keeping you safe."

I understood where she was coming from, but unfortunately we were still at odds, because my biggest concern was finding Dare.

CHAPTER 16

WHEN WE got home, Mom gave me five minutes with my phone to see what assignments I'd missed, since we'd spent the entire school day at GPD. I was pretty sure this wasn't going to be an excused absence.

I first looked to see if Dare had called or messaged me. Nothing. Same with his social media—it was a virtual black hole. The free-floating anxiety I'd been dealing with all day threatened to bloom into panic, but I wouldn't be any use to Dare if I was freaking out, so I told myself to settle down and concentrate.

I had a text from Tameka that said *Call me* and three missed calls from her as well.

"I need to call a friend from class," I told Mom.

She looked at me warily. "What class?"

"AP English," I told her on a whim. I was getting better at lying, or perhaps I was just that desperate.

"Make it quick."

"Can I take it to my room?" I asked when she made no motion to leave.

"Nope. I want to make sure this is a school-related call."

I worried briefly she'd never trust me again. I pressed Call, and Tameka answered on the second ring. "Hey," I said. "I called to catch up on what I missed in class."

It took Tameka a beat to respond. "Gotcha, Dick. Here's the word. Gundry hasn't been at school, but he has an alibi. Turns out he was at Spurs the night of Mason's murder. And get this… he's dating Tyler Kim."

Spurs was the only gay nightclub in town, west of Gainesville proper on the Alachua county line. Geographically it was on opposite sides of the county from where Mason was murdered. Tyler Kim was a wrestler who'd graduated a couple of years back. Was that the secret Coach Gundry was keeping? That he was gay?

"Why would he lie about that?" I asked Tameka. Mom shot me a look. "I mean, he can't just change due dates around on us like that."

"Maybe he didn't want the student body knowing his business. Or the other teachers."

I was conflicted about that. Coach Gundry could be a real role model for us queer kids, but maybe it wasn't any of our concern how he spent his free time. And dating a former student probably wouldn't go over well with some of the parents.

"Did I miss anything else?" I asked Tameka.

"Girl, I haven't even told you the half of it. Did you hear about Dare?"

"Yes, he's missing." And it's my fault.

Mom cleared her throat and made a motion for me to wrap it up.

"He's a lot more than that. There's something you need to see, Dick. Immediately."

I held the phone to my chest. "Can Tameka drop off some notes from class?" I gave Mom my best pretty-please face.

"Notes?"

"Yes, notes," I repeated, trying to keep my impatience out of my voice. Every second I spent arguing with her was a second I wasn't devoting to finding Dare.

"Fine, but it better not take long."

"Can you come over this afternoon?" I asked Tameka. "I got into a bit of trouble, so I'm grounded. But I'd like to see your notes, unless you think it can wait until tomorrow."

"This can't wait, Dick," she said with a twinge of worry in her voice.

"I'll text you my address, then."

"I'm on my way."

I ended the call and followed it up with a text.

"What are the notes on?" Mom asked.

Lying was never easy, especially to my mother, but I needed Tameka's information, anything that could lead me to Dare. "We're reading *Macbeth*. So much betrayal." I cringed inwardly and waited for Detective Mom to poke holes in my story, but she only yawned. She hadn't gotten much rest these past couple of weeks. I supposed one advantage of being kicked off the case was that she could catch up on her sleep.

I texted Tameka *Remember to bring your notes for Macbeth*, hoping she wouldn't respond with something snarky and blow my cover. She texted back with a winky face and that was all.

Mom held out her hand for my phone. I made one last attempt. "What if Dare texts me and I'm not there?"

"I'll answer it."

"But what if you're sleeping?"

"I'll keep the volume on."

"Mom...."

"No, Charlie. Enough is enough." Her tone told me not to argue, so I reluctantly passed it over to her. It felt like I was cutting off my own hand. "Keys too," she reminded me.

I dug them out of my pocket and placed them in her other open hand.

"I'm going to bed," she said. "I haven't slept in two days. Make it quick with your friend. I don't want you going anywhere, not even into the woods to walk Boots."

I kneeled down to properly greet my best friend. Boots was a little out of sorts, not having seen me for almost twenty-four hours. I tried not to stress about Dare, but it was impossible. What if he was being tortured at this very moment? What if he was dead? I didn't want to imagine it, so of course my mind was flooded with all kinds of terrible scenarios. I had to keep a level head. That was the only way I could find Dare.

I waited for Tameka out on the porch so as not to disturb my mom or have her know what we were discussing. Soon enough I saw Tameka coming up the road. I met her in my driveway. She climbed out of the car carrying her laptop with the cord dragging like a tail. I took the laptop from her arms so she could fend off Boots's affections. She knelt down to give him a quick pet and then strode with purpose to my front porch.

"My computer's dying. You have someplace we can plug it in?"

I grabbed an extension cord and ran it outside from the living room. Tameka powered up, explaining as she went. "There's this whole subReddit, *Who killed Mason Chalmers?* I discovered it in Techno this morning, and I've been going over it ever since school got out. Charlie, they think Dare did it."

She hadn't called me by my nickname, which meant she was too worried to tease me.

"Do they have any evidence?"

"Take a look at this." She angled her computer screen toward me. "It's a screenshot from a posting on Vent, dated minutes before Mason's murder."

I angled the screen so the sunlight wouldn't obscure it and read the message:

My brother is the most selfish, self-centered bastard I've ever known. He's always ditching me and canceling plans last minute. Our parents think he's Mr. Perfect and I'm the bad one because I don't conform to their social-climbing, vapid lifestyle. They're all phonies and fakes. My brother is far from perfect, and one day I'm going to prove to them he's no better than me. Phantom4eva 7:27 p.m.

"Is this Dare?" I said aloud to Tameka.

"Mmm-hmm. It was posted on the night of Mason's murder but deleted the next day. One of the drama kids at Gainesville High took a screenshot and posted it here."

I scanned over the upvoted comments, most of them theories as to how Dare did it and with what weapon. There were so many pictures of Dare posted to the thread, showing his array of characters over the years, ranging from his debut role as Tiny Tim in a community theater production of *A Christmas Carol* when we were still in elementary school to his most recent performance as the Phantom. The most popular theory as to why he did it was for the inheritance, of course.

"Tameka, this is just gossip and hearsay," I said, not wanting to give too much credit to armchair sleuths.

"There's something else, Charlie."

Tameka clicked on one of the top-rated comments titled "Kiss and Tell." It expanded to show a short, grainy video of two boys kissing. Even though some of the furniture was different, I recognized it as Dare's bedroom. One of the guys was clearly Dare, and the other…

…the other one was Peter Orr.

"This isn't possible," I said to Tameka, unable to tear my eyes away. The video was playing on loop, so that as soon as the clip ended, it restarted from the beginning. Judging from their body language and the soft moaning sounds I recognized as belonging to Dare, both of them seemed to be enjoying it.

"Peter Orr is gay?" I said aloud. It probably shouldn't be the most alarming piece of information, but it made me stumble. I also didn't care to see evidence of Dare's affections for another man. "Do you know when this video was taken?" I asked Tameka.

She studied the clip of their exchange with a scientific eye. "Must be from last year. Dare does his hair differently now."

She was right. Sometime around the Phantom production, Dare changed his hairstyle. The exchange between Peter and Dare when we questioned him suddenly made sense—the two had history. This must be the "prank" Peter was referring to and the reason Peter and Joey got into a fight last spring. Before I could come up with any reasonable explanation for what she'd shared with me, Tameka presented a theory of her own.

"They did it, Charlie, and they're pinning it on you. The two of them are going to sail off into the sunset with the Chalmerses's fortune and let you be the fall guy."

Tameka's face blurred, and I recalled every shy look, every vulnerable plea and tender gesture from Dare in the past two weeks. Had Dare Chalmers played me this entire time?

"Makes sense, doesn't it?" Tameka said gently. "To go from hardly knowing each other to friends with benefits in such a short amount of time? I'm not saying you don't have it going on, Dick, because you do...." She continued boosting my ego, which was nice of her and completely unnecessary, while I drifted into the tragic theater of my mind where I was the foolish mark and Dare Chalmers the murdering seducer. It was practically Shakespearean in its design.

But you know Dare, said a tiny voice. *You know he didn't do it.*

Was two weeks long enough to really know someone? Even though we'd gone to school together all these years, I'd only ever admired him from a distance. Could I have been so blinded by my affection for him that I ignored the evidence of his guilt as it was piling up around me? Was he really that good of an actor all along?

"Shit, Tameka." I handed the laptop back to her and collapsed into the lawn chair on our front porch. It felt as though I'd taken a soccer ball to the gut. She sat down beside me, giving me some time to collect myself. "There has to be a reason for this. Why would Dare kill Mason? Was it only for the money?"

People have killed for less.

"Maybe he was worried his inheritance would go to Mason, or maybe Mason didn't agree with his sexuality and who he was dating. Or maybe he's just a psychopath, Charlie. You never know with people."

But I'd seen him at his very worst. I'd been his shoulder to cry on while he grieved. I'd felt the pain in his voice when he spoke of his brother and how much he missed him. It had to be real because it felt so much like my own feelings of loss for my father.

Dare may have been faking his affection for me, but I couldn't believe he was faking his love for Mason or that he could be so callous as to murder his own twin in cold blood.

Maybe that's where Peter came in.

A new scenario took shape in my mind, like a blob of clay being molded on a potter's wheel. Dare, bitter about not getting his inheritance and fed up with competing with his beloved brother for their parents' affection, linked up with Peter Orr, who was also sick of Mason getting all the glory. Together they planned the perfect murder and executed a coordinated attack. Dare followed Mason to a desolate, deserted road, where he dropped Peter off to do the deed and then returned later to pick him up. That would explain the lack of a second set of tire tracks on the side of the road.

But if they were working together, it would make more sense if they acted as each other's alibis. And there was no way Dare could have known Mason was meeting Ms. Sparrow because they were communicating on a second phone. Unless Mason told Dare himself. But even Mason didn't know his tires had been slashed. Daniela did that on her own, independent of Dare and Peter, so the only way Dare and Peter could have been working together was if Daniela was in on it too. But Daniela had only just found out about Mason's affair with Ms. Sparrow, and ten minutes later she was slashing his tires—not exactly enough time to plot his downfall with Dare elsewhere and Peter suiting up to run the track.

"Something's not lining up for me, Tameka."

Tameka, however, was engrossed in her phone and some exchange happening via text. "Daniela needs to talk to you. It's important." She handed me her phone with Daniela's number already loaded. I pressed the Call button.

"Charlie, have you heard?" Daniela said, breathless. "Dare's missing."

"I know." I didn't have time to go into everything that had happened since that morning. I cut to the chase. "Do you know anything about it?"

"No, but I got this really weird text last night."

"From who?"

"I don't know. It was an unknown number."

"What time?"

"It says 2:21 a.m. but I didn't see it until this morning."

That was about an hour after I'd fallen asleep, when Dare was supposed to still be in my arms.

"Read it to me," I said.

"It says 'I know you did it. Meet me at Waffle Kingdom at 8 a.m. with five thousand dollars or I'm going to the cops.'"

Now that was a legitimate threat of blackmail.

"Did you go?" I asked her.

"No, I just thought it was someone playing a cruel prank. Joey got the same text, only with a different time. A couple other people got it too. Nobody knows who it's from."

"Was Peter Orr at school today?" I asked.

"Yes. At least, I think so. Charlie, what's going on?"

I knew who sent that text. Only one other person wanted to find Mason's killer desperately enough to do something so reckless and stupid. Dare, assuming GPD had the wrong guy in custody and impatient with how the investigation was going, had gone out in the middle of the night and purchased a burner phone. He sent all of our suspects an ultimatum with the hopes that one of them would present themselves as the killer. I'd bet Ms. Sparrow had received the text as well.

With Dare missing it meant that one of them—the guilty one—must have met Dare this morning at Waffle Kingdom.

Dare was innocent.

And he'd been kidnapped by Mason's murderer.

"Where are Peter and Joey now?" I asked Daniela impatiently.

"I don't know. I haven't seen them since school got out."

"And where are you?"

"I'm at work."

"Don't go anywhere. Have someone walk you to your car. Go straight home. Understand?"

"Yes, I will. What are you going to do?" she asked desperately.

"I'm going to find Dare."

I ended the call and turned to Tameka.

"Whatever you need," she said.

"Take me to Waffle Kingdom."

IN ADDITION to breaking the terms of my grounding, I did something else I felt bad about. I snuck into my mother's purse and lifted some of her cash. Hanging around Dare had taught me you get answers faster with a little green to grease the wheels, and we had no time to waste. I was glad I'd made that decision when Tameka and I approached the counter of Waffle Kingdom. I was wired and stressed as I forced myself to sit down and act normal. We had to get the servers of Waffle Kingdom to trust us if we wanted answers.

"What'll you have?" said a woman not much older than us. Her name was Juliet according to her nametag. I slid a twenty across the sticky counter. "I need some information." Juliet glanced between Tameka and me and slipped the money into her apron.

"Yeah, what is it?"

"Were you working here this morning?"

"No, but Shelly was." She pointed to a middle-aged woman who was pouring cups of coffee at a four-top.

"Could you ask her to come over here?"

"Hey, Shelly?" Juliet called across the restaurant.

Shelly came over, thinking we wanted coffee, and seemed put out when we didn't. I showed her a picture Tameka had taken at Mason's funeral. In it were Dare, Daniela, Peter, Joey, and me.

"Did you see any of these people come in here this morning?"

She studied the photo, somewhat impatiently. "Nope."

"Are you sure? Take another look." This was the key to finding Dare. She had to have seen something.

"Look, honey, I just got sat and I'm a little busy right now. I didn't serve any kids this morning. I'd have remembered."

She walked off. Meanwhile, Juliet was still studying the picture.

"I recognize these three," she said, pointing to Dare, then Joey, and then Peter. "They're regulars."

I switched tactics. Instead of starting at the end, I started at the beginning. "By any chance, were you working Friday night, two weeks ago?"

She narrowed her eyes and thought about it for a minute. "I wasn't supposed to, but I ended up covering a shift for someone who was sick."

"Did any of them come in?" I turned Tameka's phone toward her to help jog her memory.

"Yeah. Both of them did."

"Can you point to the two you mean?"

She pointed to Dare and then Peter.

"Were they together?" I asked as my stomach sank.

"No, separate."

I glanced again at the picture. "When did they come in?"

She pointed to Dare. "He came in around 8:30 and he…." She pointed to Peter. "He came in around eleven, right before closing."

I tried to temper my enthusiasm. This could be the breakthrough I'd been looking for. "Can you tell me what they ordered?"

She tilted her head and gave me a quizzical look. I slipped her another twenty. "Fine, but it's going to take me a minute," she said and sauntered away. I should have given her another twenty and told her to hurry.

"What does it matter what they ordered?" Tameka asked in a hushed voice. I explained to her about Peter having to lose weight for the upcoming wrestling tournament and how he'd claimed to be running the track that whole night to burn calories.

Juliet came back a few minutes later with printed receipts. Dare's order was just as he said it was: waffle fries with a side of bacon and sausage and a two-egg breakfast.

"He ordered all that food," she said, pointing to Dare's receipt, "but he didn't eat a thing. I had to throw it all out. What a waste."

I pointed to the other receipt. "And this one, did he eat everything he ordered?"

She nodded. "Every last bite."

I produced another twenty. "Thank you so much for this, Juliet. You are an angel."

She grinned. "So, did you all want to order anything or what?"

"Nope, this is all we need." I stuffed the receipts in my pocket and motioned for Tameka to follow me outside.

"Can I use your phone again?" She produced it for me and with shaking hands, I dialed my mom's number. I waited while it rang, but she didn't pick up. I also couldn't leave a voicemail because her mailbox was full. She was probably still sleeping with the ringer turned off. In as few characters as I could, I laid out my theory in a text. I glanced at my watch. Nearly 7:00 p.m.

A receipt wasn't going to cut it, and I couldn't rely on a hunch. I needed proof to bring Mason's killer to justice. I needed to find Dare.

"Where to now, Dick?" Tameka asked, already sensing my next move.

"Eastview High."

CHAPTER 17

IT WAS dark by the time we reached the high school. An ominous fog obscured the building. That meant the cameras might not pick up footage as well, a mixed blessing since I planned on breaking in if I had to. There were only a few vehicles in the parking lot and none that I recognized. I instructed Tameka to park outside the scope of the surveillance cameras and told her to wait in her car.

"But it's dark out here," she whined, looking a bit fearful.

"Lock the doors. If you see anything suspicious, call 911."

I left her there with the windows up and the doors locked and headed straight for the Athletics building that housed the wrestling room. The exterior doors were unlocked, but the door to the wrestling room held fast. Inside the lights were off.

"Damn."

Above the knob was a small, narrow window. I glanced around and spotted a camera aimed in my direction. I could wait for Hartsfield and the rest of GPD to catch up, but by then it might be too late for Dare.

I'd have to take the risk.

I found a nearby fire extinguisher and used the butt of it to break the glass pane, then carefully reached through to unbolt the lock from the inside. I waited for an alarm to sound but heard nothing. Gundry's classroom was pitch-black as I ran my fingers over the rough cinder block wall, looking for a light switch. There it was. Once illuminated, I headed straight for the wrestling room, intent on finding those sauna suits. I searched through the closets, pushing past warm-up outfits and singlets, stacks of mats, and piles of ear guards. I was sweating, out of breath, and frantic as precious seconds slipped by. They had to be here somewhere.

Thump, thump, thump.

It sounded like someone was knocking on the door. I froze and turned a full circle, assessing dark corners of the wrestling room. I grabbed the nearest weapon I could find—a baseball bat—and returned to the classroom to find it empty. I scanned the places where furniture obstructed my view, then locked the door from the inside, even though anyone could reach through the broken window as I had and unlatch it.

Having completed another visual sweep of the classroom, I went back into the wrestling room when I heard the thumping noise again, followed by a muffled scream. It was coming from one of the man-sized trunks in the back of the classroom.

"Dare?" I called. Someone was kicking the trunk from the inside. I dropped the bat and grabbed the fire extinguisher. With the blunt end of the canister, I slammed the padlock with all my might. The metal jumped on the latch but stayed firm. The screams from inside grew louder and more desperate. I hit the lock again, and again. Finally I was able to break it open. I unlatched the metal clasp with fumbling hands.

Inside I found Dare, lying on his back with his knees slightly bent. His wrists and ankles were tied, his mouth was gagged, and he was blindfolded. He must have been banging against the inside of the locker with his knees.

"Dare," I cried with a joyous exhalation that I wasn't too late. I quickly undid his binding and hugged him to me. "Are you hurt?"

He clung to me, the grip from his fingers cutting into the muscle in my back. "Who did this to you?" I asked, checking him all over to make sure he wasn't cut or bleeding. No open wounds and no broken bones, thankfully. There were some marks around his neck that looked as if pressure had been applied there recently. I didn't know from what; I only knew they weren't mine.

Dare started talking at last. "I was in my garage, getting into my car early this morning, when someone came at me from behind, and the next thing I knew, I was locked in this trunk."

His kidnapper must have hid his car elsewhere.

"You were trying to smoke out the murderer?" I asked, and he nodded. "Who else did you send that text to?"

"At least a dozen people, including my parents."

He didn't send it to me.

"Why didn't you bring me with you?" I scolded, the panic having subsided to give way to anger. "We were supposed to be in this together."

"I didn't want to get you in any more trouble."

I glanced around, realizing our vulnerability. To stick Dare in such a public place meant the killer must be nearby guarding him; this could be a trap.

"We've got to get out of here," I told Dare. "You have your phone on you?"

He shook his head. "You?"

"No, my mom took it. I'm grounded." Even though it shouldn't matter at that moment, I did worry about breaking the terms of my punishment. My mom was going to be pissed and probably ground me again.

Dare rose shakily, and I helped him climb out of the locker. Once back on solid ground, he clung to me like a child and seemed to not want to let go.

"Let's go," I told Dare. "We're going straight to the police."

"You're not going anywhere."

We swiveled around to find Peter Orr, wild-eyed, as we stared down the barrel of a 9mm handgun.

CHAPTER 18

"PETER?" DARE asked, confused.

"Don't look so surprised to see me, Dare. I know you think I did it."

Peter eyed us with a deranged look. His stance was wide as he balanced on the balls of his feet. His shoulders hunched forward and his free arm was spread wide, as though he were about to challenge us to a wrestling match. I wondered if he'd appeared the same way to Mason the night of his murder.

"We have no real evidence, Peter," I told him, which wasn't a lie. Of course I wanted to ask Peter about what he'd done, but my most immediate concern was getting out of there safely with Dare. I pushed Dare behind me a little, blocking him with my body. "You can let us go now, and there would be no way for us to prove it."

Meanwhile Dare had collected his courage. He shoved past me to confront Peter. His eyes turned hard and flinty as he stared down his brother's murderer. "Did you do it, Peter? Did you kill my brother?"

Dare was taking a completely different approach—a confrontational one—and it was going to get us both killed.

Peter shook his head. His face had a pale, sickly pallor. Droplets of sweat clung to his forehead and ran down his neck, disappearing into the sweat-soaked collar of his shirt. I'd bet his grip on the gun was slippery at best. The gun wobbled in his fist as he wiped the sweat from his brow. "It was an accident, Dare."

"How do you *accidentally* decapitate someone?" Dare spat with all the condescension he could muster. His nostrils flared and his body was completely rigid as he regarded Peter with utter hatred and disgust.

"I didn't…." Peter faltered and glanced around as if someone could back up his story.

"He choked him out first," I said. I'd seen the red marks around Dare's neck, signs that Peter had done the same to him. "It was an accident," I continued, hoping my sympathy would encourage Peter to lower the gun. Meanwhile I grabbed Dare by his elbow and tried to guide him back behind me. Dare shook me off like I was a mosquito. "You didn't mean to kill him, did you Peter?"

"No, of course not," Peter said, practically singing his defense. "It was supposed to be a prank. A stupid prank, Dare. That's all it was."

"My brother's dead," Dare roared, "and you're the one who killed him." Dare pointed accusingly at Peter and I gently steered his finger downward, aiming it at the floor instead. I tried to catch Dare's eye to convey to him that we should be calm, but his attention was focused solely on Peter.

"Why don't you tell us what happened, Peter?" Partly it was my curiosity, but I also wanted to keep him talking in the hopes that Tameka would get worried and call 911.

"I heard him arguing with Daniela and figured he was going to Ms. Sparrow's house after practice. I was going to catch them on video and spread it around the school. A prank. That's all it was supposed to be."

"That's the reason there were no tire tracks," I said. Suddenly everything clicked into place. "Because you were in Mason's truck the whole time, hiding in the bed."

It wasn't trash bags I'd seen in the surveillance footage; it was Peter Orr's sauna suit. And he came back to the school wearing only his singlet, which meant he'd discarded the suit sometime between Newnans Lake and his arrival back at school. If Peter hadn't already destroyed it, it was probably covered in evidence, perhaps even traces of Mason's DNA. That was the proof I'd been looking for: Coach Gundry's inventory, minus one sauna suit.

"Mason's tire went flat," Peter continued, "and I knew he'd find me and wonder what the hell I was doing there, so I jumped out and acted as if I'd been running along the road. I told him I'd help him change it. We pushed the truck off the road. Except now, I wouldn't be able to follow him to Ms. Sparrow's. And then I thought, wouldn't it be hilarious if Mason missed his own surprise birthday party? Wouldn't that be just what he deserved for being such a prick to me all these years? Get him back for all the stupid pranks he's pulled."

Peter turned from beseeching to enraged. I suspected some kind of personality disorder or intense anger issues, both of which convinced me it would be a bad idea to provoke him. I stepped sideways so Dare was once again behind me. "You should know what that feels like, Dare," Peter said, perhaps referring to their clandestine kiss.

"Fuck you, Peter," Dare hissed. "Fuck you and your stupid fucking ego."

"That video ruined my life," Peter sneered. "Mason thought it was hilarious, me and you being caught like that. All my friends thought I was a homo after that."

"So fucking what?" Dare challenged. I was out of the loop on that scandal, but I sensed it would be a bad idea to hash it out while Peter had a gun in his hand.

"He should have never filmed us, and you know it," Peter said resolutely.

"So you went and killed him, you fucking psycho," Dare roared. His face was red, except for one blue vein in his temple, straining from the effort.

I had to get Peter to give up the gun, and Dare wasn't helping.

"Put down the gun, Peter," I said in a calm voice. "You'll be in a lot less trouble if you stop now. Like you said, it was an accident."

"But it wasn't," Peter moaned, suddenly remorseful again. "He was jacking up the truck and I reached around his neck to choke him out, but I… I snapped. I wanted to hurt him. It was only a few seconds too long. He stopped breathing, and I…." Peter ran a meaty hand through his short, stubby hair. "I panicked, Dare. He was dead. I didn't know what else to do."

"You are a pathetic excuse for a human being," Dare said. I reached for his hand to settle him, but he yanked it away. "And a goddamned idiot. You should have called an ambulance, Peter. You shouldn't have just let him die there. Like a goddamned animal. And then you…."

Dare started bawling and went down to his knees, covering his face with both hands. The gun wobbled with Peter not knowing where to point it, and I helped him decide by stepping fully in front of Dare. I was taking over this negotiation.

"You didn't mean to kill him, Peter. I understand. Dare's upset, but he gets it. But if you hurt us, then everyone will know it wasn't an accident, and you'll be in a lot of trouble."

"Fuck you, Dick." Peter shambled forward and pointed the gun at my face. With my mom being a cop, I'd been around guns my whole life—I knew how to handle one too—but I'd never had one pointed at me before. A primal fear tore through me as my breath went shallow. My knees felt like jelly, but I steeled myself where I stood and widened my stance ever so slightly, preparing for a takedown.

"Looks like you got your nose into the wrong business this time," Peter said in a mocking voice.

"Go ahead and kill me," Dare snarled from behind me, glancing up with a tear-stained face. "Then there's no way you can worm your way out of this. I hope you die for this, you fucking piece of shit."

"Dare, be quiet," I said sternly. I laid a hand on his shoulder, trying to pacify them both. I hadn't given up on diplomacy just yet. "No one has to get hurt. Like you said, Peter—"

"And fuck Mason too," Peter interrupted, ignoring me entirely. "Your brother's always had it out for me, Dare. You know that. My whole wrestling career, I've had to stay one step ahead. Training harder, eating better, lifting more. Running that goddamned track every day. And this summer I find out he's been cheating by taking steroids. He doesn't even need the scholarship money like I do."

Peter was in a volatile emotional state. So was Dare. Neither wanted to listen to reason, but that was all I could think to offer.

"You may be able to get away with manslaughter," I told Peter, "but if you hurt us, then you can't say Mason's death was an accident. That's three counts of first-degree murder, Peter. You'll be in prison for life." Or on death row, since Florida had the death penalty, but I didn't want to say that and heighten his desperation. If Peter were to panic, we'd be doomed.

"Not if I put it on you." Peter wiped his nose with the back of his hand and focused his cold glare on me. "Everyone knows you've been stalking Dare since eighth grade."

"I have not," I argued without thinking.

"Have you?" Dare asked.

"Yeah, he used to bike by your house all the time," Peter said. "And once he realized you didn't love him back, he killed you, then killed himself."

Peter, in his arrogance, thought he could get away with something like that. What an imbecile. Well, I was done with the nice guy approach. Peter was going to get the cold, sobering truth.

"That will never work," I told him. "The evidence doesn't support it. Besides, I've already told my mother you're guilty." And Tameka as well, but I didn't want to put her safety at risk, just in case Peter decided to follow through with his murderous plan.

He glared at me, not believing it. "You're lying."

I pulled the receipts from my pocket. "You went to Waffle Kingdom the night of Mason's murder and ordered a shit ton of food. Two plates of waffles fries with extra sausage and bacon? Why would a wrestler trying to make weight do that, unless he knew his competition was out of the running?"

I threw my receipts at him. They fluttered to the floor like moths. It was weak as far as evidence went, but I knew there'd be more, and I hoped I'd be alive to see Peter brought to justice. I wanted Peter to reach down and pick up the receipts, giving me an opportunity to charge him, but his gaze remained focused on me.

"I told my mom everything," I continued. "GPD's probably on their way to your house right now to arrest you." And, maybe they could hurry it up a bit.

"That means I still have time to kill you both."

"The gun residue will be on *your* hand, not mine." I tried to stay patient, but I felt like I was arguing with a toddler.

Peter shook his head, refusing to believe it. "Not if I choke you out first."

Peter was intent on violence. I could see it in his eyes and the way he clung to his fantasy in the face of reason. He was desperate, scared, and hell-bent on vengeance for whatever slight he'd manufactured to justify his actions. There would be no negotiation. We were going to have to fight for our lives.

Peter trained his gun on Dare where he knelt behind me as he approached me from the back, with what I assumed was the intent to choke me out. At that point I'd be defenseless and Dare would be in even more danger. I turned slightly and stole a purposeful look down at Dare while waiting until Peter had circled behind me. He blinked, his eyes focused, and I recognized this look as Dare gearing up for a fight. I saw Peter's arm coming up around my neck, and when it was fully extended, I struck him violently in the gut with my elbow, so hard it felt like I'd dislocated my shoulder.

Peter keeled forward a little and groaned, but he didn't lose control of the gun, and even when I bumped him backward with my hip, he barely budged. I knocked his arm so the gun was no longer pointed at Dare, and the two of us wrestled for control. Even though Peter and I were about the same size, he was a far better grappler than me. He was strong and fueled by adrenaline as we fought for control of the gun. But Peter had the use of only one hand, and it was enough for me to grab him around the torso and ram him backward into the cinder block wall. A gunshot rang out, and I felt a stab in my shoulder, but I could still use my arm, which meant it probably wasn't fatal. Then the lights cut out, Peter tackled me to the hard linoleum floor, and we rolled around in the pitch-black. At any moment the gun might go off again and kill one of us, but I couldn't back down now. I heard nothing save for our ragged breathing and the cold smack of flesh against flesh.

Then I heard the metallic *thunk* of the gun hitting the floor, followed swiftly by an awkwardly placed blow to the side of my face. My cheek went numb. Then the lights came back on, and Dare was holding the gun. His hands were shaking as he pointed it at Peter.

"Get away from him," Dare screamed at Peter, but it was me who scrambled backward and away from the scuffle. My upper arm was bleeding—a surface wound, it appeared to me. I ripped off a strip of my shirt and tied it up, using my teeth to cinch the fabric.

Peter only knelt there on the ground with a cruel sneer on his face.

"Go ahead, Dare," Peter mocked. "Shoot me. What a bonus it would be if you went to jail. The Chalmers twins, ruined."

Dare tightened his grip on the gun—two hands, his whole body shaking so hard his teeth were chattering. I stood and came around the side of Dare, so he could see exactly what I was doing.

"Dare, give me the gun," I whispered.

"He shot you and he killed my brother," Dare said in a pleading voice. "He admitted to it, Charlie. He wanted to kill us too."

"You're right, but don't you see, this is what he wants? He wants to ruin your life too."

"He already has," Dare said viciously. "And I'd rather go to jail than see him get away with what he did."

Peter smiled like he was psychotic. "They'll offer me a plea bargain, and I'll be out in a few years. I'll handle it. Mason had it coming, and honestly, so do you."

"What's your game here, Peter?" I asked, sheer curiosity getting the better of me. He was not acting like a man who wanted to live. Had his jealousy and vengeance so consumed him that he'd rather destroy Dare's life than save his own? "Are you really willing to die just to punish Dare?"

"Dare doesn't have the balls to do it."

Dare racked the gun, which rang as clear as a dinner bell in the quiet classroom. I laid a hand gently on his shoulder, which was stiff as iron. I was careful to move slowly so as not to startle him. "Come on, Dare, give me the gun. Peter will suffer for what he did to Mason, I promise."

"Not enough," Dare's hands weren't shaking anymore as he took a few calming breaths. I didn't know his experience with firearms, but it seemed he was preparing to pull the trigger as he steadied his hands and took aim on Peter's torso. His eyes had a look of steely determination in them, as if he'd already resigned himself to whatever fate awaited him as a result of this action.

"You still haven't asked me why I chopped off his head," Peter said, taunting Dare still.

"Shut up, Peter," I barked.

Dare's face twisted up. His upper lip curled into a snarl. His eyes held so much pain and anguish. "Why?"

Peter smiled sadistically. The man was deeply disturbed. "To help him make weight."

Dare recoiled, and I swung around so that I was standing in front of the gun.

"Charlie, move," Dare shouted.

I shook my head slowly. "Give me the gun, Dare."

"Charlie?" he pleaded. "Please? I need to do this. I wasn't there for Mason when he needed me, but I'm here now. I can end this."

"This won't end anything, Dare, only cause you more pain." I spoke slowly and with purpose. Dare was good at getting what he wanted from me, but I wouldn't allow him to do this. "Mason wouldn't want you to ruin your life for an asshole like Peter Orr. Mason loved you, and he'd hate himself if you did this. And he'd be pissed at me too. I never told you this, but he came to me that afternoon after the pep rally. He got into my car and he made me swear that I'd never hurt you. And I never will."

"He did?" Dare asked, wanting to believe me but skeptical still.

"I swear to you he did. You've got to trust me on this, Dare. I've never lied to you before." I placed my hand gently over Dare's grip on the gun. His eyes shifted up to meet mine. "You're sad and angry, but you're not a killer, Dare. You're not."

"Charlie…." Dare's shoulders slumped. Finally, after one last torn look, he relented his pressure on the gun. It dropped into my hands and felt like it weighted about fifty pounds. I unloaded the magazine and shoved it in my pocket. Peter scrambled up and sprinted for the door, fleeing the scene like the cowardly piece of shit he was. Dare looked like he was about to chase after him. I grabbed the inside of his elbow.

"Don't worry, they'll catch him." I stuck the gun in the waistband of my jeans and hugged him to me with my good arm. Dare leaned against me, and I gave him what remained of my strength.

Then I crossed the room to the telephone on Coach Gundry's desk and dialed 911.

CHAPTER 19

THE PARAMEDICS cleaned my wound and bandaged me up properly. I was right in that it wasn't anything more than a surface wound, which made me one lucky bastard. They gave me a shot to numb the pain and another to ward off infection. The gunshot was a painful inconvenience, but it meant more evidence with which to charge Peter Orr when GPD caught up with him. And they would.

Since I'd given her the situation in the wrestling room, Mom was back on the case and in pursuit of Peter Orr with Lieutenant Hartsfield and the rest of the force. I didn't think Peter had the resources, mental or material, to outfox them.

Tameka, who'd called 911 when she heard the gunshot, offered me a ride home, but Dare insisted his parents bring me back with them to their house, so we sat side by side on the sectional sofa in their grandiose living room and waited for updates on GPD's manhunt. Daniela and Joey stopped by for a spell with hugs, tears, and well-wishes, but after a short visit, the Chalmerses ushered them out. Their lawyer was on his way and wanted to hear the story of our encounter with Peter. I let Dare do all the talking, holding his hand and offering comment when it was requested. Dare didn't hold back in his retelling, and I was proud of him for having the strength to relive it. I offered to leave after that, but Dare insisted I stay until they heard from GPD. Mrs. Chalmers wasn't entirely on board with that plan but grudgingly agreed, right after Dare told her I was a "goddamned hero."

I also didn't turn down the pot roast and potatoes their housekeeper had left warming in the oven, though I did feel a little bad for Dare, who could only pick at his dinner despite the fact he hadn't had much in the way of food or water all day.

After interviewing us, their lawyer set up camp in the adjoining study to discuss matters with Mr. Chalmers. I assumed it was in regard to what the punishment for Peter Orr would be, and whether they might also bring a civil suit against either him, the school, or GPD. With grieving, angry parents, it was hard to tell their target. I only hoped my mother survived the Chalmerses's wrath with her position at GPD intact.

Around two in the morning we received a call from Hartsfield, saying GPD had apprehended Peter just this side of the Florida-Georgia line. A gas station attendant called him in for stealing gas. GPD set up checkpoints with undercover cars and caught up with him in a Walmart parking lot.

The Chalmerses seemed relieved that Peter was in custody, but Dare only stared off into the abyss. He'd been mulling over something ever since I took the gun from him back at the high school, and because we were never alone, I couldn't ask him about it.

I received a text from my mother a little while later. *On my way to come get you and bring you home. No arguments.*

This was my chance to have a word with Dare.

"Mr. and Mrs. Chalmers, my mother's on her way to pick me up. Would you mind if I talked to Dare privately for a moment?"

"What would you need to say to Darren that we couldn't hear?" his mother asked, still suspicious of my intentions.

His father laid a hand on her arm. "Come along, Darla. Nick needs us in the other room, anyhow."

Mr. Chalmers led his wife away. Dare turned toward me but seemed to have trouble focusing.

"How you doing, Dare?"

He shook his head. "I failed him."

He could only mean Mason. I couldn't argue him out of his feelings; I could only try to understand. "In what way?"

"If Peter doesn't take a plea bargain, then it goes to trial. You and I are going to have to give a statement, maybe even testify. There are a million ways this thing can go wrong and Pete can get off. I pointed a gun at him, Charlie. That isn't going to be good for our case against him."

Dare was also abducted and kept in a storage locker for most of the day. I'd been shot, likely with a firearm that wasn't registered to Peter. He was in a mess of trouble. Regardless, there was nothing we could do about any of it now. At least Dare made the right decision and gave up the gun.

"We can't worry about the things that are out of our control," I told him, wishing I could follow my own sage advice. "I'm here for you, Dare. We're in this together. Whatever I can do for you to make it better, just let me know."

He grabbed my hand and brought it to his lips. He didn't kiss me, only rested his mouth against my knuckles. "Thank you for agreeing to help me on this, Charlie. You saved me back there at the high school. I might be dead right now if it weren't for you. Or a murderer."

I took another deep breath. We could both be dead right now. At that moment our lives seemed as arbitrary as that *Price Is Right* game, Plinko. You drop your disc in the top slot, and there's no telling where it will come out. I was utterly depleted of anything profound, so I relied on a rather trite expression that still held a lot of meaning for me, especially after my six months of exile. "That's what friends are for."

He glanced over at me, his eyes wide and a little wounded. "Friends?"

A blush rose in my cheeks. "At the very least."

He nodded but still looked troubled. "I thought I'd feel better after Mason's murderer was caught," he said softly. "But I still feel like shit. And Mason is still gone. He's not coming back, is he, Charlie?"

"No, he isn't." I didn't want to tell him the truth, that it would take a lot of time and therapy for his misery to fade, if it ever did. I put my good arm around him and drew him to me, kissing the top of his head.

"We'll get through this," I said and hugged him to my chest. I'd do whatever I could to help him for as long as he'd allow it.

THE RIDE home with my mom was a series of apologies and admitting I was wrong and stupid, beginning with getting involved in this case and ending with tracking down Peter Orr by myself.

"I wasn't looking for Peter, though," I clarified. "I was looking for Dare."

While keeping both her hands at ten and two, my mother shot me a brutal look that said my caveats were weak and not getting me out of anything.

"I told you from the beginning you were not to get involved in this case, and despite my warnings, you persisted. I grounded you and you went behind my back and put yourself and Dare in danger. You went and got shot like an idiot, so don't you go making excuses now, Charles Scott Schiffer. You knew exactly what you were doing. Any number of terrible things could have happened to you. I could be visiting you at the morgue right now instead of driving you home." She sniffed ferociously, which meant she was sucking back tears. I felt like a total asshole.

"I also stole some money from your purse," I added, figuring it better to confess it all at once.

"Yeah, I noticed."

"I'm really sorry, Mom. I shouldn't have done what I did. I let my worry over Dare totally make me lose my mind."

Her tone didn't soften in the least. "If you think for a minute this means you're not grounded, you are wrong, son."

"Whatever you want. Until I'm eighteen. Or until I move out. I'm sorry, I really am."

The thing I didn't tell my mom was that if I could do it all over again, I wouldn't change a thing, because Dare was safe and Mason's murderer was in custody. Mom was right, though. One or all of us could be dead right now.

It was nearing 4:00 a.m., and we were both exhausted. I thought she was finished, but she started up again, only without the edge of anger. "Even though I'm very angry and upset at you, I want you to know I'm proud you did all that to help a friend. I only wish you would let us do our job, so none of this nastiness had to happen."

"We were idiots. But thanks, Mom."

She pulled into our carport. I could see Boots's shadow in the front window and hear him barking wildly from inside the house. "He must really have to pee," I said.

"He loves you, Charlie," Mom said forcefully. "He was worried about you."

I reached over and squeezed her hand. "I love you too, Mom."

CHAPTER 20

IN THE weeks after Peter Orr's arrest and leading up to winter break, I hung around Dare and his friends at school, mostly to keep an eye on him, but it felt a bit like a theater production where the cast was all overacting. Dare was forcing himself to be normal, and his friends were playing along with it. It was like they all took part in this charade of the happy high schoolers, and only on occasion would one of them break character and mention Mason. It wasn't like it was taboo; it just seemed they were all wary of bringing each other down or wounding Dare all over again.

I kept my thoughts on the matter to myself.

This first time Dare appeared at my bedroom window in the middle of the night, it startled me, even more so because Boots didn't warn me with his usual guard dog growl and three-bark warning. Instead, I found Boots standing by the window with his tail wagging. On the other side of the glass pane, Dare looked uncertain. And lost. I quickly lifted the window and let him inside. He said he was having nightmares and couldn't sleep at his house, so I invited him into my bed, where we were content to share each other's warmth and a few hours of shut-eye.

It became a thing between us. I was still grounded for the foreseeable future, and both of us had a lot of schoolwork to catch up on, which limited our time together during daylight hours. Dare's first Christmas without Mason was approaching, and he was dreading the extra time with nothing to do but think.

I began leaving my window unbolted so Dare could lift it and climb in without waking me. Most nights I'd stir in the middle of the night to find Dare in my bed. My arms always went around him instinctively to comfort him. Sometimes we talked about our day or how the case against Peter Orr was proceeding, which was painfully slow. Dare talked a lot about Mason too. In the darkness of my room in the early hours of the morning, he could tell me everything that was too painful for him to deal with in the daytime. He was always gone by the time my alarm went off, so some mornings I had to wonder if I'd only dreamed him.

About two weeks into this ritual, Dare came in one night restless. The moon was full, which probably didn't help, and it was this day only a month ago that Mason had been murdered. Dare was likely feeling the weight of the anniversary.

Boots, having been disturbed by Dare's tossing and turning one too many times, opted to make camp on a pile of my dirty clothes. I kissed the back of Dare's neck and whispered so my mom wouldn't hear us, "What is it, Dare? What do you need?"

He stilled for a moment, then rolled over so he was facing me. "I need you, Charlie."

The look on his face was one I recognized, the same as when we'd returned from dancing the night before he went missing—desire with a desperate, wild-eyed edge to it. He needed a sexual release or a bodily connection, or maybe it was only a momentary distraction from the pain. Whatever it took to silence his thoughts, even temporarily.

We kissed until my lips were raw. Our touching was on the gentle side of mauling. Dare left scratches on my back and bruises on my arms. It seemed he wanted me to restrain him, as if he was testing the boundaries to have me pull him back. I was reminded of Daniela's observation that I was his anchor, and I believed in that moment without me to tether him, Dare would be in a free fall.

When at last he calmed down, he became as pliable as sculptor's clay. I explored him with my hands, fingers, and tongue, taking my time with him, savoring the taste of his skin. In the dark I no longer felt shy or awkward, and Dare's quiet moaning urged me on. Our bodies just synced up together. We tried to keep the noise to a minimum, but I wasn't too worried because my door had a lock, and my mother slept like the dead.

"Here." He guided my hand to the bulge in his sweatpants. I stripped them off him, marveling aloud at the fact that he never wore underwear. "I'm the eternal optimist," he said with a lazy smirk.

I squirted some lotion on my hand and worked him over until the bedsprings shuddered and he gasped with pleasure. When he groaned in that deep melodic baritone, my heart skipped a beat and my whole body felt as though it was perched on the edge of a high dive, my toes curling over the very edge of it, my arms spread wide and ready to leap.

Dare grabbed my forearm, interrupting my execution. "I want you inside me," he said with urgency. He looked a little desperate, and I didn't know if it was only his libido. "I want you to split me wide open and take out all the pain and emptiness and fill me with you."

And then he looked away as if he was trying to hide something from me. He bit down on his lower lip to keep it from trembling. I lifted his chin, and he stared up at me with so much vulnerability—and so much trust—as though he really believed I could do that for him.

Without pulling away, I rearranged our bodies so he was secured in my arms again. I kissed him with all the ardor pumping through my veins. "I want you, Dare," I whispered. "And I want to make you feel good, but I can't take away your pain, and I'm afraid that if I try, you might feel even worse afterward. Like I've taken something from you."

He whimpered softly, like an animal in pain. His warm cheek pressed against my chest. "I don't know who I am anymore. Without Mason, I just don't know. I'm a ghost. I float through the days. I need you to tell me who I am."

Dare had to rediscover himself in Mason's absence. A lonely solo in what had always been a duet. I knew from experience there were no shortcuts. I could help, but I couldn't take over that job for him—he'd end up hating me for it. Instead I gripped him tighter, my heart breaking for him all the same. "You'll find yourself again. There's no deadline and no expectations. Just take it slow and know that we're here for you. Me and Daniela and Joey, your parents… your therapist. We want you to heal in your own time."

I stroked his hair and placed a tender kiss on his temple. He nodded even though I could tell he was disheartened. He curled up against me but didn't initiate anything sexual. My balls were aching something fierce, but I powered through. Boots jumped back on the bed and settled in the valley of blankets between us.

"And Boots," I added. "Boots loves you too."

"Well, I love him more." Dare smiled, looking a little less tragic, and Boots, knowing his name had been mentioned, took the opportunity to lick Dare full on the face. After a few minutes Dare said, "I do want that, Charlie."

"Me too. When you're ready." I kissed the tip of his nose. "I'm sorry if I killed the mood."

"One of these days, your sensibilities will be overwhelmed by my sexual magnetism."

I chuckled at that. He was absolutely right. "I look forward to that day."

He sighed softly as he relaxed against me, a crescent moon against my chest. Dare closed his eyes, and I thought from the regular rhythm of his breathing, he'd fallen asleep. I startled a little when he turned around and asked, "How'd you know it wasn't me?"

Even though neither of us had mentioned Mason's murder specifically, it was always lurking in the shadows. It was the catalyst to our coming together, and in a way it defined our relationship, because Dare was different now than he was before it happened. We all were.

"You're not that good of an actor," I said in response to his question.

His gray eyes widened, and a scowl settled over his handsome features. "That's a rude thing to say to an aspiring actor, Charlie-bo-barley."

If he was using my nickname, he must not be too mad at me. "You're a better singer, in my humble opinion."

He nodded, mollified for the moment. "Well, that's certainly true." He rolled onto his back and stared up at the ceiling. "I miss him."

"I know you do."

"Will it ever stop hurting?"

I'd sworn to never lie to him, and I wasn't going to start now, but that didn't mean I couldn't still hope for the best. "I think it will, eventually, but these things can't be rushed. There's no fast pass to grieving. At least, there hasn't been for me." And some days you could go all day thinking you were happy when a memory suddenly stabbed at you like an ice pick to your heart and brought you to your knees. I didn't say that, though. I wanted to keep it positive.

"I thought when we found Mason's killer, something would change. The universe would right itself again or something."

I could help solve his brother's murder, but I couldn't take away his pain.

"But it hasn't."

"No."

He rolled over all the way and pressed his back against my chest. I trailed my hand along the shape of him, memorizing his contours with my fingertips. I fell asleep soon after and stirred only once more. Dare, still naked, was sitting in my desk chair facing the window. Moonlight silhouetted his long, lean frame as I watched him from where I lay still half-asleep in bed, Dare flicking his silver lighter with a rhythm as regular as a heartbeat.

"Aren't you cold?" I said while holding up the blanket for him. My mom didn't run the heater much in the winter. She said that was one of the perks of living in Florida.

Dare turned around and looked at me like he'd been caught. He snapped the lighter shut and laid it on my desktop.

"Want to talk about it?" I asked when he was nestled in my arms again, his nose just inches from my own and the comforter pulled up so we were safe and secure.

"We still haven't watched *Jocks on Cocks*," he said.

I chuckled at that, and even though I knew he was dodging my question, I didn't push it. "I bet there's some really good acting in it," I said.

"I wouldn't know," he said loftily. "I'm a better singer, after all."

I pinched his side, and he squirmed in my arms. His naked body thrilled me. At the foot of my bed, Boots snuffled at us to be still. I regretted not bending the truth on that particular comment. "You're going to throw that in my face forever, aren't you?"

He nodded. "Of course I am. That's what couples do."

I squeezed him a little closer. My cheeks felt tight with a smile that stretched my entire face.

"What?" he asked, his smile mirroring my own.

"You said we were a couple."

"If that's what *you* want." The tender note in his voice when he asked made me melt. "I have some demons."

I brushed away the lock of hair that had fallen over his forehead. "I want to be your boyfriend, Dare. Obviously."

"Obviously," he echoed and pulled me in for a kiss.

Boots, resigned to the fact he wasn't going to get any sleep, lumbered up and flopped between us, then rolled onto his back so we could scratch his belly. It seemed Boots approved.

Then the three of us burrowed together under the blankets like bears denning down for winter. I had a cozy house, a mother who loved me, an awesome dog, and now I had Dare.

I was confident I could handle whatever Dare threw at me, demons and all.

ACKNOWLEDGMENTS

FIRST AND foremost, I'd like to thank my daughter for helping me plot this mystery using only the lyrics to one of our favorite songs, "Where Did You Sleep Last Night" by Nirvana, which is a cover of a much older song with a somewhat sordid history. Needless to say, we took a few liberties. I also credit my daughter for her consultation on teen slang, the ever-changing beast of social media, high school trends, and wicked burns. She's also really good at telling me when I'm "trying too hard to be cool." It's hard to put a price on that kind of honesty.

Thank you to: my writing group Pen Ten for their feedback on a few pivotal scenes; Heather Whitaker for keeping our pens sharp and our wits sharper; Dr. J. for being so generous with loaning out her lake house to us starving artists in need of a place to hole up and write; and my wise readers Sarah, Sky, and Ashley, experts on the mystery genre, for their feedback on *In the Pines*.

Thank you to AngstyG for her brilliant cover artistry, to the Dreamspinner team for growing my readership, and to the community of readers who continue to support my work—you are what makes my writing world go 'round.

And finally, thank you to my darling husband and delightful son. These two, along with the little miss, keep me on the sunny side of life.

LAURA LASCARSO wants you to stay up *way* past your bedtime reading her stories. She aims to inspire more questions than answers in her fiction and believes in the power of storytelling to heal and transform a society. When not writing, Laura can be found screaming "finish" on the soccer fields, rewatching *Veronica Mars,* and trying to convince politicians that climate change is real. She lives in North Florida with her darling husband and two kids. She loves hearing from readers, and she'd be delighted to hear from you.

Website: lauralascarso.com
Facebook: www.facebook.com/lascarso
Twitter: @lauralascarso

LAURA LASCARSO

ANDRE
IN FLIGHT

When up-and-coming Miami painter Martin Fonseca encounters youthful pretty boy Andre Bellamy washing dishes in the kitchen of La Candela, he swears he's known him before, intimately. But Andre only arrived in Miami weeks ago, after running away from small-town Alabama and his abusive father. When Martin discovers Andre trading sexual favors for a place to stay, he offers him a room in his studio apartment. As roommates only.

What starts as a playful friendship turns into something more as Andre begins posing for Martin, whose true passion is painting fantastical portraits. Martin's obsession with Andre grows until they are sharing more than just flirtatious conversation. But when an eccentric art collector buys one of Martin's paintings, Martin's past jealousies resurface and threaten to destroy what he and Andre have so lovingly built.

www.dreamspinnerpress.com

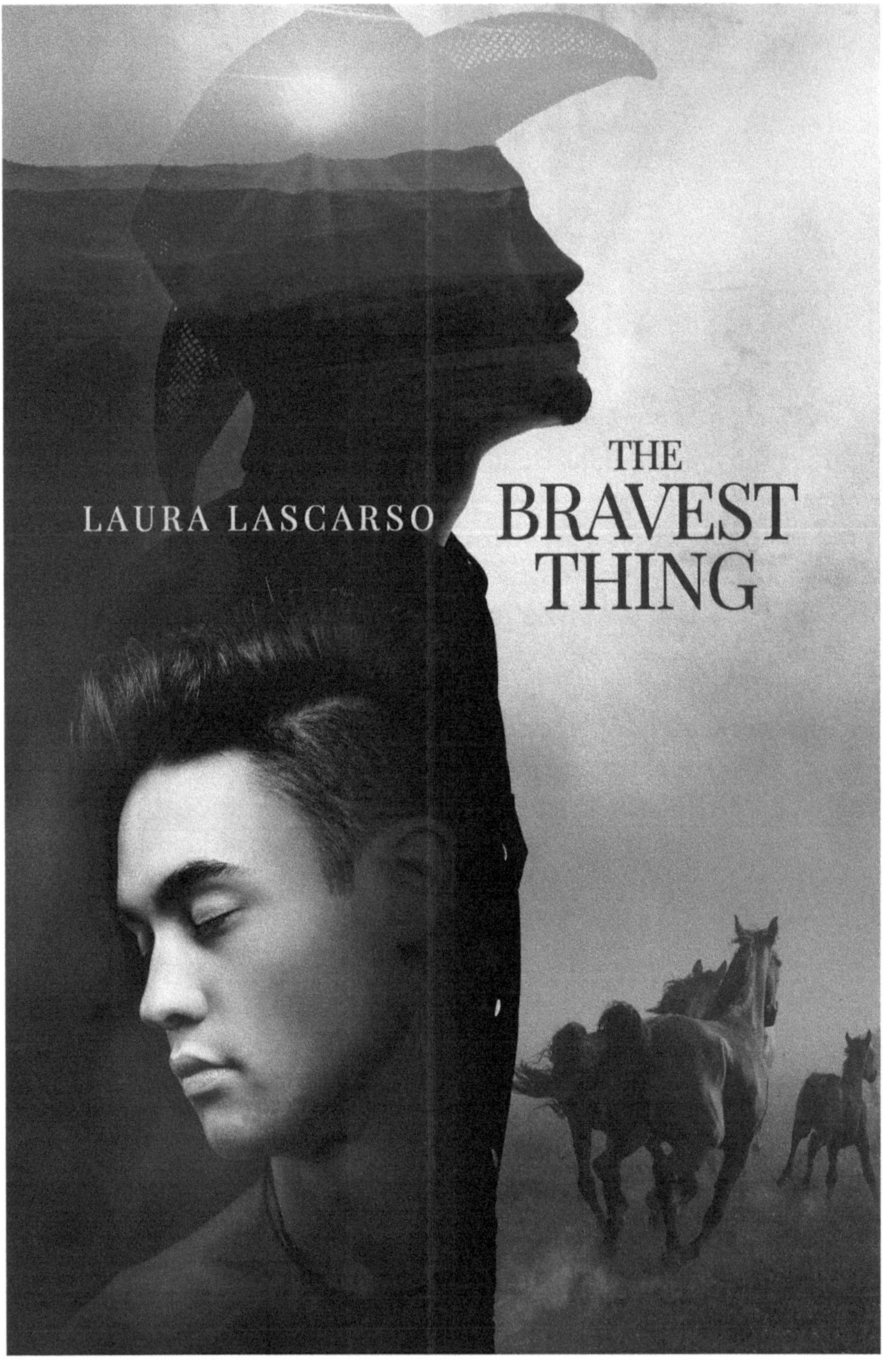
LAURA LASCARSO
THE BRAVEST THING

High school junior Berlin Webber is about to reap the fruits of his hard work and land a football scholarship—if he can keep his sexuality a secret from his best friend, Trent, and their homophobic coach. Then Hiroku Hayashi swerves into the high school parking lot on his tricked-out motorcycle like some sexy comic book villain, and Berlin knows he doesn't stand a chance.

Hiroku is fleeing his sophisticated urban scene to recover from drug addiction and an abusive relationship when he arrives in Berlin's small Texas ranch town. Initially sarcastic and aloof, Hiroku finds in Berlin a steady, supportive friend who soon becomes more. As Hiroku and Berlin's romance blossoms, they take greater risks to be together. But when a horrific act of violence tears them apart, they both must look bigotry in the face. While Berlin has always turned to his faith for strength, Hiroku dives into increasingly dangerous ways of coping, pushing them in opposite directions just when they need each other most.

Two very different young men search for the bravery to be true to themselves, the courage to heal, and the strength to go on when things seem darkest. But is it enough to bring them back together?

www.dreampsinnerpress.com

WHEN EVERYTHING
IS BLUE

LAURA LASCARSO

Sometimes the people we need most aren't bonded by blood but by something deeper.

When they were kids, golden boy Chris Mitcham rescued dweeby Theo Wooten from the neighborhood bullies and taught him how to "be cool." Now, years later, Theo's developed romantic feelings for his best friend that "arise" at the most inopportune times. Theo hates lying to Chris, but in coming out, he might lose the one person who understands him best, a risk he's not willing to take.

When a relationship with another young man goes south, Theo is forced to confront his own sexuality along with his growing attraction to Chris and the stunted, tenuous relationship Theo has with his father. Will Chris abandon Theo when he learns the truth, or will he stand by him in this tumultuous season of self-discovery?

In this quirky coming-of-age romance, Theo's path to manhood is fraught with several awkward firsts, a few haters, but also the tender comfort of an unexpected lover.

www.dreamspinnerpress.com

Lightning Source UK Ltd.
Milton Keynes UK
UKHW010439180119
335758UK00006B/562/P